VAMPIRE-TECH 2
INFESTATION

Bryan Romer

VAMPIRE-TECH 2
INFESTATION

Fiction4All

Chapter One

Sitting on the patio of Seward's penthouse apartment, Tara Harker stared up into the sky. With her newly amplified vision, there seemed to be far more stars, and each one bright as a diamond in a showcase. "I wonder if they're still up there?"

"You mean the ones who created the nano-biological things in us?" John Seward replied, less impressed by the view of the night sky, having had hundreds of years to become accustomed to it. When she nodded he frowned. "If your father's theories are right and we are possessed of a military version of their medical AI nanites, it might not be as peaceful as it looks up there. Sadly, it seems that war might be a universal constant, or at least more common than we would like to think."

"Says Vlad Tepes, the warlord."

John sighed. "We are what our times make us. I tried to be a good ruler and the defender of my people. The fact that some English hack of an author made me into a romantic monster is neither here nor there. At least there are still some in my ancient homeland who remember my name fondly."

"I thought you said you paid that so called hack to write the book … Dracula?"

He chuckled at her use of his alter-ego's name. "The perfect example of the law of unintended consequences. I wanted to ridicule the idea of vampires and to make it a joke in the mind of the public. How was I to know that it would end up with young women swooning over sparkly anaemic looking young men in books and in entertainment mediums that had not even existed yet. Streaming video!" he shuddered. He sipped what looked like a Bloody Mary and smiled at her with red stained lips. "On a brighter note, you're looking very fit and trim," he said, twirling an imaginary moustache.

Tara looked down at her rippling, washboard flat abdomen. "I do feel like a bit of a cheat. Most women who look like this have to spend hours a day sweating in a gym."

The youthful industrialist and ancient vampire laughed. "And you don't?"

"Well it's for a different reason. Just having these nanite things in me don't automatically create the right reflexes and muscle memory. If I hadn't been into combat Tai-Chi in the first place to keep fit and help my mental focus, I'd probably have been hopeless in a fight and been torn apart by Viktor. As it was I barely survived our last encounter."

He nodded. "I discovered the same thing, a very long time ago. In fact, being super strong and fast ruins all your existing reflexes. It's like those astronauts trying to walk on the moon. They bounced all over the place in the low gravity."

"That's exactly right! Half the time I feel like someone fooled into picking up a supposedly heavy box that's actually empty." Then she smiled. "But I do enjoy learning to use the sword from a true master," she said, fluttering her eyelashes at him coquettishly.

"Flattery is the first thing a ruler learns to ignore, that is if he intends to live to be a ruler for very long," he said with a laugh. "But I have always loved the sword, and the alien reflexes to fight with claws blends in very well indeed – with sufficient practise. You're lucky you know, with that nano-interface your father invented, you are learning to use your new abilities far faster than I did. And with vastly fewer innocent casualties," he added with a trace of bitterness. For years he actually had been the vampiric monster of legend, with no control over his lust for blood.

She sipped her glass of red liquid and sighed. "I know, I know, back to the gym in the morning for more training." Then it was her turn to frown. "I wonder how

Viktor is doing. He doesn't have a mentor or helpful interface nanites to help him adjust.

"He seemed to be doing well enough, too well for my tastes. I fear we haven't heard the last of your former co-pilot. Or of that bloody American corporation."

Tara shook her head. "It seems unbelievable that he is what anyone today would call a werewolf."

John touched the strange alien cross-and-disk medallion that he wore under his shirt which was actually a used and empty medical nano applicator. "And vampires are not?" He pointed at her glass. "Finish your synthetic blood substitute. Your father wouldn't be pleased if you bit him on the bum."

"Emily might like it. She seems to be in for just about anything."

"Don't let her dumb-blonde persona prejudice you. She's very intelligent, even if a trifle over-sexed."

***

"It's at least semi-intelligent, an AI or even a quasi-biological life-form, I'm sure of it. The latest test results you obtained from Seward and Tara show – " Rowland Harker abruptly stopped speaking when he felt his new lab assistant and girlfriend Emily Palmer press her body against his back. From the way it felt, she wasn't wearing anything under her white lab coat.

"And those results and their intelligence will still be there in the morning, but you might not be if you don't get some rest. Now be a good dirty old man and take me to bed."

"I resent that 'old' part, although I confess there is more than a modicum of truth in the 'dirty' part…" Once more she cut him off by spinning him around and kissing him passionately. He still found it hard to believe that a beautiful young woman like her could be attracted to a mad scientist type like himself, especially given their age differences, but she had proven her devotion and capabilities, both in the lab and in the bedroom more than adequately, and he had no intention of performing dental examinations of gift equines. "I suppose you're right. I do need to get some sleep."

Now pressed tightly against his front, Emily smiled. "Who said anything about sleep?"

**

Viktor Tiranul swore as he dabbed at the deep claw mark on his cheek that was already starting to close and heal. The sound of the roaring and crashing of what sounded like a large animal through the hedgerow and bushes faded into the distance. "Damn! That's the third one this week. I thought we had finally managed to work out a selection process that worked."

"I'm beginning to think it's not possible to predict, not without a much better understanding of this … this thing that's inside of us," replied Jenny Smith, formerly the unwilling test subject of the UK biological laboratories of Werner Aerospace and Robotics and now Viktor's devoted follower. Unlike Viktor, she had been deliberately infected with the alien nano-biological system that he and Tara Harker had accidentally discovered after he had tried to hijack Rowland Harker's latest experimental aircraft, and fatally shot Tara in the process. Unfortunately the alien medical technology was species specific, and the two pilots had received treatments intended for two very different alien species, giving rise to some rather dramatic side effects.

Viktor nodded, pounding a fist against the bole of a tree in frustration. "I think you're right. We may have to reconsider our recruitment strategy. We might have already attracted too much official attention. Perhaps it would be wise for the pack to move on from this area."

Micki Benini whistled as she opened up the back of her white panel van. Since the police didn't deal with random wild animals unless they were proven to be rabid, the pest control business was good. Mostly they were stray dogs, foxes and badgers and the like, although the reports often referred to "hairy monsters". Urban residents were just not used to live animals and would often panic at the sight of a chicken or small lizard. Her heavy leather work gloves and thick sleeves of her jacket were sufficient to handle most encounters, but she pulled the steel shafted noose stick out of the van and clipped on an illegal pepper spray dispenser onto her belt. Better safe than sorry. The occupants of the house that had engaged her had pointed out where they had last seen the animal, so she stopped whistling and headed in that direction. The day was overcast and a little chilly, with threat of a drizzle later, basically par for the course. She shook her head as her experienced eyes searched the grass for spoor or droppings. You would think that people living this distance from the main city areas would be used to a few wandering animals. Then she slowed and frowned. She had spotted a paw print in the ground, although the grass made it indistinct, unlike the nice clear shapes you always saw on TV. But it was large. Impossibly large. Her frown deepened as she began to suspect a hoax or someone trying to make a "found video" film with her as an unwitting actor. She shrugged. The company charged both by time and number of animals captured, so if they wanted to play silly buggers they would have to pay for it, and a long walk was better than struggling with an angry ferret.

The spoor continued to lead off in a nearly straight line towards a stand of trees and a mixture of brambles and nettles. Once again her heavy work clothes would protect her from these minor hazards and she continued walking, using the noose pole as a walking stick. A deep rumbling growl made her pause and then grin. It had been too loud and deep chested for anything short of a lion or some other major predator, and both she and the company kept careful watch on all reports of escaped zoo animals and specially licensed pets. To her ear it had sounded more like a dog than a large cat, but from the footprints the dog would have to be bigger than her. Of course there were some people who kept stupidly big breeds of dogs, so she approached the trees cautiously. "Here Rover, nice doggie," she muttered, still following the prints. If it turned out to be some kid with an MP3 player and speakers she swore she would pepper spray the little bastard, male or female.

The growls grew louder and changed in rhythm, sounding almost anticipatory, eager, and there was a crackling and crunching of something large moving through the undergrowth.

Micki stopped just short of the trees, hand on her hip. "Oh come on now! This is too fucking much. No wild animal would make that kind of noise, not even a stray dog. Come out of there right now. I'm warning you, I'll be really pissed if you make me play hide and seek." She smiled when she saw an upright figure moving towards her through the trees. "I'm glad you've decided to be sensible. I might not even report you to the police if you…" She trailed off when the figure stepped out into the open, and then started to laugh. "Really? A werewolf suit? What is this, some kind of TV – "

The werewolf bared its fangs in a hungry snarl, saliva dripping from its open jaws. It extended its arms and long wickedly hooked claws appeared. Then it raised its muzzle and roared.

Shock and experience warred in Micki's brain even as her hand drew the pepper spray from its tiny holster. She still wasn't sure it wasn't a prank, but the thing looked far too realistic to be a man in a suit.

Standing her ground she extended the noose-pole to hold whatever-it-was (her mind refused to use the word werewolf) off and raised the pepper spray. She had used it often enough to automatically adjust her position to take account of the direction of the wind so the eye searing liquid wouldn't blow back into her face, and she held down the trigger button. She grunted in satisfaction when the stream of liquid hit the thing squarely in the face.

If it had been a true member of the alien species, the eye searing spray might actually have worked, since their biologies were not so vastly different from human, but the creature had barely begun to feel the sting of the capsaicin spray when the alien medical nanites within its body efficiently neutralised it, so all the spray did was anger it even more. It roared again, louder this time, and sprang at her jumping so high and long that it almost seemed to take flight.

Micki just had time to realise that things were going very wrong indeed before the pole was wrenched out of her grip. She screamed when claws like curved steel nails raked her hand and arm, making her drop the pepper spray projector. Blood spurted from flayed flesh and she was still screaming in agony when the hairy body of the creature slammed into her, knocking her onto her back and sending her skidding across the damp grass. She had time for just one more horrified scream before the impossibly large jaws closed over her lower face and throat, crushing bone and ripping flesh.

***

Tara held her father's hand as they watched the news on TV, sitting side by side on the sofa. "It's times like this that I miss mum the most," she said, leaning against his shoulder.

"I would have thought it was when you were in

11

the cockpit. That's where the two of you seemed to spend most of your time together," he said tartly.

"She didn't die in a crash just to spite you, you know," Tara said. She hated it when the subject of flying and her mother came up. It always made her father upset. To her surprise, this time he sighed and nodded.

"Of course I know that. She loved flying. In a way I was jealous, because sometimes it seemed she loved it more than me. I think that was what made me resist your becoming a test pilot. Not the possibility of an … an accident, but of losing you to a greater love. After everything that's happened lately, including Emily, and how many times you could have died, I've come to realise that life's too precious to waste on anger or resentment."

Tara saw the way he glanced at her when he said Emily's name. She squeezed his hand. "I'm glad for everything we have, and if Emily makes you happy, I'm happy about her too."

"Really?" His face brightened. "I've been so afraid that you would think …."

She kissed him on the cheek. "The only one who needs to be afraid is her if she hurts you."

Rowland shook his head. "No fear of that. She's a good woman, Tara. I'm sure of it."

"You're sure of what?" Emily asked, walking into the living room. She was wearing glasses instead of her contacts and a cashmere cardigan over a blouse and tight jeans.

Avoiding her question, Rowland pointed at the wide screen LED TV. Isn't it amazing how little mention there was on the news about the massacre at the Werner Biotechnologies Labs or the people living in the area who were killed.

John, who had discreetly seated himself in an armchair across the room from Tara and her father to give them privacy, even though he could hear everything they were saying as if they were shouting in his ear, said, "Werner did a good job of cleaning everything up. From confidential sources I hear that it was treated as a chemical leak caused by a disgruntled employee, who also shot several of his colleagues and attacked more with a fire axe. The relatives were paid large compensations and signed non-disclosure contracts." Then his eyes swivelled towards the TV and his face slowly darkened into a frown as he listened. "Damn that Viktor! I had hoped he would be satisfied with his powers and the companions he had gathered."

"What's happened?" Tara asked, turning from her father.

"There's been a death, an animal control specialist. She was ripped apart by what the news is calling an animal attack. This was not the first, but this latest is one too many too soon. There are rumours of rabid dogs, and DEFRA, the Department for Environment Food and Rural Affairs as well as the Police are being called in to investigate."

"But if Viktor is trying to make more werewolves, they won't find any rabies," Emily said. Her eyes widened. "Oh!"

"Oh indeed. If they are unlucky, there are going to be a whole lot of dead medical workers and policemen if they run into one or more werewolves," John said grimly.

"But why would Viktor want to draw attention to himself like this?" Rowland asked, puzzled.

"It's not Viktor. Not directly, anyway," Tara said, understanding John's concern. "He's trying to make more followers, but from what John tells me, very few humans who are turned are capable of any coherent thought or self-control when in their werewolf form. It requires incredible strength of will and character. All the others simply adopt the base alien form, like a human baby suddenly given the body of a full grown adult. All they

13

know is hunger and self-preservation. Basically the werewolf of legend. Viktor was incredibly lucky to find the few followers that he did."

"And now he's making more and just turning the rejects loose on the countryside," Rowland said, nodding thoughtfully. "We have to do something. Can't you warn the authorities?" he said to John. He shook his head and slapped his forehead. "And tell them to look out for werewolves – of course not. But that means…" His eyes went to Tara and his face paled. "No … can't John just…"

Tara just stared silently at him.

Rowland sighed. "Of course not."

Emily squeezed his arm. "She'll be all right. John will protect her, and they'll be doing the hunting. It won't be like the other times."

Rowland laughed. "I would never have imagined that I would be depending upon Count Dracula to look after my daughter."

For a moment a looked as if John would take offence, his face darkening and subtly shifting into a more angular, almost inhuman form, and Tara tensed, preparing to leap to her father's defence.

Then John laughed, and he looked like the urbane young industrialist and billionaire once more. "I was always known as a lady killer, even in my younger days, but I have never deliberately harmed a lady who had not tried to attack me first. Even during that period when I was … not myself, I tried my best to restrain myself from fatally draining my female victims, as my old friend and companion Mina can testify."

Tara gasped. "Mina Harker? She's a real person – and a … a vampire?"

Her expression made him chuckle. "Yes she is very real, and one of the few people that I infected that remained in control of herself, or perhaps I should say regained control of herself with my help. Her inclusion and starring role in the novel was my little tribute and joke. She was no longer using that name by the time the book was published, so it didn't put her in any danger." He raised an eyebrow. "And no, you are not related to her, or to me. I took the liberty of performing a DNA test. Naturally I would have informed you if the test had been positive. You surnames are simply an incredible coincidence, or perhaps God's little joke."

Tara was tempted to ask him if he had any children, but something in his eyes made her hold her tongue. Instead she kissed her father on the cheek, and followed John out of the living room. Behind her, she heard the news announcer talking to a supposed expert on rabid animals.

***

"It were a bloody great wolf, I tell you!" the old man shouted into the camera before the lens switched back to the mock sympathy of the newswoman. "Authorities are calling for calm and not to listen to unsubstantiated rumours. There are no wild wolves in this region of England, especially not rabid ones. All necessary measures are being taken..." Ian Werner cut off the news feed with a touch of a button, his expression wavering between a smile and a frown. "Internal Audit, did you see that?"

The Corporation's security and unofficial trouble-shooters, otherwise known as "Internal Audit" had a person on this line twenty-four hours a day, every day of the year including holidays, ready to respond to a call from Werner. The security desk had an automatic link to any news item or communication flagged by Werner. "Yes Mr Werner. Mr Jackson has been alerted."

"Inform him he has my authority to use whatever influence and contacts we have in Britain to locate and destroy any Infected at large. Exclusive ownership of all samples is critical until we can find a way to patent whatever it is. Only Viktor Tiranul is to be taken alive if possible. Reports from the earlier incident indicate that another party is interested in the product. Maximum force is authorised against any such unofficial interference. Inform the British authorities that credible terrorist threats against the Corporation and its staff have been received, although no specific group or persons have been identified as yet."

"Yes Mr Werner."

"Keep me informed of progress," Werner said, cutting off the line before the other party could answer.

***

Dan Jackson, head of Internal Audit for the Werner Corporation had been in London for over a month now, establishing contacts with the people in the various British government organisations that were friendly or controlled by the Corporation one way or another. He had also been recruiting and carefully accumulating an arsenal of heavy weapons for the team he was assembling. Because of his orders, he couldn't risk using his own people. He was hiring mercenaries, even criminals, all of whom could be written off and who could not be traced back to Werner if captured or killed. Given their intended prey, he expected casualties to be high. Naturally none of his recruits were being told the whole truth, just that they were going to be sent after very dangerous targets. So far, there had been no trace of the supposed werewolves or of the people who had fought them. Someone with as much or even more influence as the Corporation had been very effectively covering their tracks. But the news article and Mr Werner's agreement gave him a definite lead and course of action at last. If he could kill or even capture this supposed rabid animal he might be able to trace its movements back to the others and ultimately to Viktor Tiranul. The Corporation was generous with its expense accounts for people like him, and he called for room service, ordering a good lunch and an expensive bottle of wine before making the calls that would assemble a strike team and their equipment. Truth be told, despite the video evidence and the reports, he still had trouble believing that he was really faced with howling at the moon werewolves. Something, or more likely someone very dangerous was definitely out there, someone capable of taking out an entire "Internal Audit" team and the security staff of the UK office, but the market was full of ex-special forces soldiers of all nations who could do things that would look miraculous to an ordinary security guard, even well trained ones.

***

"What on Earth is that?" Tara said, examining the rifle that John held out proudly like a new child.

Patting the futuristic looking weapon he said, "The automatic shotguns with silver shot worked well enough, but they lack range and are dangerous to use in a crowd. We can't afford to mow down some innocent bystanders, especially not with silver bullets. These are prototypes my labs have been working on. Electromagnetic propulsion, quiet, fast, and capable of using a variety of ammunition types from silver pellets suspended in silver nitride, silver impregnated slugs, to .50 calibre armour piercing ammunition and micro-grenades throwing silver shrapnel."

"Rail guns?" she said, raising an eyebrow. "You've been reading too much science fiction. No one has been able to get one of these to work."

He grinned. "And for the average soldier or policeman, they still don't." He held it out for her to take and smiled at her expression when she felt the weight.

"Much too heavy, about eight kilogrammes unloaded, for a man or woman to comfortably carry. The battery is new. Something we learned from the alien technology salvaged from the spaceship you discovered. Enough power in a single charge to fire thousands of rounds without recharge. Ten minute charging time, and exchangeable battery."

"But not too heavy for a vampire," she said, understanding.

"The mass still gets a bit of getting used to, but with intelligent sights that adjust to the ammunition type and because of the ultra-high velocity of the rounds, you get a nearly flat trajectory at all useful ranges. You could take down an attack helicopter or a charging werewolf with equal ease."

"It would be nasty if Viktor's people got hold of these. They're strong enough to use them too."

"But so far they seem to lack the intelligence and self-control in werewolf form to use complex equipment, even Viktor. But just in case, the handle has a DNA detector built in. Only you or I can use them."

"And the authorities?"

He shrugged. "Field tests of a prototype. I have all the permits."

Tara had always been a gun freak, much to her pacifist mother's disgust. She grinned. "Can we try them out on the range?"

John nodded. "We should have time while our gear and the helicopter is being prepped."

"But I still want my silver coated sword and dagger," Tara said.

His grin was feral. "Of course. How could any warrior go into battle without her blades."

***

An armoured and fully equipped SUV was waiting

for them at the airport. John drove, since oddly enough for a test pilot, Tara didn't like to drive. John's network of corporations had its own satellite and drone supported navigation system, so they didn't have to use GPS and thus had a reduced signature should the authorities or Werner via the US military and security agencies were watching out for activity in the area. It wasn't world wide, but it was more than adequate for the UK. The vehicle itself was registered to an industrial pharmaceutical chemical company's research division, giving it a reason to be moving around the area. Moulded compartments built into the vehicle allowed all their weapons to be discreetly concealed from view. Long logo covered jackets in corporate colours concealed their unusual clothing.

"What do we do if we run into a police or animal control unit?" Tara asked.

John shrugged. "I managed to wangle a permit from the Home Office to observe the proceedings, but weapons are out – except in emergencies."

"But..."

"I know. People might get killed. But we can't protect or save everybody. I'll try my best to warn them, but I fear they won't listen to advice from civilians especially when I can't mention werewolves."

Chapter Two

"Fresh out of the labs," John said proudly, waving his hand at the full body suit that Tara was wearing at his insistence. "It will stop an armour piercing round and still resist piercing and ripping beyond the maximum specifications presently in use. Note the flexible hardened plate over the abdomen. Overlapping layers of a new flexible ceramic, harder than steel and impregnated with a force distribution network that will reduce transmission of point impact force. It will stop a .50 calibre round from a Barret. Still not very useful for the troops because even though it stops the penetration, some of the impact and shock still gets through. Too much. But useful for people who happen to have special advantages."

"Such as me," Tara said, feeling the strange, almost skin-like texture of the silvery material of the suit. "Isn't it a bit gaudy?"

"Once you activate it with that control on the edge of the armour plate, it can be set to adjust surface reflectivity to match surrounding light levels. It can change and adapt to surrounding colours and patterns too. Not perfect camouflage, but better than anything on the market. Anyway, these corporate jackets only leave your trousers and boots showing."

Tara remembered the feeling of Viktor's claws ripping into her side and breaking her ribs and nodded with a shudder. "Any advantage would be welcome. We don't know how many of them we might be facing. And Viktor is smart and dangerous."

"I have the feeling it won't be Viktor or his followers we'll be facing this time, and I'm not sure if that's good or bad. They won't be as smart or logical, but they'll likely be more reckless and aggressive."

***

"Bloody heck, there are uniforms crawling all over the place!" Mario exclaimed, scanning the area with his tripod mounted spotting binoculars. He was on a hill half a kilometre away from the scene of action, so there was little chance of being spotted unless he was careless.

Lying prone behind his AS50 sniper rifle with the long tubular suppressor attached, the team's sniper Peter Walker tracked a uniformed female officer through his telescopic sights, imagining the effect of the .50 calibre round hitting the policewoman. They were both wearing ghillie suits, which rendered them nearly invisible from a distance so long as they didn't make any sudden movements. "I don't see anyone in a fur suit," he grumbled. "How long are we supposed to wait?"

Mario stared hard at his partner. "As long as we have to. The people who hired us don't fool around. You know that."

Peter sighed. "I know, I know, it just feels fucking stupid lying here waiting for … a target to turn up." They had been shown the photographs of what they were hunting, but no one had actually used the word "werewolf".

"We're being paid well either way, with a bonus if we actually kill something, so shut the fuck up and pay attention," Mario said. Actually he knew that his partner was an absolute professional and that his attention never wavered from the kill area, but he was feeling the oddness of the situation too and it was making him edgy. "Hello… there's another vehicle approaching, and it doesn't look official." He glanced at Peter. "Remember, if it's those mysterious others, they're secondary targets and only to be engaged if the primary target or targets appear and are taken down."

"Yes, yes, I know. You can stop nagging any time now," Peter said, his voice low and almost inhumanly toneless as he concentrated on what he was seeing through his telescopic sight and mentally compensating for temperature, wind direction and strength, and the height of the hill they were on.

***

The werewolf, who used to be Wilhelmina Brown, manager of a fast food restaurant, sniffed the air and growled softly in anger. It was hungry and she had totally embraced her werewolf nature, and would turn back into human form only when she was fully sated and fell asleep. It could smell and hear the men and women stumbling about clumsily around her, and it retained enough of its human mind to understand from their words that they were hunting her. She felt no fear or even alarm, only raw deadly desire for bloody flesh, and lots of it. The change had used up a lot of the human body's reserves and it had to be replaced. She had also caught to scent of other humans, two of them, but they were much further away and were less of a threat. But its mind noted the scent of their fear and aggression, which marked them as possible enemies – and prey. The alien medical nanites had boosted its senses and its strength far beyond even the formidable natural abilities of the alien species it had forced upon the human form in order to save its life, and the hybrid creature moved like brown and grey blur across the terrain as it tracked one of the humans.

***

Standing beside the parked SUV, John's head turned from side to side like a hunting predator. "There's at least one of them nearby. I can sense it."

Simply by willing it, her HUD, the Head Up Display that was originally part of the experimental flight control and integration system, appeared as an overlay in front of her field of vision. Without her conscious input or that of her father who had invented the system, the alien medical system had been steadily adapting and modifying it for its own purposes, allowing it increasingly greater ability to communicate and interact with its host. Unlike John, who possessed a full military suite of nanites just like hers but who had only learned to use them through trial and error both on his part and those of the intelligent alien nanites in his body without the benefit of a HUD, the werewolves who were within an as yet undefined range, appeared as a marker tagged initially as a yellow "civilian". If the system detected hostile intent the marker would change to a red "enemy" symbol. One yellow marker showed clearly on her HUD. She frowned when she saw another marker fade in and out right at the edge of the visual display. "I think you're right. There's another one out there, further away at four o'clock."

John was too experienced a warrior to simply turn his head to stare. Instead he willed his vision into a long distance focus like a hunting hawk and slowly scanned his surroundings, leaving the indicated direction nearly for last. The direction matched what he vaguely sensed himself, but had to suppress a frown at what he actually saw. He smiled and turned casually towards Tara. "There are people on the rise at four o'clock. They are wearing military sniper camouflage, one spotter and one shooter, but they're not wearing British standard issue and neither is their equipment."

Making sure her face was turned away from the hill, Tara said "They have to be Werner's people. We knew they would be back and that news article must have brought them here. Since neither of us have been shot even though we've been standing still in the open long enough, they must be after the werewolf."

The ancient enemies of Vlad Tepes would have recognised the smile that crossed his face. "It appears that the hunt may not go quite the way they expect."

Tara raised her eyebrows. "You think the other werewolf is going after them?"

"I'd bet gold on it. One is acting as decoy, as well as hunting the supposed wildlife experts and coppers, while the other goes for the kill."

"Should we try to warn them?" Tara asked.

"I wouldn't bother, but even if we could, our priority should be to try and protect the servants of the law here who have chosen to ignore my unofficially forwarded advice. You'll notice that no members of SCO19 or the military are present, just a few AFOs with shotguns."

"But you said no weapons," she protested.

"We'll just have to try to distract the werewolf's attention. Fortunately they can't sense our presence, although from experience they seem to recognise from my scent that I'm different somehow and more of a threat than a run-of-the-mill human."

"So we act as unarmed bait?" Tara said without enthusiasm, remembering the fear and pain of her last werewolf encounter.

John grinned. "I didn't get to live so long by being insanely self-sacrificing. We turn the SUV around and drive back down the road as if we were warned away by the police. Then we lay out our weapons in the back covered with a blanket, and return here on foot. If we manage to get the werewolf's attention, we lead it back to the car."

Tara's smiled happily. "And blow the bastard to bits – assuming we can get to the guns or swords before it catches us."

"If that happens, I'll hold it back while you get the guns. Just watch who you shoot."

Tara blinked innocently. "Why, anyone would think you didn't trust my aim."

John's laugh had an edge to it. "I've been

accidentally shot in the back more than once in my life by supposed allies – or so they claimed just before I ripped their throats out."

His expression made her shudder. It reminded her that the man she was with had killed countless men and women, and that was before he became a vampire. "I'll be very careful to hit what I aim at then."

Her ambiguous answer made him laugh even harder, with real amusement this time. "I'm sure you will." His eyes flicked sideways to indicate the snipers on the hill. "Watch out for the shooter. He might change his mind and go for one of us instead. With luck we'll spot the muzzle flash in time to dodge. If he's using a subsonic round, we might even hear the shot." One advantage of their vampire status was greatly accelerated reflexes and increased strength, suited to a creature that was originally a gliding predator and amplified by the military grade alien medical nanites.

"And hopefully dodge it," Tara added feelingly.

"Even if you or I don't, the suits will prevent penetration unless he goes for a head shot."

"Somehow that isn't very comforting," Tara said as they began to jog back towards the search scene. However, as they neared the search site again, she realised that the sniper position had been automatically marked and tagged as a threat and her senses were monitoring it without her conscious intervention, just like the anti-missile system of her fighter jet. The alien system was getting more intelligent and able to interpret her needs by the day.

***

The female werewolf sniffed the air and its ears twitched. Somehow it could sense the general location of its pack mate and that it was unhurt and in hunting mode. Its jaws opened in a carnivore's grin. It darted

25

from one hiding spot to another, deliberately showing itself for fleeting moments to keep the attention of the distant threat while it hunted the closer and much less dangerous prey that crashed through the shrubbery all around it. Soon it would feed. Despite its resemblance to a bipedal wolf, it was no mindless animal. It had all the intelligence and cunning of an adult human, but lacking any trace of conscience and driven only by the most basic of desires. It would kill and eat and reproduce, and to do so it would fight with everything it had to survive against all threats. Because of the imperfect integration of the medical nanite system, only the simplest of the human's memories and education were available to it. For instance, it recognised that the metal and plastic implements held by the men around him were weapons, and that the fact that they wore uniforms meant that they were a greater threat than a person in civilian dress, although it could not explain why. It's incredibly sensitive sense of smell detected the gunpowder in the shotguns as opposed to the chemical tranquillizer in the dart rifles carried by the animal wardens and it understood the difference in the threat they presented. In fact, the tranquillizer was no threat at all because the medical nanites would counter their effect almost instantly while the shot shells would still injure it, even though it would heal at an incredibly fast rate and could continue to function as a deadly killing machine even when severely wounded. The alien werewolf-like species had risen to the top of its planet's food chain in part by being extremely hard to stop or kill, as well as because of its intelligence and ability to work in social groupings the same way humans had. It sniffed again, and steel hard claws extruded from its fingertips. The human had drifted away from the others and was vulnerable. Unlike Earth wolves, it could climb quite well using its claws and it picked a suitable tree and sprang up onto a lower branch like a hunting leopard, a single bound lifting it high enough for its claws to grip the branch and to lift it up into the air, where it crouched, waiting for its approaching prey.

**

"Damn! I lost it again," Walters whispered. "Whatever it was, it appeared in the gap between the trees for just long enough for me to see it, and then it was gone. It was almost as if it was …." He took his eye from the telescopic sight and twisted his head around to look at his partner.

Mario's eyes narrowed, his lips a tight line. Smoothly, almost casually, he unsnapped the catch on his holster and drew his pistol even as he began to turn towards their rear. But it was far too late. "What the fuck..." His hands snapped up, lifting his gun into firing position even as his face twisted in shock and horror. His pistol roared, a double tap fired in quick succession, and he felt a fleeting satisfaction when he saw them hit the thing leaping towards him. He realised that the 9mm bullets had not affected the creature when it smashed into him. Claws raked the wrist of his gun hand and his pistol flew off into the distance along with several fingers. "Rifle! Use the rifle!" he screamed just before fang-filled jaws closed on his throat, silencing him.

Walters didn't question his spotter's instruction. Hugging the high powered sniper rifle to his chest like a lover, he rolled to the side and away from the attacker, came up on one knee and raised the stock to his shoulder. The target was much too close to require or use the telescopic sights, but he felt confident of the ability of the heavy calibre round of the rifle to stop whatever it was. His hands and arms were rock steady as he levelled the rifle and squeezed the trigger. The hammering recoil was almost a surprise, but he grinned when the impact of the .50 calibre round hit the fur covered creature's torso and sent it tumbling off of his partner. "Gotcha!" But his jaw dropped when the thing rolled onto all fours and sprang over Mario's blood soaked form, moving in a brown and grey blur low across the ground towards him. He was unable to lower the long barrel of the rifle in time and burning agony made him drop his weapon when the creature's claws raked across his lower abdomen, disembowelling him like some kind of shredding machine. Unable to scream, he watched in wide eyed terror as huge jaws closed over his face.

***

The animal warden frowned when he heard the shouts and gunshots in the distance. He had objected strongly when the armed policemen were assigned to accompany him and his team. Rabid animals or no, they were the experts, and they didn't need or want a police escort with shotguns who were more likely to shoot innocent cows and deer than anything else. Some poor farmer's dog had probably just been a victim of a trigger happy copper. He had managed to lose his own assigned police companion. The thing he was tracking had left unusual spoor, with resemblances to a large dog or wolf, but not quite. Perhaps some idiot had smuggled a hyena or something into the country as an exotic pet and then dumped it when it proved to be too aggressive to be kept around the house or farm. But whatever it was, he would tranquillise and safely restrain it for blood tests for diseases and then it would probably be have to be humanely put down. He stopped when the trail suddenly came to an abrupt halt and he glanced to either side, searching the ground for sign. It didn't occur to him to look up until he heard the rumbling, almost amused growl. He lifted his head to see the impossible sight of the wolf-like creature crouching upon its hind legs on the branch nearly ten feet above him. His last words were

"That's not possib...."

***

The blood curdling screams erased the annoyance from AFO Constable Smith's mind. It was obvious that something had gone very wrong and his training took over. He ran in the direction of the sound, shotgun loaded and held across his body as he pushed is way through the shrubbery and branches, ignoring the thorns that ripped at the skin of his hands. The bulky stab resistant vest suddenly felt very comforting. He had already radioed in a report and other constables should be converging upon his location at that very moment – assuming they could find him. He stepped into the clearing and came to a skidding halt. He raised his pump action shotgun to his shoulder even as he fought the possibly fatal urge to bend over and hurl up his last meal at the sight of what remained of the warden, who somehow was still screaming in unspeakable agony. But it was the blood splattered creature crouching on the screaming man's body that made him want to lose control of his bowels. His trigger finger jerked spasmodically, and he knew that he had failed to deliver a fatal or stopping shot even as the shotgun slammed against his shoulder. The creature seemed to grin mockingly at him as its hind legs flexed and thrust with impossible speed and power, throwing the hairy, gore covered body towards him even as he desperately pumped the fore grip of his shotgun for a second shot. Terror gripped him and he felt a liquid warmth run down his leg. An impact that folded his arms like they were straws crushed his shotgun against his chest, and claws pierced his supposedly stab resistant vest like it was paper and dug into unprotected flesh, making him shout in pain. Hot foetid breath bathed his face and he knew for certain that he was a dead man. Even as the jaws turned sideways to close around his throat, there was a strange vibration, a rumble so brief that it was almost imagined, followed by the whiplash crack of a supersonic projectile. The wolf-monster-thing was slammed sideways, the wet liquid coated fangs snapping shut so close to his throat that the hairs of its muzzle brushed his skin. The creature howled, an unmistakable sound of pain, and then its head shattered, literally exploding from the ultra-high velocity impact of round after round of silver impregnated slugs. Shards of flesh and bone and a spray of blood hit Constable Smith in the face and he staggered backwards, his face twisting in disgust. Training made him turn towards the direction that was the source of the strange gunfire, but all he saw were moving leaves and a flash of greyish silver. Remembering the more immediate threat, he spun back towards his monstrous attacker, only to be hit by another mind jolting shock. Instead of a fanged, clawed, fur covered monstrosity, the near headless body of a naked woman lay on the ground, her hands still outstretched as if to rip at something and he wondered if he was going mad.

***

Tara stepped back into the shrubbery, touched a button and her suit changed from silver grey to a mottled green and brown that closely matched her surroundings. Even with all the damage she had done to the werewolf's head with the ultra-velocity silver slugs, there was a chance she would eventually regenerate if her head was not completely severed from her body. But other officers were closing in and she had no intention of staying around to be questioned, especially while carrying a technically illegal firearm. Their plan to serve as bait had not worked out the way she had expected, and when she had seen the attack on the animal warden she had dashed back to the SUV for her rifle, returning just in time to save the policeman. John had gone after the other werewolf and now she headed off in his direction just in case he needed help. She had done all she could here.

***

Like Tara, John had armed himself and headed towards the hill, going around its base and ensuring that he was downwind of the werewolf's approximate position, giving himself every advantage. He had hunted too many of these deadly creatures to be careless or over-confident despite his modern weaponry and armour. Without Tara, he allowed his form to subtly twist and change, making him a blend of human and the alien bat-like species. This was an ability he had developed over the long years and one that he had not informed Tara or her father of as yet. From experience, most humans reacted badly to his hybrid form. With the change came greater speed and agility, as well as greatly enhanced senses. His torso lowered and bent, and he ran across the fields at a speed impossible for the fittest human. It was this change that had given rise to the legends of vampires changing into wolves when spotted by ignorant medieval peasants. He could smell the sharp copper tainted scent of fresh human blood and he knew he was too late to save the assassins even if he had been so inclined. As far as he was concerned, anyone who fought for Werner deserved to die. Allowing his enemies to live had rarely worked out well for him during his times as Voivode of Wallachia, even when that enemy had been his own brother, although he had been as merciful towards his subjects as any other ruler in those harsh and dark days. He had even accepted that the Turks of today were no longer the ravaging conquerors of his youth, although he still could not bring himself to like them. The memories of his childhood captivity and tortures at their hands were still as fresh in his memory as they had been two hundred years ago, and Dracula did not easily forgive such insults and abuse of his person and dignity. But right now, he had a true monster to deal with. He crept silently up the slope of the hill, all the while hearing with his superhuman senses the sound of fangs ripping at human flesh. He also heard the agonised moaning and heartbeat of a seriously, probably fatally injured human. One of the sniper team was still alive. He also detected the scent of werewolf blood. The sniper must have managed to hit the creature at least once with his heavy calibre weapon, drawing the werewolf's fury upon himself. This meant that it was probably the spotter who was groaning out his last moments of life. John had learned that unlike the vampire species, the werewolves naturally produced a paralytic toxin in their saliva, which helped them take down their prey. Unfortunately it also allowed viable specimens of the alien nanites to be injected into the prey before they were dead. This meant that each victim was a possible new werewolf if he or she was not totally ripped apart by the werewolf's attack. Like the unfortunate spotter whom he would have to deal with after he had disposed of the werewolf. The thought of defeat never even crossed his mind. Tara and the other werewolf had provided a convenient distraction, and he had no desire to draw the attention of the police and animal hunters again, so he drew his sword and slung his rifle across his back. In the past he had favoured the heavy hand-and-a-half bastard sword that had been the weapon that he had carried in the wars against the Turks, but lately he had been experimenting with a shorter, heavier blade more suited for close in work. It was patterned after the traditional Chinese Dao, a slightly curved single edged weapon with a heavy point, built for slashing but still possessing a point suitable for thrusting and stabbing. It also worked well to block such things as a werewolf's claws and fangs. An intricate silver pattern had been hammered into the surface of the fine steel, and most would assume it to be a decoration, a touch of ostentation suitable for a rich collector. But the werewolf species had a violent allergy to silver, and it interfered with the integration of the creature's cells with the medical nanites, at least for short but very painful periods. His body resumed its fully human form and he strode towards the top of the hill. "Ho! Monster. Come and face one who knows your kind!" he called, knowing the creature would hear him even though he hadn't shouted.

The werewolf lifted its gore soaked muzzle and snarled. Despite the direction of the wind, he caught the scent of this new challenger. He had never met a vampire, but its instincts flared in warning of another predator although it bore the shape of the easy prey that it had just taken down. It growled and heavy muscles rippled on its arms and shoulders as it rose onto its hind legs and turned to face this new threat. Its claws extended, like steel hard meat-hooks with serrated and sharp edged inner surfaces. It roared and charged forward, teeth bared and dripping toxic saliva.

John's lips curled and twisted as fangs extended from his upper jaw and his eyes took on a reddish tinge as he braced himself to meet the charging monster. Although it looked terrifying and had just ripped apart two trained Special Forces soldiers, he knew that it was one of Viktor's new spawn and had barely had time to learn about its new abilities and was acting on sheer instinct and traces of its human memory. His feet tested the firmness of the ground even as he prepared to meet the creature's attack. He stood still as a statue, the only movement being the tiny rippling of his hair as the wind blew into his face, capturing and analysing in those brief seconds the way his opponent moved, the hand and leg it favoured, and the length of its impossibly fast strides. It was only when the werewolf raised its paw to rake its claws across John's face and neck while the other drove forward towards his belly that he moved. Werewolves were fast, but vampires, especially the vampire the world knew as Dracula, was faster. Much faster, and centuries more experienced in combat. None of which meant he couldn't be hurt. John ducked and swivelled at the same time, his right foot moving back to brace his body as he raised his sword vertically in front of him, point down, his left hand supporting the unsharpened back of the blade. Instead of ripping open John's belly, the werewolf's left hand collided with the razor sharp edge of the sword, steel meeting hairy flesh at the wrist.

The very power that would have torn into John's flesh drove the silver plated and inlaid sword into and through the werewolf's flesh and bone, cleanly severing its paw from its arm. The monster howled in agony, the silver preventing it's almost instant healing ability from working as it should, and a bright fan of blood sprayed out into the air. The wound would still heal and the lost limb would regrow, but it would take hours, perhaps days instead of the minutes of an ordinary wound of that nature.

John grimaced when the werewolf's blood splattered across his torso, a fine crimson mist staining his hands and cheek. He allowed the force of the werewolf's blow to spin him around and his wrist twirled the sword blade around for a cut at the back of the werewolf's leg. If it had struck home, it would have severed its hamstring, crippling the creature and basically ending the fight. But the creature was faster and more agile than he expected and his blade only managed a cut across the back of its thigh before it had darted past him. He sprang upright, the silver patterned sabre in front of him even as the injured werewolf whirled around, the claws on its feet sending soil and grass flying as it fought its own momentum. This time John didn't wait to be attacked and darted forward, closing the distance between them even while the bleeding werewolf was recovering its balance. He dodged to the side when he was two paces away and slashed out at the creature with the silver coated blade as he ran past. He felt his sword bite into flesh, but the werewolf dropped and lashed out with a hind leg, catching him on the hip. The high-tech chain mail and body armour saved him from the claws, but the impact, as powerful as a glancing blow from a passing car, sent him tumbling through the air. He hit the ground and rolled smoothly to his feet, annoyed at himself. He had made one mistake, which was one too many in deadly combat, and he did not intend to make another. Ignoring the pain of the blow, he sprang into the air just in time to avoid the three legged charge of the enraged werewolf. His body twisted in mid-air with the power and grace that would have made an Olympic gymnast green with envy and landed on both feet, facing the direction from which he had come. This time his sabre did not miss, cleanly severing the creature's hamstring.

The wound would have healed in seconds if it had come from an ordinary steel weapon, but the silver of John's sabre crippled the monster. Even so, it tried to turn and use its jaws and fangs, but the edge of the heavy sabre caught it in mid-turn, and driven by the power of the vampire's superhuman strength, it severed the creature's head from its body, sending it rolling across the ground. A jet of blood shot into the air from severed veins and arteries, and then the creature's body toppled bonelessly to the ground, already changing back into its human form as it thudded against the bloodied earth.

John flicked the blood from his sabre and returned it to its sheath with a single fluid motion of his arm and wrist. He could hear the spotter's heart still beating and the sound of his laboured breathing so he strode quickly to the dying man's side.

"Th-thank you," the man whispered, blood

gurgling in his throat. He knew he was dying, but he was a warrior and had the satisfaction of seeing his killer join him in death. "We were supposed to kill you too," he said, repaying his avenger with the only thing he had left, which was the truth.

"I know. Were you sent by Werner?"

The man nodded, conserving his failing strength. "There are more of us." His breath rattled and his dying body convulsed. "Dan ... Jackson ... Werner's ... man ...." His eyes froze and the breath hissed from his lungs.

John made the sign of the cross over the man's body. He had been an enemy, but he had honour and had died well. Now there was one last service he could perform for him. He had survived long enough after being bitten for the medical nanites carried by the werewolf's toxin laden saliva to possibly be transferred to his body. If so, the man would rise again as a werewolf. John drew his sabre and the silver flashed bright in the sunlight as the blade came down in a glittering blur to sever the dead man's neck. He cleaned the blade on the man's bizarre looking camouflage suit. A sound made him whirl around, although he already knew who was coming up behind him.

Tara studied the carnage and deliberately looked away as John's fangs gradually retracted. The sight still disturbed her, although her own teeth did the same when she was angered or frightened – or hungry. "I should be sad that you were unable to save them, but I'm not. Is there something wrong with me?"

"They would have killed us without a second thought if they had the opportunity. Save your sympathy for those who deserve it like the innocents who are going to die under the fangs and claws of Viktor's creations."

Tara sighed. "I suppose you're right. There are going to be more of them, aren't there," she said, her words more a prediction than a question.

John nodded. "Viktor isn't going to give up, and

the ones he has already unleashed are going to create more spawn of their own. I fear we may be unable to stop this from turning into a plague."

"Werner seems determined to destroy them," Tara said hopefully.

John nodded at the two dead mercenaries. "He isn't telling them the whole truth." He picked up the sniper's rifle and extracted the magazine. "Ordinary bullets. They don't know about using silver either. They won't stand a chance. What they will do is alarm the authorities. Teams of mercenaries roaming the English countryside shooting at all and sundry won't go unnoticed forever."

"The press and news bloggers are going to catch wind of this soon," Tara said, nibbling her lower lip as she thought. "There could be a panic. Even more people are going to get killed just because they act strangely or have wrongly shaped eyebrows," she said, referring to the folklore that said that werewolves had eyebrows that met in the middle of their face.

John nodded. "The torch and pitchfork bearing crowds who hunted vampires and werewolves in the past were always more of a threat to their own neighbours than to us."

"Just like the witch hunters," Tara said grimly.

"We need to return home and rework our plans to account for an infestation, and I'll need to reach out to my government contacts to see how they are going to respond," John said, nodding towards the SUV.

"Should we do anything to hide this..." she waved at the carnage at their feet and the naked, headless man who had been a werewolf.

"Men with guns the police and other agencies can understand. Let them puzzle over that," John replied, nodding at the headless corpse. How did you do down there?"

Tara bit her lip. "I managed to save a policeman

and took down the werewolf, but I didn't have time to decapitate her. It was a woman."

John put his hand on her shoulder consolingly. "You did well. If we're lucky the nanites won't take."

"If they're lucky you mean. If it regenerates in the morgue, the staff will be slaughtered."

John ran his fingers through his hair. "We can't risk a battle in the middle of the city. There are too many security cameras for me to take out. They'll just have to take their chances. This thing will escalate soon enough. When it becomes public and there's enough pressure on the authorities I can volunteer a research team. If they accept my offer then we will have official approval to wander around in public wearing funny looking suits and even carry weapons."

Tara kicked at the grass in frustration. "I know you're right, but it just doesn't feel proper to stand back and do nothing when .... "

John's fingers tightened on her shoulder. "Remember, as far as everyone else is concerned, we are monsters too, not superheroes."

Tara sighed and nodded. "We better get out of here before they send someone up to investigate."

John studied the scene with narrowed eyes. "They're going to notice the extra footprints. Hopefully they'll assume we were more of Werner's mercenaries."

Chapter Three

"It's beautiful," Emily said, leaning gently against Rowland, deliberately letting her breast press against his upper arm. She enjoyed teasing him like that, especially since she knew he was too much of an old world gentleman to take advantage of her, not that she would have minded if he did. She truly liked the slightly unworldly scientist and engineer despite their age difference and she had always viewed sex as something to be enjoyed, much like a sport, although she was very selective of whom she slept with, despite her empty-headed demeanour. They were looking at the nearly finished second prototype of Rowland's revolutionary aircraft, the first of which had been destroyed when Viktor, Tara's co-pilot at the time, had attempted to hijack it. John had provided a new facility so that he could continue his work, although it was supposedly for the design and production of high powered airships, after Rowland had been forced to abandon his own facility by Werner's attacks.

Rowland put his arm around her waist and nodded. "That she is. And faster, more agile, and more powerful." Although most of the scraps of alien technology they had found in the crashed alien ship were far too advanced to even consider reverse engineering within any practical time frame, he had been able to adapt certain concepts in both electronics and materials simply by knowing they were possible, and these had been incorporated in the new prototype. He knew John's researchers were using those same discoveries, but he considered the ancient vampire turned industrialist a partner and perhaps even a friend. He was confident that unlike Werner, John would allow the world to quickly benefit from their discoveries rather than keeping them closely guarded, tied up with mountains of patents, and used mainly for military purposes. "And if Tara and

John's predictions are accurate, we're going to need something like it to keep up with what is about to hit the world. Viktor's selfish, narrow minded actions are going to bring disaster to this country, and I have no doubt Werner will unleash the same or worse in America and soon the rest of the world.

"Can't you warn someone? Surely not all scientists are corrupt." Then she thought of the staff at the Werner biotechnology facility that had recently been destroyed by werewolves unleashed by their experiments on the alien artefacts and her face turned gloomy. "On the other hand .... "

"I've tried, and I'll keep on doing so, but what can I say to convince them. That we have alien technology that turns people into werewolves and that my daughter is a vampire?"

Emily sighed. "I guess that might be a bit hard for anyone to swallow without proof."

Rowland laughed bitterly. "Well thanks to Viktor, they're certainly going to have proof of the existence of werewolves soon enough – although I'd wager my last penny that the government will try to suppress that knowledge until it becomes too blatant to deny."

"But ... but hundreds, perhaps thousands of people are going to die if they don't do something to control it," Emily protested.

Rowland nodded. "Perhaps that's exactly what Viktor wants. If everyone is too busy chasing monsters in the street, they'll be distracted from noticing a more organised, controlled group of werewolves forming right under their noses."

***

"If we can't predict who will be successfully converted, we'll just have to go with whatever we can get," Viktor said, as he watched their latest test subject change.

"That means an awful lot of feral ones running around the countryside," Jenny said doubtfully. "Won't that draw unwanted attention to us?"

"They're going to find out that werewolves are real no matter what. So if we can't hide, we'll lose ourselves in the crowd."

Jenny grinned. As a former prostitute, she had little love for society anyway. "Let 'em chase the wild ones, while we recruit the ones that can control themselves," she said, nodding her understanding.

Viktor stroked her hair and grinned. "I like your idea. The police won't care about a few drug dealers getting ripped off, not when they have the bigger problem of rampaging werewolves in the high street. Tara and her new friends won't be able to stand by idly either, which will keep them off of our backs too. The gangs and cartels may frighten the normals, but they won't stand a chance against our people. We can take over entire gang territories. We'll live like kings."

"And queens," Jenny added with a vicious smile. Like Emily she pressed herself against Viktor. Unlike Rowland, he had no scruples about using her body, nor was he a gentle lover. But her wounds and bruises healed quickly now, and it was a small price to pay to stay at the side of the strongest protector she had ever known. Even with her new powers, she was no match for his strength and ruthlessness, and she liked strong, ambitious men. To her, sex was a currency, and she was willing to spend as much of it as necessary to remain his favourite companion.

Viktor nodded his head slowly. "For a start. First we get money and somewhere to base ourselves. With large sums of money comes power – a lot of power. Then we'll see what else we can accomplish." He was strongly aware of Jenny's sexuality, and he was fully aware of why she clung to him. But she was skilled and willing in bed, and totally ruthless towards his enemies, so he was content to have her close to him and in his bed – for now.

**

A rap on the door made Dan look up from his notebook computer and the report he was preparing for Werner. "Come," he barked.

The appearance of the man who entered positively screamed "military", from the cropped hair and hard fit body to his rigid, square shouldered posture. It was obvious that he longed to salute, but instead he said, "Sir, we've lost contact with team Alpha."

Dan's eyes narrowed. "What do we know?"

"Their last report was that they were in position and had a possible sighting of the target. They also reported the presence of armed police. It's possible they were spotted and clashed with the police, but our police band scanners don't indicate it although there has been a reported police casualty and a dead unidentified naked woman. Police radios were supposedly encrypted, but the NSA had back doors and other methods of defeating the cryptography, all of which was available to Werner who supplied much of the equipment used by the NSA in the first place.

"That still doesn't explain the loss of contact with Alpha team. We need to know what happened to them."

"I'm on it, sir."

"You'd better be. In the meantime I'll try to find out what happened to the body of the woman. Orders are that all kills are to be destroyed or at least beheaded."

The mercenary lowered his gaze to his employer's face for just a second. "Do you really believe in ..."

Dan's knuckles rapped the table like a gavel. "What I believe in is obeying orders," he said, his words a challenge.

The mercenary stiffened, his gaze returning to the wall straight in front of him. "As do I, sir."

"Then get your ass back to work." Dan watched as the man spun on his heel and marched out of the room, silently closing the door behind him. He didn't care if the werewolves were real or men in fur suits. Mr Werner wanted them dead and out of the hands of the British or anyone else other than the Corporation, and he had worked for Werner long enough to know that his employer never did anything without a good and profitable reason. He had come to his position by giving his boss whatever he wanted, and he didn't intend to fail this time.

Chapter Four

Rowland peeled the electrical contacts from his daughter's forehead. "The ... whatever it is in you, doesn't seem to have affected your ability to link up with the aircraft control and feedback system. But I'm still worried that in mid-flight..."

Tara put her hand on her father's arm. "Don't be. The alien system understands what you're doing. It even changed some of its display elements on the HUD as you were testing it so that they didn't conflict with your configuration. John believes that the alien system is at least semi-intelligent, and I think he's right." She sprang off the wire festooned seat. "If I'm done playing lab rat, I have an appointment with John to work on my sword technique. I have some pretty impressive claws when I'm ... changed, but they don't compare to those of a werewolf."

Rowland hesitated and then said, "Tara, you know I like John, and I think I even trust him, but don't get too um, involved with him. You know he's ...."

"A monster? A mass killer? Perhaps. But he's saved our lives more than once and he's risking a lot to protect us. Besides, if he's a monster, then what am I?" She kissed her father on the cheek. "Don't worry father. I won't do anything silly like falling in love with him," she said lightly as she headed for the door.

Rowland sighed and shook his head.

"Don't worry. She's a big girl. She can take care of herself," Emily said.

"Ordinarily I'd agree. But John – Dracula – is the only person on Earth that is anything at all like her, and you have to admit, he's a charming devil."

Emily grinned. "That he is. He's also had centuries of experience in dealing with women. He's rich and he's handsome. He doesn't need to seduce Tara when he could have any woman in the world that he wanted."

"I hope you're right," Rowland said doubtfully.

***

The impact of John's stroke staggered her and Tara was forced to skip back to avoid his follow up stroke.

"Tilt your blade more, direct my blow away from you. Don't meet it head on. You may be strong but there will always be someone stronger. Fight smart. Now let's try that again." He was teaching her to use the customised version of the Dao for infighting, blocking and slashing at the same time, and keeping the blade swirling around the body like a web of steel and silver.

It was very different from Western sport fencing and Tara was having to learn a whole new set of moves and reflexes. Fortunately, one of the changes the alien nanites had made to her body was the ability to develop muscle memory literally in a single pass, so techniques that should have taken years to learn were being absorbed and perfected within days. The new style also meant being much closer to her instructor and she felt herself reacting to his scent, his power, his very aura, and she was beginning to wonder if she had been lying when she had told her father that she was able to resist becoming emotionally entangled with this strange, ancient, and deadly man – if he even was a man any longer. But she was changing too, perhaps faster than he had because of the implanted nanite control interface that her father had developed. So far she was the only one who had survived the implantation process, a fact she knew weighed heavily upon her father's conscience. The two other pilots had been volunteers and had known the risks. All prior tests had shown positive results, but for some reason when the pilots attempted the actual interface, they had both died some days after what had appeared to be successful link-ups with the aircraft systems. By that time Tara had also been treated with the nanite interface system. Her father had been panic stricken as they had waited for the fatal symptoms to appear in her, but to their amazement, nothing negative happened and the interface system had grown in her brain just as it was designed to do. The alien nanite AI was growing increasingly adept at using the interface both to work on her physiology and to communicate with her, the user. It was as if the system had learned English as well as the differences between her body and its intended recipient, a bat-like alien life form. Because it was a military version, it was seeking out ways to optimise and strengthen her body based on the abilities of the alien species it was designed for and the combat enhancements its creators had included. To an ordinary human, the two of them would have appeared to be whirling blurs of flesh and steel, their sabres touching, sliding, and rebounding so quickly that the sound was like that of the ringing of an old fashioned alarm bell, until at last John broke through her defences once more, the edge of his blade touching her throat and the claws of his other hand poised to drive up and under her ribs. She froze, their faces inches apart. She felt an involuntary thrill at his strength and maleness, as well as the sheer indomitable will that seemed to blaze from his eyes.

John's claws disappeared and his fingers brushed her bare, sweat slick belly before he stepped back, his sabre swirling into a safe position. He smiled, well aware of her reaction. "Don't let anything distract you during combat." His fingertips kissed her cheek. "Anything."

Tara started to deny her visceral attraction to him, but remembered that his senses were just as sharp and wide ranging as hers. She knew her arousal had to be as obvious as a glowing mist around her. Instead she smiled and nodded and used her new found control over her body to dampen those responses and return her mental focus to what she was doing. "I'll remember that."

He chuckled. "I'm sure you will." He approved of

her self-control as well as her intelligence, strength, and beauty. Then as if a switch had been thrown, his own warmth and attraction disappeared, and the cold deadliness of a master predator shone like black light from his eyes. "It could save your life one day."

Tara had to force herself not to step back, when every instinct told her to run. Just as suddenly, he was John again, the charming, urbane industrialist with a reputation with the ladies. Slightly shaken she said, "Do I look like that?"

"At times, when you're hungry and not paying attention," John replied.

She nodded. "I'll be more careful," she replied, understanding that his warning was two edged. To many she was now a monster, a thing to be hunted and destroyed. She needed to be constantly aware of those around her, and of how she appeared to others.

"Take a shower and get kitted up. We need to get to the morgue. We can't go in to protect the staff, but we can watch from outside and stop the werewolf if your head shots didn't do enough damage to prevent healing and regeneration and it gets out of the morgue." With the shots to the head with silver bullets, even the werewolf's incredible augmented healing would take close to a day to repair the damage, and John estimated that they should get there just before the earliest possible time that the werewolf would re-awaken.

Tara paused at the door to the showers. "Werner's people will be there too you know."

John smiled, allowing a trace of his fangs to show. "Perhaps we can take a prisoner this time and find out where the Werner group is laired."

***

The police forensics teams were unable to explain the extreme mutilations and bite marks on the corpse of the animal control officer, nor could they later identify the foreign DNA that they found on the corpse which was assumed to have been corrupted since it didn't match any known human or animal species. The testimony of the police officer who had been first on the scene was incoherent, which was put down to the shock of coming upon the mutilated officer and the unexplained naked corpse of a woman who appeared to had suffered fatal wounds from a heavy calibre weapon, but they were at a loss to explain why no one had heard the multiple shots. The police officer was sent for a medical check-up and trauma counselling, and the corpses to the local morgue for autopsy.

About two hundred metres across the street from the morgue was an old office building, and a lavish outlay of Werner's money through an anonymous intermediary had allowed Audit Team Beta to obtain the temporary use of an upper floor office with a clear view of the main entrance to the morgue. The sniper team, sans ghillie suits this time, set up with the rifle muzzle just behind the open window so that they would not be easily spotted by nosy passers-by. After they had discovered and cleared up the remains of Alpha team and the beheaded naked man, Beta team had been reinforced by two more mercenaries armed with FN P-90 PDW compact submachine guns to watch their backs. The team, who were not in any way traceable to Werner, were bored.

"This is stupid. We're supposed to watch the morgue in case the dead come back to life like zombies? Really?" one of the guards grumbled. "I could do with a beer."

"Shut your trap. We're being paid premium for this job, and if they want us to watch for the entire cast of Star Wars, that's what we'll do," said the other.

The spotter for the sniper team peered through his tripod mounted binoculars. "The medical examiner's staff are working overtime, so something must be going on in there. Go get some Indian take-away and stuff your face if that will keep you quiet. No one's going to find us here. At least not until we take a shot."

The guard let his compact weapon hang from its sling under his civilian overcoat and zipped it up. "Good idea. I can smell the curry from here and I could use a bite. I'll get some for everybody." He went to the front door of the office, peered through a gap to make sure there was no one around and slipped silently out into the hall. The old building had no security cameras and only an old watchman downstairs at this time of night, who had been well paid to turn a blind eye and warned of the consequences of a loose tongue, so he simply pressed the button for the lift rather than creeping down the stairs.

***

"There! That man that just came out of the building, the one with the red painted door. He's carrying a weapon under his coat," John said, pointing. He clung to the wall of the building with the claws of his other hand and those from his feet, which extended from specially designed slits in the toes of his boots. He and Tara were twenty metres above the ground, hidden by the shadows and the adaptive ability of their suits.

Tara followed his pointing finger and her eyes zoomed in on the distant building. "I see him." She chuckled. "I think he's going for curry."

John grunted softly. "That's where I would have chosen for a sniper nest too. Now we have a problem."

She nodded. "Do we take them out first and risk missing the werewolf or risk being shot if we go for the werewolf first. We could split up again, as we did at the other site."

"They'll be ready for an attack this time. One of us could pick them off one at a time, but it would be messy

49

and risky," John said doubtfully.

"So what's your preference, oh master of the night?"

John winced. "I never liked that one. I always faced my enemies in the daylight if I could." He looked around, and then up. "Two can play the sniper game. Think you can hit him from the roof of this place? Or you could go around the back of the morgue and get up on its roof. If something happens, take out the sniper and join me in chasing down the werewolf."

Tara squinted, her vision zooming in to the maximum as she stared at the open window. "There's a bit of an angle from here. On the other hand, all hell will break loose in the morgue if it does wake up. Greater risk of running into someone who will remember me. I'll do it from here." She didn't suggest that they exchange roles because she was under no illusion as to who was better at fighting a werewolf, or anyone else for that matter.

John nodded, knowing that she could see him even in the darkness. "You'll have no trouble finding me at this range. Be careful. A .50 cal bullet in the eye is hard to recover from, even for us. Don't let them see you. Stay back from the edge of the roof and don't let your outline show against the sky. Dark as it is, they'll be good and they'll likely spot you." With that it seemed as if he simply let go and fell. In reality he controlled his fall by briefly catching hold of every hand or foothold, slowing his fall just enough that he landed lightly on his feet at the end with only a slight flexing of his knees. The ability to move faster than anyone believed possible had saved his life more than once and he had worked hard to discover the limits of his abilities, or lack of them. Tara still had a lot to learn, but he would teach her – if they survived what appeared to be coming. Now that it appeared that Viktor was deliberately creating uncontrolled, feral spawn instead of putting them down when they demonstrated a lack of control, he was endangering everyone. There had been a few werewolves around as long as he had, but the ones that had survived had adapted, hiding amongst the ordinary humans just as he had. They even policed themselves when they could, hunting down and destroying those who would not or could not control themselves. He had even helped them on occasion. But if Viktor created them faster and over a wider area then anyone had done before, the public and the government were going to find out the truth, or part of it. Monsters were real. In the past, people had believed in monsters, vampires and werewolves, demons and dragons, and it looked like they were going to again very soon. He had hoped if he and Tara could find and stop Viktor and Werner from creating any more werewolves the situation could be controlled, but he feared that it was too late. Vlad Tepes was not a superhero. But he had always fought to protect those who believed in him and had looked to him for leadership – and he would do so now. But first, there was the current situation to deal with. He had hopes that the corpse would not rise again, but the medical nanites had already been active in its system. The silver had slowed but not stopped them from working, and autopsies did not begin by severing the head from the body. It would be soon. He picked a hiding place, out of view of the sniper and waited for the inevitable.

***

Viktor looked around Paddington Station and grinned widely. He and a few of his followers had just stepped off a train, and now they were in London. So far, his spawn had attacked people in the countryside, and the authorities had blamed it on some kind of animal attacks. But now he and Jenny were in London, while more of his pack were in Manchester and Birmingham.

He could hardly wait to see what would happen when his feral children struck in Oxford Street and Trafalgar Square. People with cameras were everywhere. They would not be able to deny the truth this time. Most of his feral children would undoubtedly be killed or captured. But it did not matter. The people of Britain would know that the age of the Werewolf had returned. There would be terror and panic, and with that, opportunities for him and his new family to grab power in the underworld. Wolves hunted best in the darkness, and in the cities, that meant the dark underbelly of thieves, murderers, drug dealers and organised crime. He would use the terror that his sacrificial creations instilled to take over. First London, and then the other cities, until he ruled them all from the shadows. There would be total confusion and no obvious enemy to hit back in revenge. Viktor wondered if the Prime Minister would even dare to stand up in Parliament and say the word "werewolf". He hugged Jenny and kissed her fiercely, ignoring the stares of the surrounding travellers and commuters. What better place to start out than from one of the main travel hubs of the city. It would be easy to find an unobserved corner and make his first kill. If he was restrained and did not do too much damage, the victim could rise again in less than an hour. Together with Jenny, they could easily create at least half a dozen spawn in a short time. Who knew, he might even find one who would possess the strength of mind and will to become a pack member instead of a mindless killer. This was going to be fun. He led Jenny across the Lawn, the great concourse of the station and wandered through the shops, cafés and restaurants. He bought two travel bags and filled them with an assortment of T-shirts, jackets, caps, and scarves. They would need a change of clothing after each kill. He wasn't worried about DNA because he had learned during his time with Werner Biotech's people that it no longer resembled that of Viktor Tiranul, and his blood when he was in his werewolf form did not resemble anything human. "Let's go hunting," he said, placing a "I Heart London" cap on her head and kissing her nose. Soon his children would be spreading out all over the city and the country from this starting place, spreading terror and death.

***

Tara peered through the electronic gun-sight which presented a high resolution image from a micro camera mounted on the barrel of the rifle. Because of the extreme high velocity of the bullet projected by the weapon it flew in an almost perfectly flat trajectory for most practical distances so there was no need for windage or drop compensation, although the electronics in the sight were capable of that too. The camera also recorded in a much wider light spectrum than normal humans could see and amplified it. Tara, like John, could see well into the ultraviolet and infra-red spectrum so she could see the target even in what would have been near total darkness. Her modified nervous system allowed her to hold the rifle completely steady, unaffected by her breathing or pulse. She stood about two metres back from the edge of the roof and her suit rendered her a sooty black. She was standing in front of the raised block of the access stairwell, which also helped to conceal her outline from the slightest trace of light in the night sky. She didn't require a bipod or support to hold the rifle perfectly steady, and she saw the other sniper in her sights with crystal clarity.

As she waited, Tara wondered what her mother would have thought of her now. Her deceased parent had been strongly pacifistic, and the possible military applications of Rowland's work had bothered her intensely, but she also loved and trusted her husband to do the right thing with whatever he built. Yet her daughter was now a blood sucking vampire, and preparing to kill a man in cold blood. She wondered if her mother's possible disapproval or the fact that she felt no qualms about what she was about to do disturbed her more. As a test pilot she had always had a tight control over her emotions, especially her fear, but she worried that the changes to her body had also made her mentally less human as well. Only John's centuries long survival and seeming normality prevented her from going mad with apprehension. Then a sudden tiny movement of the sniper's body, indicating that he was pressing the stock tight against his shoulder, as well as muffled sounds coming from far below her told her that something was happening.

***

The medical examiner was tired. There had been several suspicious deaths within the past few days and she had been hard pressed to keep up with the demands of the Police and the Crown Prosecutor's office for an official confirmation of unnatural death for each of them, and to know if there was anything she could do to aid in their investigations. She sighed as she washed down the operating table and prepared it for the female cadaver with the spectacular apparent bullet wounds. She had never seen damage like that before from any kind of firearm, not even a military rifle firing a .50 calibre round which she had seen images of at a convention. It seemed unlikely that anyone would be driving around the English countryside with an anti-aircraft cannon, and the police and animal control teams would certainly have noticed it being fired. It was this unusual and puzzling aspect of the cadaver that gave her a second wind and she actually felt eager to get to work on the remains of the poor woman. She changed her gloves and then turned towards the bank of huge steel drawers. However she had only taken two steps forward when she stopped, startled by the sound of pounding coming from the drawers. The thought of a body rising from the dead never even passed through her mind and she looked around in annoyance, expecting to see a repairman or clumsy cleaner. More muffled pounding and a strange clattering sound made her frown and move towards the drawers. "I swear if that stupid git has locked a cat in there ...." she muttered, referring to her assistant who had inconveniently gone for a toilet break. Suddenly there was a tremendous crash which rattled all of the very heavy metal roller mounted steel tables behind the polished steel doors and she stared in disbelief when there was another crash and a corner of one of the doors bent outwards. Even if that horribly mutilated woman had somehow awakened, no human had the strength to do that. Thoughts of zombies finally came to her mind, but her medical training refused to allow her to step back. "No. There's no such thing as..."

But then it was too late. The spring mounted lever handle exploded from the door and flew across the room to smash into a glass cabinet and the square steel door slammed open. A horrific roar issued from the cloth covered form on the slab and a dark hairy form shot out of the chilled storage space as if propelled by an explosion.

The medical examiner only had time to realise that the thing was not a reanimated corpse or a trapped cat before it slammed into her with irresistible force, knocking her backwards and onto the floor. She tried to scream, but powerful jaws crushed her larynx before she could gather her breath. Blood sprayed outwards from her throat, and a cold clinical part of her mind made a note. "The victim's internal carotid artery and jugular vein were severed by a creature of unknown orig...." Then everything went black and she was dead before her brain could even acknowledge the terrible pain.

The regenerated werewolf was famished due to the use of her body's reserves by the alien nanites to repair her injuries and she tore madly at the dead examiner's body, her jaws cutting through the spine and sending the head rolling across the formerly spotlessly clean floor. The remnants of the silver in her wounds still hurt like fire and she was in a foul mood.

Still tugging at his fly, the assistant medical examiner stepped through the automatic door. "I'm sorry. It took longer than..." Even though he was used to dead bodies, kicking his boss's head while seeing a hairy monster ripping at her body was sufficient to render him into a state of mindless panic. Uttering a shrill scream, he turned and ran.

The annoying noise stabbed at the werewolf's sensitive ears, aggravating her headache, and the man's running form triggered her hunting instincts. Tossing back a final chunk of the medical examiner's flesh, she rose up in pursuit. The automatic door was unable to respond quickly enough and she slammed into the tempered glass and aluminium, shattering it into diamond-like fragments and twisting the metal frame into a piece of modern art. A quick sniff of the air told her that her new prey had turned left and she sprinted on all fours in pursuit. She skidded around a corner, her claws cutting furrows in the polished vinyl floor, and her jaws opened in a grin when she spotted her prey who was swiping his access card through the reader with shaking hands.

There was a private security guard near the main entrance which was equipped with a security scanner gate. There were also a number of administrative staff who were also working late on the paperwork required to process the cadavers brought to this facility. The assistant medical examiner had begun screaming again, a mixture of warnings and pleas for help, and more and more of the staff as well as the guard were gathering in front of the entrance to the autopsy rooms. He shouted in relief when at last the door began to slide open, and he felt a warm wetness in his crotch and running down his leg when he heard the growling and clicking of claws growing close behind him. "Run! Get the fuck away! There's some kind of..." That was as far as he got before the werewolf landed on his back and shoulders, claws digging deep into his flesh.

For long frozen seconds the crowd of office workers and the lone security guard watched as what appeared to be a werewolf tore into its victim's back. Then when the werewolf realised it was not alone and lifted its head to snarl and roar, panic struck the crowd as if carried by the spray of blood and they turned to run. But there was a chest high barrier across the lobby, the only access being the narrow scanner gate and another locked security gate. Unfortunately for the guard, he was standing right in front of the only exit, torn between the desire to do something to help the still screaming man and the instinct for self-preservation. The terrified office workers converged on the opening, first pushing the guard backwards and then knocking him over and trampling him in their desire to be next through the gate.

Once again the sight of fleeing prey triggered the werewolf's instinct to attack. The wolf-like alien race hunted by catching and biting its prey, the toxin in its bite paralysing its victim, allowing it to go after more game and return to feast and feed the rest of the pack at leisure. That's what it did now, leaving the already bitten medical examiner on the floor, it crouched and sprang into the air to land upon the tangle of bodies jammed together at the security gate. With such an abundance of prey, it reverted to instinct and bit and slashed all around itself, knocking each new victim to the ground and biting it.

The logjam finally broke and the survivors ran screaming into the street, most driven half mad by terror, pursued closely by the blood soaked werewolf. The human flesh it had eaten had been rapidly metabolised with the aid of the alien nanites and used to complete the repairs to her body and to strengthen the hybrid creature, now a single blow from her arm broke a man's back and flung him against a parked car, denting the metal and shattering the glass of the windscreen and side window.

***

Tara saw the flash of the sniper's rifle muzzle and a fraction of a second later she heard the crack of the shot. Even from that distance she clearly saw the surprise on the sniper's face, mirrored by his spotter who said something to the gunman, who nodded and fired again and again, a steady chain of shots. The tiny earbud radio crackled and she heard John's voice. "The sniper is shooting through the crowd! He's killed two people already and the shots are just making the werewolf angrier. Take him out, Tara!"

She had already been taking aim as John spoke, and her finger squeezed the trigger when he said her name. There was no flash of exploding gunpowder, although the rifle kicked hard against her shoulder and there was a sharp crack as the projectile went hypersonic as it left the barrel. She was using non-silver ammunition, a needle slim tungsten penetrator wrapped in lead and wrapped again by a magnetised sabot that allowed the rail gun to accelerate the armour piercing round to incredible speed. The bullet was moving so fast that the sabot began to burn and the bullet itself glow like a tracer round, although it moved so fast that there was barely a flicker of light before it struck the sniper's forehead just above and to the side of the telescopic sight of his rifle. The energy and heat was so great that his skull exploded as if a bomb had gone off inside his head. The bullet fragmented into a cloud of lead powder and only the tungsten needle continued on to bury itself in the old red brick of the wall behind the sniper, leaving a tiny needle sharp point protruding from the other side. The hole was so small and clean that the Crime Scene Examiners, SOCOs, didn't spot it during the examinations.

Tara fired again even as the sniper's skull was shattering, and hit the spotter's binoculars, driving them back against the man's face with such force that the eye pieces drove into his eye sockets and smashed his face as if he had fallen from a building. This time the needle continued on to pierce the door and buried itself into the wall on the opposite side of the hall. She would have shot the two guards as well but they had dropped to the floor, and though she could see them via her infra-red vision she decided to ignore them and to change her magazine back to silver rounds. She slung her rifle and ran to the side of the building. She peeked over the edge and immediately spotted the werewolf. "The sniper and spotter are down," she said, knowing the microphone and bud radio would recognise her voice and transmit the message to John. "I'll try to catch up with the target by going across the rooftops as far as possible before going down to street level."

"On my way," John replied, darting down the opposite side of the street which was relatively unobstructed by shocked and terrified victims. The air was filled with screams, most from those injured by the werewolf, but also from the two who had been wounded by the sniper who had shot through them while firing at the creature.

***

"The sniper team is down sir. The other side must have had a counter sniper team covering the area," the mercenary said into the radio while brushing skull fragments from his jacket. "Must have been damned good to. We didn't see or hear a thing until both of them er, sort of exploded."

"Exploded? Were they using rocket grenades? No, couldn't have been or you to morons would be dead too. Where are you now?" Dan demanded, pounding his fist on his thigh. He didn't look forward to report another failure to Werner. He only maintained his position by failing less than anyone else and this wasn't going to help his record.

"On the way downstairs, sir. The sniper managed to get off five shots, but he didn't bring the… the er, target down, so we're going to finish the job close up."

"Some brains and initiative at last," Dan said, feeling a trace of hope. They might recover from this balls up yet. "Don't fail me. Take that thing out, or I'll have you taken out instead."

Although the identity of their client had not been revealed, both mercenaries had a good idea who was paying them and what would happen if they failed. "Yes sir. Leave it to us, sir. We won't let you down." The mercenaries and the sniper team had not even known each other's names. The sniper and his spotter were just Beta One and Two, he was Beta Three and the other gunner was Beta Four. Only code names were ever used over the radio and they couldn't be made to talk if they didn't know anything.

Beta Four had been listening and nodded towards the side door that would let them out of the building. He thought regretfully of the curry that he had never had the opportunity to eat. But he knew if they fucked up, eating would be the least of their concerns. He hid his P90 under his coat and examined his partner who had done the same. "You're good to go."

Beta Three nodded back. "You too. If we cut across the road there we should be able to catch up to the thing without being noticed. Then we can take cover behind those parked cars and open fire. The people in the street won't see anything except our muzzle flashes. When it's down, we move along the road and wait to see if the secondary targets turn up."

Beta Four slapped his concealed weapon. "I'd like a chance at the bastard to took out Beta One and Two." After checking that the street in front of them was momentarily empty, he stepped out into the open and strode briskly across the road. Even from this distance the night was filled with screaming, roaring, and the sickening sound of tearing cloth and flesh.

Lights were coming on in the windows all around them and Beta Three said, "Slow down. Keep it casual. Witnesses will notice two men hurrying towards the noise rather than away and so will the street cameras." Both had the hoods of their jackets up over their heads and were wearing wide brimmed caps underneath which would make them hard to identify in any surveillance videos that happened to catch them.

***

Tara leapt across to the next building, practically flying, ran to the parapet and glanced over and down to the street. "I can see it, and I can see you as well. The think has killed or injured at least seven people already. God knows how many of them are going to turn, and we can't go around chopping off heads in the middle the street especially not with police cars and ambulances approaching from all directions. I'll bet some of them are special anti-terrorist units too."

"Can you get a shot at it?" John asked.

She peered through her rifle sights. "No. It's moving too fast and there are still too many bystanders around to use automatic fire. I don't intend to gun down innocents like that Werner sniper – what the hell?" She saw the werewolf flinch and roar and even from the

61

distance she clearly heard the submachine gun fire. It didn't go down, but two people on either side of the creature cried out in pain and clutched at a wound, one falling to the street. "Bloody hell! It must be the remaining Werner gunmen. You're closer to them, so why don't you take care of them and I'll handle the werewolf," she said into her radio.

"Agreed. But be careful. This one is more experienced and appears to be pretty pissed off from being shot with silver bullets. You surprised her the first time, but she's already been shot now and she'll be ready this time."

"I will," Tara replied, slinging her rifle across her back. John had anticipated the need to remain anonymous even in public, and her suit included an expanding ski-mask like headpiece rolled into the collar. To make recognition even harder, it had thin moulded pieces of silicone rubber built in that changed the contours of her face, and black streaks on the face like a painted mask. It made her feel silly, as if she was on the way to a costume party. It would also reduce the amount of biological material such as loose hairs that she would leave behind. She ran across to the other side of the building and rapidly crawled down the side, her eyes scanning for security cameras and all her senses alert for the werewolf. She landed on the top of a concrete ledge above a side door, and when she was sure the coast was clear, she sprang onto the ground and ran down the alley towards the roaring of the infuriated werewolf.

***

John also pulled on his mask and then replaced the hood of his jacket so that he would not look like some overdressed bank robber if he bumped into anyone or was somehow caught by a mobile phone camera. The rifle was too long and hard hitting for his new targets, so he sprang up into a tree and left it there securely hanging by its strap from a branch. He would do this the old fashioned way. Immediately he felt his body beginning to change, preparing for combat. Razor sharp talons grew from his fingertips and his fangs extended past his lips. Muscle and sinew began to shift and change as he became the being the world knew as Dracula. He slid through the shadows like a ghost, silent and deadly, a perfect killing machine, a weapon honed by centuries of tempering, fighting in wars, against assassins, against monsters, werewolves, and even his own kind, vampires who refused to live in the shadows and openly killed and stole, and even occasionally raped. Tara and her father would be shocked to learn just how many vampires actually existed all around the world. Most had the wisdom to stay out of sight and to drink blood of animals or at least not to kill human prey and infect them. Unlike werewolves, vampires did not exude a poison from their fangs, and they had to feed a dying victim their own blood in order to create a new vampire. It never happened by accident. Those who would not control themselves he had taken upon himself to punish and discipline, and in some cases, kill. In some cities they even formed clans or families, aiding and supporting each other. But none were as strong and deadly as Dracula, just as he dominated his lands when he lived as Vlad Tepes. All who had opposed him had lived to regret it – or simply died. He sniffed the air. He could smell the two men, hear their breathing and heartbeats, and each movement that they made, the tang of oiled metal, and the odour of recently fired guns. Warriors defended their people. These two killed anyone for money. He did not feel the slightest trace of doubt or regret at what he was about to do. Only the bole of a tree separated him from one of the men, the one he had heard named as Beta Four by the other. He waited until the other, Beta Three pointed and raised his weapon, then he twisted his body around the tree and hooked his long clawed fingers around Beta Four's throat while his other hand clamped down upon the mercenary's wrist, crushing bone and preventing him from firing his weapon. Effortlessly, he lifted the big powerful man off of his feet and pulled him into the shadows and ripped his throat out.

But Beta Four's convulsive struggles had brushed a twig and the snapping sound made Beta Three spin around. He saw the movement of more than one body and he opened fire, uncaring of the fate of his companion, fearing a second werewolf.

Most of the bullets struck the already dying Beta Four. Unlike the werewolves, vampires did not almost instantly heal, but Dracula was blindingly fast and twisted out of the way of the bullets even before Beta Four's body had begun to fall. Only one bullet struck his side. Although the P90's ammunition was designed to penetrate body armour, his new body suit shrugged off the round, although it did not stop all of the energy of the high velocity bullet. Dracula hissed in pain but he was otherwise uninjured by the impact which would have cracked the rib of an ordinary person, but which only left a deep bruise which would fade in minutes.

Beta Three, horrified at the sight of his partner's bloody corpse dancing under the impact of his bullets, wildly sprayed the surrounding area at waist level, shouting incoherently.

But Dracula had dropped to the ground and changed further towards his bat form and scuttled rapidly along the ground until he was at the mercenary's side. His body reforming into a more human shape even as he rose, he sprang into the air, bounced off of a tree trunk and landed upon the panicked mercenary's shoulders. Both hands gripped the man's head with taloned fingers. He hissed "Who is the monster, you or me?"

Beta Three felt his head being pulled upwards

with irresistible force and for a second he felt unbearable agony as the flesh and tissues of his neck and spine began to tear.

Dracula leaped off of the man's shoulders before he could be sprayed with blood, still holding the mercenary's severed head in his grip. "For the murder of innocents, I sentence you to death," he said to the head before tossing it away. Now he needed to deal with the far greater danger of the werewolf. Tara was far more skilled and accustomed to her vampire powers than in her last encounter with the creatures, but enraged werewolves filled with the flesh and blood of freshly killed prey were unbelievably strong and resilient, and he had never been one to leave an ally to fight alone if he could help it. Dracula ran through the night like a pale shadow, moving with the speed and power that even Hollywood had never been able to accurately portray with all its CGI and camera tricks. The oldest living vampire was on the hunt.

***

The people behind the rampaging werewolf were running away from it, so Tara was forced to dodge and weave around witlessly terrified men and women as she neared the creature she needed to stop. She could see several security cameras within range, but unlike John, she had not yet developed the skill to disable them using her mind and the electronic capabilities of the medical nanites alone, so this time her actions were going to be recorded. Her camouflage unit was still on, so she was a shifting grey and brown shadow hard to see even by infra-red cameras. If she could quickly take the creature down without displaying too much of her inhuman powers, her actions could still be explained away as those of a particularly skilled martial artist or Special Forces soldier. Her mask would hide her fangs unless

65

she lifted it to above her mouth, superhero style, so hopefully there would be no talk of vampires. The last thing she needed was the government and vampire lovers and hunters stalking her – or John. But when she finally pushed through the last of the screaming, yelling, crowd stampeding towards her, the werewolf was nowhere in sight. She could sense that it was near, and its general direction, but although there were several bleeding bodies lying around, she didn't see any sign of it. She frowned and dropped into a fighting posture. The thing must have recognised her scent from their last encounter and gone into hiding. Then she thought … any sign of … she simultaneously looked up and sprang to the side, out onto the road. This abrupt movement saved her life. The werewolf, who had been perched on top of a shop sign jutting out perpendicular from the wall like a hairy gargoyle, leapt down and landed with a heavy thud on the spot where she had been standing. She sprang up into the air in a somersault, leaping over the creature's slashing claws. There was no time to unsling her rifle, so instead she reached for the handle of her short sword in mid-air and landed with the sword in her hand. She dropped and spun with blinding speed, the blade blurring into a horizontal silver disk like the blades of a helicopter.

The werewolf attempted to imitate Tara's jump, but because it was charging forward it didn't gain enough height fast enough to completely avoid her sword and it shrieked in enraged agony when the silver coated blade slashed across the front of its thighs. The wound wasn't deep, but the silver made it extremely painful and slow to heal.

Once more Tara darted to the side, aiming a cut at where it would land, but her sabre hissed through empty air when the werewolf landed on all fours, limbs splayed and bent like an impossible looking lizard. It scuttled towards her faster than any Earthly animal, but when she tried a vertical cut down at its head, she was caught by surprise when it reared up at the last moment and batted her blade aside with its claws and crashed into her, knocking her off of her feet with the creature on top of her. Slavering, poison coated jaws darted towards her throat and she instinctively threw up her left forearm. Its jaws closed around her arm and she shouted in pain. The sleeve of her jacket ripped but the suit beneath prevented the werewolf's fangs from penetrating her flesh. It was like having her arm caught in a vice and she clenched her fist to tense her muscles, fighting against the crushing pressure. Her flesh and bones were inhumanly tough, but the creature was much stronger and it might break her arm or even rip it from her shoulder if she gave it the time. Ignoring the agony of the bite, she twisted her head to avoid the claws aimed at her face and brought the pommel of her sabre, also silver coated, up and across like a sledge hammer, slamming it into the creature's temple with a bloody crunch.

Stunned and blinded with pain, the werewolf released Tara's arm and rolled off of her, shaking its head rapidly from side to side as if it could throw off the pain in its head as well.

Tara rolled backwards, her booted foot coming up to kick the werewolf under its jaws, slamming its mouth shut and somersaulting backwards and away from to creature before springing to her feet and charging forwards. If she was going to win this she had to go on the attack and not simply keep defending and responding to the werewolf's moves. Her sabre weaved a glittering figure eight pattern in front of her with the main cuts on the upstroke, the blade going in under the creature's arms and threatening its wrists, belly, and throat. As they came together she felt the silvered edge of her sabre bite again and again, not inflicting any deep fatal wounds but leaving a mass of painful bleeding cuts that threatened tendons and arteries, while forcing the werewolf to keep its muzzle raised and away from the threat, preventing it from using its fangs as a weapon.

The werewolf countered by scuttling sideways around her and towards her left, away from her blade. Each cut burned like fire and weakened it, blood flowing and soaking its fur into a matted red coat. Goaded beyond bearing, it threw itself forward, ignoring the punishing blade and reaching for her tormentor with fangs and claws.

Tara attempted to spring up and over the monster again, but her timing was just a fraction off, and the werewolf's claws caught her calf and ankle, the impact sending her tumbling to crash painfully back onto the tarmac of the road. The suit and gloves prevented her skin from being ripped off by the rough road surface, but she was momentarily stunned by the uncontrolled impact. She rolled onto her back and saw the werewolf rear up above her. She had clung on to her sabre, but before she could use it, the werewolf's clawed foot landed on her wrist, pinning it to the road. She began to pull it free, but she knew it wouldn't be in time to prevent the creature from plunging its jaws down and biting off her face. She raised her other hand in front of her, her own claws ready to meet the attack.

But suddenly the creature arched up and back, roaring in agony, and twisted its torso and head to look behind itself.

Tara's internal HUD indicated that John was standing in that direction but she couldn't see what he had done. However the distraction was sufficient for her to pull her arm and sabre free. She dug the claws of her left hand into the tarmac to brace herself and then hacked with all her strength at the werewolf's knee. Driven by her inhuman musculature, the blade cut cleanly through fur, flesh, and bone, severing the werewolf's left leg at the knee joint. Using the same grip on the road surface, she pulled herself from under the toppling werewolf and rolled smoothly to her feet. Her furry opponent had fallen onto its hands and remaining knee, and Tara now saw the handle of a dagger buried deep in the creature's back.

Seeing her hesitate, John shouted "Finish it now! Do it – before it has time to recover." Despite the silver of her blade, he could see that the blood had stopped spurting from the stump of its severed limb, although the pain and weakness from loss of blood still slowed the creature down. The werewolf's inherent allergy to silver interfered with its body's interaction with the medical nanites rendering it temporarily unable to block the effect of the pain and shock. He raised his rifle to his shoulder just in case. The steep angle would allow the bullet to pierce the werewolf and bury itself safely deep within the ground.

However, Tara's natural ability to recover from the unexpected that made her an excellent test pilot now allowed her to shake free of her shock and relief. Moving almost faster than the unaided human eye could see, she raised her sabre as she stepped forward and to the side, and then she brought it down with a powerful two handed stroke. The impact jarred her hands and arms, but the werewolf's head rolled away from its body, cleanly severed at the neck. She looked up at John.

He waved at her. "Come on, we have to go! The police will be here any moment and I don't want to have to hurt any of them or for them to get too good a look at us. I've disabled all the nearby video cameras so your fight will be mostly a blur or just a blank in the recording, so let's get moving."

Tara nodded, sheathed her sabre and recovered her rifle, which had come off her body some time during the fight. Its finish was scratched but it appeared to be functional. She broke into a trot and then a run when she reached John's side and they disappeared into the darkness, breaking their trail by climbing the occasional building and jumping from rooftop to rooftop, which would make it hard for tracker dogs to follow their scent.

When they got back inside the modified SUV, there was a flashing LED on the dashboard indicating an urgent incoming message. John switched on the OLED video display and Emily's face appeared.

Her face pale, Emily said, "You need to see this." Then her face disappeared to be replaced by a TV news broadcast. The newscaster's voice said, "There is pandemonium in Oxford Street with people running in all directions and into shops and other buildings as well as along the road. First reports indicate that it might be some kind of terrorist attack, but … but … well just look for yourselves," he said, apparently lost for words. The image changed to what was obviously a live transmission from a mobile camera team. There were bodies and blood everywhere, desecrating the famous shopping street, and in the middle of the fleeing crowd stood three werewolves, ripping at downed victims and eating their flesh. Worse still, there were people coming out from the shops who were unaware of what had been happening outside. And even worse, many of them assumed that it was some kind of stunt or the set for a horror film and stopped to take shots or videos with their cell phones. Then the werewolves noticed the fresh and surprisingly immobile prey and they began to run. "Oh fuck!" the news cameraman shouted just before a werewolf leapt, and then the screen was washed with blood and the speakers filled with gurgling screams of agony before it suddenly cut out to return to the news desk and the stunned looking newsreaders. One of them shook her head and said, "This … this can't be real. There has to be..." Then she winced and pressed her hand to her hidden earpiece. Her mouth closed with a click of teeth and the screen blanked and the broadcast was replaced by a "Technical Error" sign.

"Shit," Tara said slowly, looking down at the

blood on her hands and body.

"Bloody hell, Viktor's been busy, hasn't he? I was afraid of this," John said calmly, his tone deadly grim. "That changes everything. I'll bet every penny I have that there will be more attacks in London and in other cities. Too many for the authorities to cover up or deny. Viktor wants panic and fear."

"But why? Why this carnage? Why pick such a crowded location?" Tara said numbly.

John frowned and nodded his head. "It's a distraction. It's all a distraction so that no one will notice when he strikes his real targets."

"Which are?" Rowland asked, his voice coming clearly over the speakers.

"I don't know. But I wager we won't like it when we find out."

***

Dan Jackson's hand shook as he dialled Werner's secure number. Not even the NSA touched this one.

"Speak."

"Sir, it seems we have lost Beta team as well."

"All of them?" Werner's voice was icily calm, which all his employees knew was not a good sign.

"Our police contacts have informed us that a sniper team was found shot dead by what appears to be a very heavy calibre rifle or anti-aircraft cannon, but .... "

"I'm not in the mood to play 20 questions Jackson," Werner snapped.

"No sir. The forensics team found no trace of the bullets, sir."

Werner didn't waste his time making the obvious comments. "Have our own people examine the place when the police are gone. And they better find something."

"Yes sir. The guards were found dead near the

scene of the um, incident. The police are working on the theory that the creature killed them. They are still waiting for DNA results. The creature itself was nowhere to be found, but the body of a recently deceased woman, the same woman who had been found at the sight of the previous encounter, was found in the street, with one leg amputated at the knee, with the rest of the body badly cut up and it had been both stabbed and beheaded. Mortuary attendants are saying the head was in better condition than when it went into the morgue, but no one is willing to officially admit this, and the police have confiscated all of the medical examiner's photographs and videos.

"Hmm. It appears that our unknown opposition has struck again. Killing both the werewolf and at least two of our team. This news does not please me, Jackson. Not in the slightest. You were supposed to be competent, but all you've done is get your ass kicked either by mythical creatures or some organisation who seems more competent than you are."

"Yes sir. I..."

"Don't bother snivelling Jackson. Fortunately for you, it seems that keeping this affair out of the view of the Brits has become impossible."

"Sir?"

"For Jesus's sake, just turn on the news. There's nothing else but werewolves on the British news reports, although the wire agencies in the US of A and elsewhere are still being careful or openly scoffing, while the conspiracy people on the Net are blaming the CIA of course, or Monsanto." For a moment he sounded amused. "No one has thought to mention Werner so far."

"Then should I continue to eliminate these creatures?" Dan said, unwilling to use the word "werewolf".

"No. Not that you've been spectacularly successful so far. The Brits are going to throw everything they have at them. Let's see how much success they have and what we can learn from their efforts. In the meantime, direct your efforts to discovering the human agents who have been interfering with our operations. Once we know who they are, I can decide what to do about them. It's possible they are some kind of Brit Special Forces unit, and I don't want Werner to get into an undercover war with the SAS or MI5. But if they're just meddling civilians or mercenaries, well then we shall see."

"Yes sir. Understood. Observe only and search out the opposition."

"For now," Werner added. "And Jackson …. "

"Yes sir?"

"I don't give third chances. Screw up again and I'll have to consult HR about a replacement for you."

Dan felt his brow grow damp and he nodded, even though Werner couldn't see him. "I understand sir." As always, Werner cut off the line first, but even then Dan didn't swear or grumble. He wouldn't put it above his snake of a boss to have had another team bug his base of operations. Instead he pulled up his tablet computer and began to search through his list of contacts for a different kind of mercenary. He needed experts at finding people and digging out secrets, not killers. He fully intended to continue breathing for the foreseeable future, and to do that he had to find whoever had helped and was helping Tara Harker and her father, both of whom seemed to have dropped off the face of the Earth. But in a modern country like Britain, no one could stay hidden forever unless they had somehow been moved to another country. They would be found, he would find them, and he would take great pleasure in killing them all when Werner gave him the nod. He didn't even care if they were MI5. Everyone was mortal and could die.

Chapter Five

Back at John's research and development facility, Tara, John, Rowland and Emily gathered in a well-appointed lounge. There was one more person present, Karen Duncan, a mercenary soldier, formerly in the employ of Werner Biotechnologies until she discovered that her employers had sent her into a warehouse to hunt down real werewolves without telling her or her companions what they were facing. In the end, only she survived, and that only because of the intervention of John Seward. She knew he and Tara were something different, more than human. They said they were vampires, but she still wasn't sure how seriously to take them. But she had seen John rip trained men apart and kill seemingly invincible werewolves. But he had also been kind to her and had taken care of her when Viktor or one of his people had shot her. She knew Werner would never forgive her betrayal, but that didn't bother her. She had chosen a side and she would stick with it until the job was done. That characteristic had made her a top class mercenary. Nonetheless, she felt flattered that they had chosen to include her in their council of war, since she would have obeyed John's orders even if she had not known what was behind them.

"Can we stop them all? Should we even try?" Tara said, looking at the others. It felt important to her that she took into account the opinions of her father and the others and not just follow John's lead, which was all too tempting given their shared unique natures.

Duncan looked around. "Without an army, how could we? And the cops and whatnot aren't going to allow a private army to run around shooting up the cities anyway. From my experience the coppers aren't very grateful when someone tries to help them. Nor the Army, unless they're ordered to."

Emily nodded in agreement and then looked at

74

John to see how he would respond. She was an engineer and not a military person, while John had more experience than all the generals in the country put together. Besides, she thought he was hot.

John grinned at their expressions. "Would it surprise you to learn that I agree too? A warrior must learn to pick his battles. I didn't live this long by charging madly at every threat. Sometimes cunning is the answer, and sometimes even politics. I fear that before we can offer our help, we must let the authorities, the police and the army learn what they are really up against. Only when they've had their noses bloodied a few times will they even start to listen. And remember, the politician's favourite choice of action is to do nothing and hope the problem goes away, despite any brave words they might spout. Only when they are backed into a corner will they do something radical and risk looking foolish to the public. The best we can do is to try and covertly help out wherever the threat is most serious, even though we might be tempted to try to save everyone.

Rowland cleared his throat. "If we're going to take on the role of firemen, you're going to need a fire engine, so to speak."

"It's ready?" Tara asked in delight.

"It's ready to be tested. Carefully," Rowland said sternly.

Duncan looked at John. "What's ready?"

Rowland stood up briskly and grinned at Emily. "Why don't you let us show you?"

***

As they approached the assembly hangar, Rowland said, "I've been thinking about the name of the craft. DNIA Mark VI just didn't have that ring to it, especially not if it's going into limited service. Therefore

I took the liberty of choosing a new name. The second and very successful jet fighter ever built in Britain was the de Havilland Vampire."

Tara looked aghast. "Father, you can't be serious!"

Rowland ignored his daughter's indignation and pressed his security pass to the lock and placed his hand to the scanner plate. The huge hangar door rumbled and smoothly rolled up. When it was high enough to step through, he led the others in and swept his hand towards the centre of the hangar. "Behold. The Rowland Industries Vampire II."

Before Tara could protest further, Emily said, "We, Rowland and I, have been thinking about this a lot. If you are going to go out to fight these werewolves, and God knows I thoroughly approve having almost been eaten by one, sooner or later people are going to hear someone in the team mention vampires. So in order to forestall any inconvenient speculation, we thought, why not name the strike team Unit Vampire and the ship The Vampire. That should provide a plausible excuse for any inadvertent use of the word, and even fangs and other physical changes could be explained away as combat make-up adopted by some in tribute to the team's name. I've even had some prosthetic fangs made up for each of you based on your dental records. If confronted by a photograph or video, just produce the fangs from your pocket and grin."

John had been rubbing his chin thoughtfully as he had listened to Emily present her case, and to Tara's surprise, he laughed. "I like it. Hiding in plain sight is an old and respected tactic. Vampire it is."

Since John had financed the entire facility and the building of the new DNIA prototype, Tara decided he had every right to choose a name; and Emily's argument did make sense. She could even imagine waving the false fangs at an over-inquisitive investigator. She grinned and nodded. Then her test pilot's curiosity and love of flying machines drew her attention back to the brand new aircraft before her. She could see that numerous subtle changes had been made to the design, including a gleaming pearl-like finish to the dark grey skin. She walked up to the Vampire and touched it. It felt slick, like the surface of a non-stick frying pan, but it clearly wasn't Teflon or anything like it. There was also a faint swirling motion to the surface as if inky fluid flowed just beneath the surface. She felt her father move up beside her and looked at him with a raised eyebrow.

"Most of the materials and engineering technology from the alien wreck was simply beyond our current ability to understand. But we did manage to get a glimmer of comprehension of the surface coating on its hull and some of the materials used in its engines. It was designed to resist the intense heat and friction of re-entry from space, as well as hypersonic flight speeds in an atmosphere, and possibly the molecular friction of dust and other molecular particles in space. It is also immensely strong. I've tested forces equivalent to multiple strikes of a 20mm cannon on it and there wasn't a scratch. Plus, it has one other feature. He produced a remote control unit from his pocket and pressed a button.

Tara stepped back and gasped in admiration when the ship faded into near invisibility, the skin matching exactly its surroundings. "Adaptive camouflage. Nice!"

Emily stroked the aircraft lovingly. "That part was my idea. The surface is capable of not only changing colours but can actually emit light, similar to the OLED screens used in some cell phones and TVs. Cameras on the ship record a spherical image of its surroundings and then a computer system based upon the brain of a cuttlefish inverts the image and projects it on the surface of the ship. This way, the surface stays matched to its surroundings even as it moves, and will not show a darker outline even when viewed against the sky."

"It's not really invisible, but it is damned hard to

see," Rowland said proudly.

"Just like our new suits .... " Tara said and looked accusingly at John, who smiled innocently back.

"Emily and I had been discussing the concept and exchanging ideas and research. However the suit's system is much more basic."

"I can see that," Tara said softly, amazed at how perfectly the ship's surface matched the interior of the hanger even as she walked around it. Only the openings of the air intakes and jet engines when viewed head on were not disguised.

"It can even display other pictures and even text, so it can send messages and imitate the colours of commercial airlines and military markings," Rowland added proudly.

"But how well does it fly?" Tara asked, her pilots mind returning to what was really important.

"Why don't you find out," Rowland suggested.

"The media and authorities have been notified of my intention to develop prototype hypersonic aircraft to match those of the Americans, Russians and Chinese. Naturally, the government and military were enthusiastic, especially since it isn't costing them anything," John said. "And we're tracking the various national spy satellites. We have about a one hour window in approximately twenty minutes time," he added, glancing at his watch.

***

Tara sat in the cockpit of the Vampire, which had been reconfigured to show the colours and markings of John's cover corporation. A tug had pulled the aircraft out of the hangar and onto the parking pad next to the runway, not that the runway was really needed since the Vampire possessed VTOL (vertical take-off and landing) capability just like its destroyed predecessor. At the moment, she was more concerned with testing her mental interface with the new aircraft, and was pleased to discover that everything worked just as it should. In fact, she realised that her control was much more precise and realised that the alien nanite system was helping her filter and focus her thoughts so that far less irrelevant thoughts unrelated to flight or control of the various systems created mental static that the aircraft's AI flight systems had to filter out. "Vampire to Tower, all systems are green. Ready for take-off."

"Tower to Vampire. The pad and runway are clear. Radar shows no aircraft or birds in the immediate area. You are cleared for take-off."

Tara willed full flight integration, and suddenly she could feel the aircraft as if it was an extension of her body. She could feel the shape and angle of the wings, the pressure of the tyres on the tarmac, the thrumming power of the engines and all the flexible thrust venturi that allowed the change from horizontal to vertical flight and back again. "Lifting to hover in full VTOL mode," she said into the radio. In addition to all the instrument displays in her internal HUD, she could see John's position in the tower as an icon when she thought about it, though it faded into the background when she did not focus on it. With her hands resting on the control studded arm rests, she willed the aircraft to lift, just as she would her body to hop up into the air. The engines roared and the wings flexed to create the maximum ground lift effect, and with the slightest rocking motion, the Vampire lifted off of the ground to hover at three metres. The undercarriage folded away, and she commanded the ship to lift higher. She deliberately looked from side to side, then up and down, but the ship remained stable, unaffected by her loss of focus. Simply by willing it, the aircraft tilted from side to side, waggling its wings, then tilted, first nose up and then nose down. A wide grin split her face. "Yes! She had her marvellous and unique aircraft back, and this one was a generation better than the one Viktor had tried to steal from her. "Vampire to Tower, commencing test flight pattern Alfa One." The ship lifted even higher, and then transitioned smoothly into horizontal flight, the wings flexing into the optimum shape. The Vampire shot forward, pressing her deep into her seat as the acceleration built up until she was experiencing 6G of continuous acceleration force "eyeballs in", meaning from the chest towards the back. Military pilots experienced as much as 9G in a catapult take-off but that was for a very short period of time. Twenty-five seconds later, she had achieved hypersonic flight. It was apparent that her father had learned more than he had admitted from the alien ship. The efficiency of the engines was far greater than anything the previous model had been capable of, or any other existing aircraft, for that matter – even better than the American's super secret SR-72. She quickly slowed to mere supersonic speed to prevent the hypersonic capability from being spotted by satellites, and continued the test flight. She and John could easily withstand such acceleration and more, but if Duncan or any other passengers were aboard she would have to accelerate at a far more sedate pace. But this hypersonic dash capability meant the Vampire could outrun even anti-aircraft missiles as well as out-manoeuvre any fighter aircraft in the world because of both its engines' amazing thrust as well as the AI controlled flexible wings that shaped and adapted to every speed and movement.

***

"She's amazing!" Tara shouted from the cockpit as she pulled her helmet off. She had downloaded the specifications and manuals of the Vampire into the artificial storage build into her mind by her father's neural interface and expanded to a ridiculous capacity by the alien nanites, and she had been studying them on the flight back. The advanced pilot controlled rail guns had been improved by incorporating John's technology and could shoot cannon shells and missiles out of the sky as well as literally cut an aircraft or any land or sea vehicle in half with a single burst. Since they were turret mounted and individually controlled by the aircraft's AI systems she could successfully attack and destroy multiple enemies simultaneously. She discovered from the manuals that her father had been working with John on various hypersonic and drone style missiles as well, with semi-biological AI controllers akin to the intelligence of a mosquito, which could recognise a target from various imaging systems. The pilot only had to select a target and the missile would relentlessly hunt down its prey and because of its extreme speed, strike from directly above or below the target, in the air or on the ground before the target could take any form of evasive manoeuvres. Neither chaff nor flares would work to fool the missile since it was smart enough to tell the difference, and it would actively avoid anti-missile missiles. The prototype missiles were ready, but Rowland didn't want the military to even get a sniff of them since he considered them too deadly and destabilising, and for the time being the werewolf problem didn't seem to warrant the use of missiles unless Viktor somehow got his hands on an air force capable of taking on the UK and US air forces, which didn't seem likely. Her father was holding them back for the eventuality that Werner had managed to salvage and study more of the alien technology than they thought. A preliminary hypersonic missile sans advanced AI had been presented to the MOD and RAF by John's sales teams and would help to mislead everyone about their actual level of development.

Her father waved happily at her. "That was a marvellous first flight. Some minor bugs of course, and I

81

need to have another look at the engine heat levels, and..." He shook his head. "But I'm getting carried away." He took Tara's helmet from her and waited for her to climb down. "Did you have any problems with the control interface?"

Tara knew he was concerned about the possible interference by the alien nanite systems with his own. "Nothing. In fact the AN seemed to be actively cooperating. They had agreed to refer to the alien AI nano implants as "AN" both for convenience and security. "I suppose we shouldn't be surprised, since the intended owner was also a military pilot." The unspoken problem that hung in the air was the fact that they had yet to successfully implant the basic Harker designed nano-interface in anyone else other than Tara, and after Viktor's betrayal Rowland was hesitant to entrust it with any other pilot outside of their immediate group anyway.

"John can fly jets you know," Emily said.

Tara grimaced. "Why doesn't that surprise me?"

Rowland nodded and pointed at the flight simulator built to test the interface. "He's willing to try using the interface without my implant. I have no idea if anything at all will happen but it's worth a try."

She nodded and ran her fingers through her hair and said, "Anything new on the werewolf front?"

"More attacks, in most of the major cities in the UK, and even in Glasgow. None in Ireland or Eire so far." Emily said.

John walked up to join them, and with his enhanced hearing he had heard what they were discussing. "They lost the Oxford Street werewolves, you know. One minute they were there, but when the armed police and anti-terror units arrived and started shooting they vanished. Everybody is puzzled and the public are demanding explanations." Of course, he and the others knew what had happened. The werewolves had been hurt by the hail of police bullets and had sprang into cover where they had reverted to their human form, becoming just another shocked and terrified victim. The fact that some were naked was just credited to the fact that they had jumped out of store changing rooms in a blind panic. Worse still, there was an attack inside a tube train on the Piccadilly line. Dozens of people were killed or injured before the train driver stopped and the passengers abandoned the train, which meant the security cameras also lost sight of the werewolf in the darkness of the tunnels. People are refusing to use the Tube to go to work until the government can guarantee their safety or at least produce one dead werewolf."

"Eventually someone with a camera will witness a werewolf changing," Emily said.

"But will anyone believe it?" John replied. "In medieval times, people were all too ready to jump to a mystical or magical explanation, but now people are so jaded by CGI that they won't even believe video or photographic evidence. Which, I admit, has been of considerable advantage to me in the recent past."

"So what do we do?" Tara asked, frustrated by their helplessness.

John folded his arms. "We need to make them believe. After a few more incidents, they're going to realise that bullets won't stop the creatures. That's when I'll have one of my pharmaceutical companies step forward with an experimental tranquilliser drug that might work."

"The drug will include some kind of silver compound!" Emily exclaimed.

"But won't the werewolves recover after a short while?" Tara said, frowning.

"They will, but not before police or army personnel see the werewolf transform back into human form," John said.

Rowland was horrified. "But when they wake up in handcuffs or in a cell, won't they change back again and tear their captors apart? Normal prison cells won't hold them."

"Perhaps. But then the government and security organisations will have to admit that werewolves exist, even if they can't explain them. You know that without the original nanite applicators, the government and university laboratories aren't going to find anything in their blood to explain their condition, since the nanites self-destruct once outside a living host as a safety measure. That's when I can step in to offer more help. After all, my company would be the first to develop something that would even slow them down."

"That's pretty cold blooded and manipulative," Tara said.

"Do you have a better idea?" John asked levelly.

Tara imagined going into a police station with the true story and sighed. She would be carted off to a mental facility. And if she proved it by changing into vampire form in front of them or demonstrated her inhuman strength and agility, they would want to imprison and probably dissect her. The authorities would never allow a real live vampire to walk free. She shook her head, angry at her inability to think of something that would mean less innocent casualties. "No, no I don't. But..." She slammed her fist angrily against a table top and was startled when the plywood cracked and splintered. She looked shocked and mortified. She was also frightened. Was the difference between her and the werewolves really that narrow?

Rowland put his hand upon her shoulder and shook her gently. "With great power..."

She nodded. "Comes great responsibility. I know. I know. It's just that ... how do I know whether I'm..."

"That is the same feeling rulers of every era have felt and had to deal with. Suddenly you are on the throne, and a careless word or loss of temper could result in someone's death. How do you know? You don't. You just do your best, and it is history that will judge how well you did. Just remember that people will rarely know why you did something. They only see the results – and even then, rarely the larger picture."

Tara remembered that she was talking to the man most thought of as Vlad the Impaler, a man many historical records called a monster and prototype for the Dracula legend. If anyone knew about the subject, it was he. Yet she and the others gathered there today trusted him and had their lives saved by him more than once. Could it all be a sham, an artifice hiding the monster beneath? It was possible, but she didn't think so. And her father trusted him too. More than that, he trusted John with Tara's life, and that said a lot. Still staring at the shattered section of the table, she slowly nodded. "We can only do what we can do. John's right. We need the authorities, the politicians to be desperate enough to be willing to listen to us."

"I'm not saying we do nothing. We'll monitor the news and police radio transmissions, those that we can decode anyway, and if an incident threatens mass casualties or Werner's people turn up and start shooting up the place, we'll try to help. We'll need to respond really quickly if we're going to play catch up, so the best thing we can do right now is to make sure the Vampire is ready for the field." The police Airwave Tetra system was a commercial product, and like any such product, its encryption was capable of being defeated by various methods, including stealing information from the makers or even getting the security protocols from John's contacts in the government.

"I'll have some modifications made to our equipment," Emily said with a mischievous smile.

***

The Deputy Commissioner of the Metropolitan

Police leaned over his desk and glowered at his subordinate. "You're being fattened up as the sacrificial lamb as well as being given an important new position, you understand this?"

Sitting stiffly upright in his chair, Commander Colin Blair nodded his head briskly. "With even the BBC screaming "Werewolves!" the chances that whoever leads this operation is going to end up with egg on his face and an early retirement is extremely high. If we fail to stop them – whatever they are – I'll be the one who is thrown to the wolves. Even if we do stop them and the result is unpalatable – if they really turn out to be werewolves – same thing. The chances are exceedingly small that I'll come out of this looking good. I understand, Deputy Commissioner."

"But you're willing to take on the job anyway?"

Colin opened up the folder that rested upon his lap and placed it upside down on the table before him. A large and very clear photograph of what appeared to be a werewolf ripping the arm off of a young girl, taken by a horrified tourist, lay on top of a stack of numerous equally horrific images. "Something is tearing innocent people, men, women, and children apart in broad daylight all over Britain. The population is teetering on the edge of mass panic. Some coordinated effort to hunt down, understand, and stop these things has to be made. At the moment we don't even know if they are humans in costume, aliens, robots, something else entirely, nothing. We've managed to injure but not kill a single one, nor have any been captured. I don't care if it ends my career. We have to stop them."

"You understand that your reports are going to have to be strictly compartmentalised. One set, which goes up the official chain will make no mention of fantastical creatures or monsters. A second set, for the eyes of myself and the Cabinet only, will contain full details. If you have to take um, unorthodox measures, no

86

one wants to know until we are sure they work and we can explain them in a reasonable and scientific manner. If drowning them in holy water and beating them to death with a cross is the only solution, it will not be recorded or considered sanctioned. Do you understand?"

Colin smiled. "I haven't even taken the job yet and they're already sawing at the plank behind me."

The Deputy Commissioner sighed heavily. "I'll support you the best I can. The Executive Liaison Group (ELG) have already agreed that you shall have access to all the hardware and specialists, scientific, medical, military, that you need. If you call for a helicopter gunship you'll get it, but heaven help you if you don't produce results."

"Yes sir. Whatever it takes."

"And Blair … "

"Yes sir?"

"No word of plague or infection is to pass your lips. Let the conspiracy nuts rant on the Internet, and leave it to the Disease Control chaps to make that call. The deaths resulting from the panic would be worse than any number of attacks."

"I understand sir."

"In that case, here are your appointment letters and letters of authority. Don't make me look foolish." The Deputy Commissioner handed over a sealed envelope and rose to shake the Commander's hand. "Good luck to you."

Colin took his hand. "Good luck to all of us if this is real, sir."

Chapter Six

Viktor decided to commence his campaign to gain power in the criminal underworld, by proving his ability to kill and his willingness to do so as often as necessary, but without stirring up the serious and organised criminals. So he target the street gangs first. Although he was unfamiliar with the gangs of London, he had several followers who were, and the Internet was a fertile source of official information. Just like in every city in the world, the gangs had their home territories, so he could attack one gang at a time. He picked east London as his starting place. He didn't care about their names or their positions in the gangs. He and his followers would simply stroll through known gang territories after dark and waited to be accosted. He had been torn between looking like a gang member himself or a potential target. Since he was unfamiliar with their dress codes, he made himself and Jenny look like European tourists, complete with cameras and shopping bags.

Three aggressive looking youths finally approached them. "Allo mate. Lost then, are we?" their apparent leader said, blocking the pavement, hands on his hips.

Victor looked about helplessly. "Hello. Someone told us that there was a good place to eat down this way. Can you point us in the right direction? I'd be so grateful," he said, allowing a trace of Romanian accent to appear in his speech.

The gang member rubbed his chin in an exaggerated motion. "Lookin' for a restaurant are you. Hmm, no, nothing like that around here. He must have been having you on. You know where you are don't you?"

"I have a map somewhere, don't I Jenny?"

Jenny nodded earnestly, amused and eager for what was about to happen. Viktor had managed to get his transformation ability somewhat under control. He only had to get angry or excited and he was able to will a change. But she was still learning, and needed a real threat or a source of pain to trigger the transformation. She had a pin in her pocket that she could use, but instead she stepped forward. "We'd be so grateful for your help."

The gang member stared at her. "You're English. What are you doing with Eastern European trash like him?" he said, being deliberately offensive just to annoy her.

"How dare you! That was rude. Apologise at once," she cried indignantly, prodding his chest hard with a finger.

The gang leader heard his companions chuckle, and his face darkened. "This is our turf, and you don't go showing disrespect like that," he said angrily, and without warning he slapped her face back-handed, knocking Jenny back against Viktor. To his surprise the woman rubbed the bruise on her face and grinned. "Thanks. I needed that."

"Wot? Whaddya mean you needed..." He fell silent when he saw Jenny's body shudder and twist. For a moment he thought she was having a fit, then he stepped back in shock when her face started to change and fur to sprout all over her exposed skin. "Fuck me," he exclaimed and reached into his pocket and produced a folding knife which he flicked open with a practised motion. "You stay away from me. There's something wrong with you. Stay away or I'll..."

"Or you what, little man?" Jenny growled just before her jaws changed so much that she was unable to speak English any longer. She was wearing spandex and other stretchable materials, so her clothes didn't tear as she changed.

With everyone's attention focused upon Jenny's transformation Viktor stepped to the side out of their line of sight and triggered his own change. He revelled in his increased strength and speed and feeling of invulnerability, although as always the effort of changing left him extremely hungry and he felt saliva begin to drip from his jaws. His fang-filled grin widened when the leader of the gang began screaming. His companions considered going to his aid, but when Jenny ripped the young man's arm off and disembowelled him with a stroke of her claws, they turned to run. But Viktor was already in a position to block their flight, and his stomach growled.

Both youths produced knives, but they were shaking with fright. This was like nothing they had ever faced before. When they realised that Jenny was coming up behind them, they stood back to back, waving their blades and shouting their defiance in high pitched voices.

This was a massacre, not a fight, but that was what Viktor had intended. He wanted his followers to experience a string of easy kills and to gain confidence in working together as a pack. It was likely that no one would even report the killings until some passer-by or dustman found them. After his planned diversions, the police would have more important things to do than to investigate the deaths of some gang members. He gorged his fill of raw flesh and signalled to Jenny that it was time to leave. He still didn't think as clearly or at least not as Viktor even now, but he retained enough judgement to carry out an attack and flee without losing control and going on a rampage. He had to be sure that his pack members could all do that before they went after more dangerous and valuable game, especially the arms and drugs dealers and importers. That was where the money and power was. Prostitution and human trafficking was much less profitable and harder work, but he would get around to them after he was a person of importance in the underworld.

Jenny followed Viktor as they raced away from the scene of the kill, mostly operating on instinct. But her awareness and control was growing and she felt extraordinarily proud when Viktor praised and kissed her after they had changed back and were safely in their car.

They had brought several changes of clothes with them and packs of wet wipes. When they were clean and changed out of their blood soaked gear, Viktor headed for the next street he had selected for the night. As they drove away there was still no sound of sirens, even though the entire street must have heard the screams. But by the time they reached the third of the chosen streets, he heard sirens in the distance. It was time to finish up for the night.

Things went pretty much as in the previous two attacks, except this time one of the youths had a gun. When Viktor shoved him, his face twisted into a cocky, confident grin and he whipped out the pistol, which was tucked in his waistband behind his back as he had seen on telly. Holding the cheap automatic pistol sideways he shot Viktor in the middle of his chest and turned to slap hands with his cronies but stopped when he saw their faces. He turned back and his eyes widened in disbelief when he saw Viktor still standing in front of him, apparently unhurt. Since they were less than two metres apart, he knew that he couldn't have missed. In fact he had seen the bullet hit and go in. He started to raise the gun for a second shot, but froze when Viktor began to change.

"Remember, we need one alive," Viktor growled to Jenny before he completed changing. The shot had hurt, but he was confident of his body's ability to heal around the bullet, especially when he changed. The fur was still sprouting when his hand darted out and grasped the gang leader's wrist. His claws sank deep into flesh, grinding against bone, and he growled in amusement when the youth screamed in agony and dropped the pistol.

The poorly made pistol went off when it struck the ground and shot its owner in the lower leg. But the youth was too busy screaming about the hand Viktor had ripped off of his arm to respond to the bullet wound. A second swipe of his claws ripped the man's torso open from neck to groin. He saw Jenny dart forward to bring down a second gang member, so he focused on controlling his rage and hunger driven mind. The third youth tried to run, but Victor caught him by the back of the neck before he had taken two steps, lifted him off of the ground, and turned the choking youth around to face him. He put the terrified gang member back on his feet and slowly drew one claw down the boy's cheek, which sliced his flesh open like a razor. He willed the change back to human form, and when he could speak he said, "I'll let you live if you deliver a message for me."

"W-wot message? T-to who?" the youth stuttered, wetting himself in absolute terror.

Viktor looked around at their dreary surroundings. "To everybody. All your gang bruvs and any other gangs that will listen." He shook the youth like a rat and said, "Tell them all that my name is Viktor, and the streets, all the streets in all the turfs, are mine." He twisted the boy's head to look at his eviscerated leader. "Tell them this is what will happen to anyone who crosses me or tries to grass me out. The gangs can't protect you. The firms can't protect you. The police can't protect you. Obey or die. Got it?"

The youth tried to nod, but Viktor's grip even in human form was like a steel vice. "I got it. I got it. P-please don't hurt me no more."

Viktor snorted in disgust and tossed the crying youth on top of the remains of his leader. "Let's go."

Jenny pulled her jaws out of her victim's torn open belly and looked up. It required a second for Viktor's words to reach her human understanding, but then she reluctantly stood up and closed her eyes. With some mental effort, she triggered the change, and obediently followed Viktor away towards the car.

They sat quietly for a moment, quelling the urge to change again, and then Jenny said, "What now?"

Viktor pulled her towards him and fiercely kissed her blood stained lips. "Now we go home and celebrate our first step towards the top."

As a prostitute Jenny had hated it when men were rough with her, but now she revelled in Viktor's strength and power, and felt an urgent heat in her loins. She grinned. "Yes, let's celebrate. After all, you took me out to dinner."

Viktor found this hilarious and was roaring with laughter as they drove sedately away, passing the oncoming police cars and ambulances going in the opposite direction.

***

As Viktor had predicted, the police were too preoccupied dealing with random werewolf attacks against the law abiding public to care too much about some dead street toughs, no matter how gruesome the manner of their deaths, especially since everyone in the area claimed not to have seen or heard anything out of the ordinary.

However, the manner of their deaths caused the cases to be flagged, and eventually made their way to Commander Colin Blair's desk. He frowned as he studied the photographs of the victims and the interesting fact that the SOCO report noted the presence of blood traces from another victim, who had apparently escaped the attack.

The other people to take notice were all the street gangs of London. Someone called Victor had declared war upon them, and each gang began to prepare to meet the threat. Some by agreeing to stick close to their regular haunts and to avoid the streets for the time being, while others started searching for heavier weapons. With the right contacts and enough cash, automatic weapons were to be had even in London, and the bigger, tougher gangs geared up for the next encounter.

***

For the next two days, Viktor was contented to remain at home, often in bed with Jenny, while his followers continued to create feral werewolves all over the country.

"Do you think the gangs will listen to you?" Jenny asked, lying nude and glistening with sweat beside her lover.

"Some. But the others will try to fight back. So I'll give them time to plot and gather, and then we'll be able to see who the most stubborn ones are. And when we do..."

"We hunt?" Jenny said eagerly.

Viktor chuckled and kissed her bare shoulder. "Yes my dear. Then we hunt." He wanted the gangs thoroughly cowed before he moved on the serious criminal mobs. They wouldn't be such easy prey, and he couldn't afford to fail when he finally struck. After all, he didn't intent to wipe out every criminal in London. No indeed. He intended to rule them – and that was just the start.

Chapter Seven

It had been another week, a week filled with carnage and increasing panic amongst the public when it became clear the authorities were unable to explain the killings or the killers, let alone stop them, and Tara was getting both depressed and angry that they weren't apparently doing anything to help. She wanted to rush to every spot, guns blazing, but she knew that she was more likely to get into confrontations with the increasingly nervous policemen and women than to take down werewolves. More constables had been killed in the line of duty since the beginning of the werewolf attacks than in the past decade combined. Something on the TV news feed drew her attention and she reached for the remote control to turn up the volume. A multiple werewolf attack near Guildford and sightings suggested that they were headed for the Royal Surrey County Hospital. She jumped to her feet. Unlike most places, many of the occupants of the hospital would not be able to flee when the monsters arrived. The death toll would be horrendous if they actually entered the hospital. She turned and pointed at the TV when John strode briskly into the room.

"I received a news flash on my phone," John said, nodding at the images of dead and wounded and the flashing lights of emergency vehicles. "I think we need to respond to this one, despite the risks."

Tara slapped her fist into her palm. "At last. I'll get into my gear." With her modified body, she no longer required a high G flight suit, so she could wear her combat gear even when flying.

Duncan came running in. "I want to go too."

John shook his head. "We may need to run from the police and we won't be able to shoot back, so it's better if you sit this one out. Besides, I need you here to lead the security team and protect the facility.

95

Werewolves aren't the only threat we face, remember."

Duncan looked disappointed, but she knew how to take orders. Besides which she knew he was right. The hospital could turn into a three way battle, or two and a half, since they couldn't fight back against any police officers who confronted them. Plus she knew that the threat of Werner's people attacking them was very real. Her ex-employers were not the forgiving kind.

Rowland and Emily were waiting at the hangar when Tara entered, bristling with weapons. "The Vampire's fuelled and ready to fly. Most of the bugs and problems have been fixed, and what remains shouldn't be life threatening. Emily's even had some um, cosmetic changes."

Despite the urgency and seriousness of the situation, Tara was forced to giggle. The name "Vampire" had been painted onto the nose, along with a stylised mouth and vampire fangs.

John rolled his eyes, but grinned anyway. "It seems my attempts to popularise vampires as romantic and non-threatening seems to have backfired on me. Hoist on my own petard."

"That sounds naughty," Emily said, smiling suggestively.

"Apply that naughtiness to Rowland. Tara and I have other matters to attend to." He and Tara climbed up the ramp that lowered from the belly of the prototype, which lifted smoothly at the touch of a large button mounted on the inside of the fuselage. Tara clamped her weapons in the racks provided for them so that they wouldn't fly about dangerously when the aircraft was manoeuvring and took her place in the pilot's seat. There was a co-pilot's seat beside her and John strapped himself in there but without activating the interface headset that was part of the seat's headrest.

With a thought, Tara connected to the ship's flight and weapons systems, the flight version of her HUD appearing in the air in front of her. She waved at Rowland and the tug pulled the unique aircraft out of the hangar while she ran over the pre-flight checklist. When everything was green she said, "Vampire to tower. Ready for VTOL take off. She had activated the camouflage system before they left the hangar, and a vertical take-off would make it harder for satellites using visual tracking to spot the ship getting off the ground. The Vampire was built to be radar stealthy as well. In addition to the usual non-reflective shapes, the ships outer coating included a radio wave frequency converter invented by John's scientists. Rather than absorbing or scattering radar waves the coating slightly altered the frequency of the incoming signal when it bounced off again, making it indecipherable by the transmitting station. This function only worked when the skin of the ship was powered up in camouflage mode and could be activated or deactivated separately from the visual elements. Tara switched to horizontal flight and sent the Vampire rocketing into the sky, the wings changing shape as the speed steadily mounted. When the ship was within the cloud layer and hidden from casual observation, she turned the stealth function on, saying "Radar Avoidance Active". She could have done it silently, but it helped her focus her mind and informed John of what she was doing. Now that the ship was nearly invisible both to ordinary vision, and radar, she activated the pre plotted flight plan and headed for Surrey. "Collision avoidance LIDAR active," she said, activating the forward facing laser based detection system. Since they had not filed a flight plan and were not under air tower control, there was the risk of collision with commercial and military aircraft. The LIDAR didn't have the range and power of ordinary radar, but it would detect an oncoming aircraft in time to avoid it while not giving off a signal detectable from the ground. "Vampire to Base. We're on our way. I'll let you know when we're nearing the objective."

Rowland's voice replied, "Base to Vampire. Roger. Be careful. Out."

***

With attacks by the UP (unidentified perpetrators), which was the officially agreed upon term for whatever was attacking the populace growing, so far no pattern or motive had been identified. The victims appeared to be selected entirely at random, although it was possible that an incredibly ruthless killer or team of killers actually had specific targets, but were killing innocent bystanders at random to hide the real motive for their attacks. Nothing had been stolen, at least not by the UP, and no ultimatums or threats had been received, nor had anyone come forward to claim responsibility. It was maddening and frustrating. Commander Blair was aware of a fact that had not been mentioned by the news media so far, and which the Government was doing its best to encourage the media not to announce, was that the attacks seemed to be spreading in two ways. First there were attacks at random locations all over the country, and then fresh attacks seemed to spread outwards from the scene of each incident, as if the violence was somehow infectious. But so far the medical experts had found no sign of a bacteria or virus in the victims. To date none of the attackers had been killed or captured. Even more disturbing was that the secondary attacks seem to originate from the places where the victims were being treated or the bodies stored, again suggestive of some kind of contagion. But even in the facilities equipped with full Biological Hazard Containment Level 4 protocols, the secondary occurrences seemed to happen with equal frequency as those held at a small town morgue or hospital. He needed to set up an organised response, both to vector heavily armed teams to the sites of specifically these attacks within the shortest possible time, and to set up recording and observation of the attack victims, living and dead, this second at the request of the Public Health England liaison.

With everyone working close to twenty-four hours a day, it was not possible to call an organisation meeting of the senior officers from every region in the Greater London region, let alone all of England, so Commander Blair decided to make a tour of the sectors in and surrounding London first to present his plans and to gather feedback. He could have simply sent out letters and emails, but he wanted to be sure that each responsible officer actually bothered to read and understand all the plans and protocols he had worked out so far. It was sheer coincidence that he was in the Guildford area when news of the attack reached him. After a moment spent studying the rather confused reports, he spotted the same trend and threat that John and Tara had. The UP were headed directly towards the location of Royal Surrey County Hospital. A quick check told him that the hospital had over five hundred beds, fourteen operating theatres, and around three thousand staff, not taking into account the daily flow of visitors, emergency outpatients, and suppliers. It would be a disaster of unprecedented scale if the UP entered the hospital. He turned to the Sergeant who was serving as his aide. "Requisition a helicopter immediately and notify the locals. I need to set up a mobile headquarters in the hospital and bring in a full AFO team. Notify the military liaison as well to stand by in case we need more men and firepower. We have to stop this attack."

***

Pat and Mike were council employees and had been engaged in trimming the trees and hedges along Egerton Road when they were attacked by one of

Viktor's pack. The werewolf bit both in the throat, but did not rip out the flesh, leaving the two men to bleed to death. The venom in the werewolf's fangs and saliva injected a huge dose of active medical nanites directly into their bloodstreams and they immediately detected the critical condition of their assumed patients. Attempts by the alien nanites to communicate with their new hosts failed, triggering emergency protocols. Despite the fact that the hosts were the wrong species, they were close enough in biology for the nanites to work, and they proceeded to take emergency action to save their lives. Unfortunately, without the ability to communicate with their host or a built in body template, the nanites were forced to revert to their default template. So instead of simply healing the fatal wounds, they proceeded to implant the entire biology of the werewolf-like species so that they could correct any damage. If the hosts had been members of the advanced alien cultures that created the nanites, their brain implants would have retained the memories and knowledge of their original species, and if too much time did not pass, the conversion could be reversed in a medical facility. But in the case of these human hosts, only a small percentage of victims of werewolf attack possessed the will and genetic disposition to allow them to gain some degree of control over their dual forms, as in the case of Viktor. The rest became essentially two beings in one. A human with little or no memory of what had happened, and a werewolf with the mind of an infant which reverted to base instincts when faced with threats or hunger. A little over an hour after the initial attack, two new, confused, and hungry werewolves stood in the trees beside Egerton Road.

Werewolf Pat sniffed the air, and his sensitive sense of smell detected the scent of blood and injury, which to his undeveloped mind, meant food. He growled to the other werewolf at his side. The original werewolf species was extremely social and their culture was based on a pack structure resembling a commune. With no other werewolves in sight, he immediately bonded with his fellow werewolf, and he pointed in the direction of the food smell.

The other werewolf, who used to be the human known as Mike, also felt the bonding, and followed the other's arm. He sniffed and also detected the blood and weakness. He growled and looked at his new pack mate, his body language and growls indicating agreement. When Werewolf Pat began to lope away, he followed, running past the road sign bearing an arrow and the words "Royal Surrey County Hospital" which of course it could not read.

As the agreed pack leader, Werewolf Pat led the way down the road. On the way they passed screaming humans, but he ignored them, drawn by the strong scent of a large gathering of prey and of fresh blood. He was starving, and he intended to feast. He was fearless, since on the werewolf's home world it was the apex predator, and the only other creatures that could resist or hurt them were herbivores, huge lumbering armoured behemoths, and a few tiny, highly aggressive hive creatures. Its ability to heal extremely quickly made them hard to kill, and with the medical nanites, they became almost unkillable unless they were literally torn to small pieces or beheaded. He was the perfect killer, and it was time to hunt.

***

The helicopter had dropped Commander Blair at the field just across the road from the hospital, and he had quickly met with the hospital's management and commenced to set up a field command post. Reports from civilians and police cars indicated that the original werewolf had torn a trail of carnage around the Egerton

101

Road area in the direction of the roundabout linking to Southway and then had mysteriously vanished. But two more UPs were reported to still be headed for the hospital. After the first attack, everyone who had heard about it had fled, and the area leading up the road to the hospital was largely empty. He was torn between the desire to evacuate as many people as possible, and the possibility of them being attacked en-route by more of the creatures. Most of the staff refused to abandon their patients, and many of the non-essential staff and mobile ill were too terrified to leave the safety of the building. In the end, he decided that his best option was to lock up and fortify the hospital's entrances as best he could and to defend it with the team of ten HK MP5 submachine gun armed police constables, with reinforcements from the local CO19 on the way.

***

The pair of werewolves arrived at the hospital after passing through a Tesco car park and crossing the circus into a stand of trees at the corner of the hospital complex. There was a service and delivery entrance just down the road, but it had been locked. But just meters away was a large square cornered spiral fire escape staircase leading up the side of the building and to the roof. The defenders of the hospital had made the mistake of assuming that the creatures were simply large animals. But Werewolf Pat had a limited access to Pat's memories if not his reasoning, and understood the significance of windows. With a soft hunting grunt, it led its companion in that direction. The smell of blood as much stronger now, and he was driven into a killing rage by his hunger. It also scented oiled metal and other smells which told it that there was danger behind the curtained windows of the ground floor. Instead he dashed along the wall on all fours below the level of the window sills and straight to the fire escape. Followed by its pack mate, it sprinted up the stairs, ignoring the locked door on the first landing and on up to the uppermost level, and from there onto the roof. It could hear cries of alarm through the concrete as it dashed across to a ventilation duct. Rather than trying to crawl into the opening, it dug its claws into the tarnished aluminium, crumpling the thin metal, and with a growl and flexing of its knees it ripped the entire structure out of the roof and tossed it aside. The inside section, deprived of bracing and support, fell down leaving a gaping hole in the roof. The werewolf that had been Pat roared with excitement and leapt head first into the hole, closely followed by his pack mate. The room was an engineering space and empty of people, but there was only one door, and the scent of prey coming through it was strong.

***

The sound of the ventilation duct being ripped from its concrete mountings rumbled and groaned alarmingly through the entire building, carried by the insulated shafts like some kind of bizarre musical instrument. Commander Blair sprang to his feet, sending a building plan floating to the floor. "What in blazes was that?" His Airwave radio crackled and he snatched it up, his heart sinking. "This is Blair, over."

Crackling and hissing because of the interference from the solid walls for the building and the numerous pieces of powerful electrical equipment surrounding them, the urgency in the Sergeant's voice was unmistakable. "Commander, a nurse claims to have seen two fast moving figures through a window. From her description they were the UPs. She says they were on the fire escape and headed towards the roof."

The sound of tearing metal made sense now and

Blair fought down a sense of chagrin over the fact that he had been outwitted by the creatures. All the APOs were patrolling the ground floor, in anticipation of an attempt to break in there. "Sergeant, get five APO headed for the uppermost floor immediately. Remind them that they are in a hospital and not to open fire unless they are certain it is safe to do so." The last thing he needed was for one of the armed officers to indiscriminately fire into a ward full of sick people. "Assume that there are intruders and that they are extremely dangerous. They are to stay together and to perform a sweep of the floor. If possible employ Tasers. If they are men in costumes, we need to question them."

"Understood sir. Five APO upstairs, Tasers if possible." There was a pause. "They're on their way sir via the stairs." Blair had ordered that the lifts be shut down in the event that the UPs entered the building so that the stairs could be used as choke points to control access to each floor.

Since it had proved impractical to evacuate the hospital safely, Blair had decided not to make a public announcement to the patients and other members of the public. Only selected senior staff and the hospital security officers had been briefed on the actual situation, while the rest were just told of an unspecified threat. Putting on his cap, he went to join the Sergeant in the main lobby of the hospital.

The Sergeant took him aside. "It's not good sir. The wing penetrated by the UPs contains the Intensive Care ward and Accident and Emergency. There'll be loads of completely immobile and very sick or injured patients."

Commander Blair nodded grimly. "Have the remaining APOs secure all the connecting exits and entrances leading from that wing to the central block. Since the central block has only one level, we can at least try to keep them bottled up in that wing if they get past our men."

The Sergeant, whose name was Murphy, pointed to the five APO. "This lot are designated Team Bravo, and the unit headed for the upper floor Team Alpha."

Both Blair and the Sergeant, just like the rest of the men were armed with HK MP7A1 PDW, a small submachine gun with ammunition designed to penetrate body armour. "We'll act as mobile reinforcements in case of need," he said.

"Should we unlock the main doors, sir? Sergeant Murphy asked.

Blair considered the question and shook his head. "While we've only seen two of them, there may be more outside. With the doors locked we have a chance to contain them inside the building."

"Yes sir," Sergeant Murphy said uneasily.

"You disagree Sergeant?"

Sergeant Murphy, who had been a soldier before joining the Police, said "We have no line of retreat, sir."

Commander Blair raised an eyebrow. "We're facing either some kind of infected animal or men in funny suits Sergeant, not an armed military force. We need to control the site, not make plans to run away."

"As you say, sir," Sergeant Murphy said stiffly and checked that his weapon had a round chambered and was ready to fire and pushed the selector from safe to semi-automatic fire, relying upon the trigger safety to prevent an accidental discharge.

Although what the Sergeant had done was against safety regulations, Blair remembered the photographs of all the horrifically torn up victims and did the same.

**

The Alpha team members were designated Alpha One to Five and they made their way single file up the staircase, their weapons covering all directions as they moved. SO15 were trained to combat terrorism, so they watched out for signs of IED and other kinds of booby traps and moved from cover to cover in the assumption that the enemy had firearms, even though all casualties so far seemed to have been inflicted by knives or some other kind of edged weapons. The rumour mill and news said that they were hunting monsters, even werewolves, and even though they still didn't quite believe it, they were all on edge as they neared the uppermost fire exit. Then they heard the screams, the kind that made hairs stand up on end. Alpha One silently pushed on the door and peered through the gap, but saw nothing but brightly painted walls. Another horrific scream rang through the corridor and the armed officer burst through the doorway, weapon raised to his shoulder, followed closely by the rest of the team and he advanced quickly down the corridor.

Moments later a hysterical, blood soaked nurse came running towards them and when she saw their uniforms pointed back the way she had come. "They're back there. Oh God, they're killing everybody. You've got to help..."

"Please calm down miss. Who is killing people, and how many of them are there?"

The nurse began to tremble violently in shock. "T-two. There are two of them. Things, horrible hairy things ...."

"Do they have weapons?" Alpha One asked urgently.

"N-no. They just ..." She shook her head violently, pushed past the Police officer and ran down the hall.

Alpha One signalled the team to advance and they moved rapidly in the direction the nurse had indicated. Moments later there was a crashing that sounded like furniture being thrown about, and a thunderous roaring. He touched his radio and said, "UPs located. No sign of firearms, but sounds of extreme violence. We are making approach now." The sounds were unmistakably coming from the next set of swing doors, which from the sign on the wall led to a ward. He pressed his shoulder against the door, took a deep breath, and then shouting "Armed police!" he burst through the portal, the muzzle of his short weapon moving rapidly from side to side in search of a target. He continued to advance in order to allow his team to follow him through the door. He jumped when an entire hospital bed suddenly flew from one side of the ward to the other, hitting the wall like a wrecking ball. He crouched, and despite his orders his finger tightened on the trigger when two nightmare figures sprang into view. He shouted wordlessly in shock and fired. His face paled when the creature didn't even stagger from the bullet that struck it right in the middle of the chest. Fighting a rising tide of terror, he flicked the selector to full automatic and started to fire three round bursts into the werewolves who were stalking towards them, jaws wide as if in laughter. He heard and felt the explosion of gunfire behind him when the rest of Alpha team opened fire as one. And still the things kept coming. He wanted to run, but he was afraid of turning his back on the blood covered creatures. The bolt locked back on an empty magazine and his hand slapped at his belt for a reload, knowing that he would never complete the action. A huge, clawed paw reached for him and he began to scream.

***

"Alpha One, what's happening? Alpha team, report!" Sergeant Murphy shouted into his radio. They had heard the gunfire and both he and the Commander had grunted in shock when the gunfire changed to full automatic. The team was inside an occupied hospital ward and they were spraying armour piercing bullets like water. Had the entire team gone mad? Both of them jumped when someone screamed into his microphone, the sound cutting off abruptly. "Alpha Team, what the fuck is going on?" He turned to look at Commander Blair. "What do we do now, sir?"

But before Blair could respond the radio crackled and a man's strained and panting voice came out of the speaker. "Th-this is ... Alpha ... Five. Can anyone ... hear me?"

Commander Blair held out his hand to stop his Sergeant, and he clicked on his own radio. "This is Commander Blair. What is your situation Alpha Five?"

"Alpha team are all dead ... except me. I saw ... saw them ripped apart. There were two of them. Werewolves. I don't give a fuck ... what anyone says ... they were definitely werewolves," Alpha Five replied, his tone rising higher and higher. "Bullets ... they didn't even ... feel them."

It was obvious that the man was nearly hysterical. "It's all right, I believe you, Alpha Five. Where are you now?"

"Back ... I'm back at the staircase. I can hear them coming after me. I'm headed down."

"That's good Alpha Five. Head for the main reception area. If you can draw them after you, you'll be saving the staff and patients and leading the UP ... the werewolves towards us. We'll take care of them."

"Main reception. I'm ... on my ... way," Alpha Five said, in between desperate rattling gasps for breath.

When Commander Blair released the talk button of his radio, Sergeant Murphy said, "Can we stop them, sir? You heard him say that bullets were ineffective."

Blair shook his head dismissively. "Nonsense, Sergeant. These small calibre rounds are not effective against large animals, you should know that. And if they are people in costume, they could have been wearing NIJ Level 4 body armour as well as being high on drugs. No matter what they are, hit them enough times with these, and they'll go down. Count on it," he said, patting his own rifle. He wished he felt as confident as he sounded. He pointed. "If they follow him, they'll be coming at us from that corridor. Call all the men in and we'll set up an ambush and kill zone right here."

"Yes sir," Sergeant Murphy replied. They were in a combat situation and it was no time to express doubts. Besides, other than to open the main doors and to run, abandoning the civilians in the hospital, there was little else they could do. He looked at his watch. Besides which, CO19 should be here in less than fifteen minutes. He called out to Beta Team over the radio and began eyeing the lobby for the best cover and angles of fire. He began to feel more confident as the men came jogging towards him. The Commander was right. Nothing could survive the concentrated firepower they represented. Alpha Team must have been distracted by the UPs strange appearance and panicked when their bullets didn't seem to have immediate effect. For all they knew, the UPs could be badly wounded already.

Commander Blair took cover behind the curved reception desk and rested his elbows upon its surface with the folding stock of his weapon pressed into his shoulder. The rest of the men including Sergeant Murphy were positioned in an arc facing the direction that they expected Alpha Five and the UPs to appear from. According to Alpha Five's last communication he was nearing their position, followed closely by whoever was pursuing him. He heard footsteps echoing from down the eerily silent hallway, clicked his weapon to semi-automatic and peered over the sights. He heard the Sergeant say "Watch out for our man. Don't shoot that first thing that moves." This was good advice and he eased his finger off of the safety trigger.

***

Tara had landed the Vampire in a large field, feeling the landing gear sink into the soft loam. The hospital was just across the road and she could see it over the tops of the trees from the height of the cockpit. From intercepted police radio messages they knew that everybody was converging on the main reception area including, presumably, the werewolves. She had joined John in strapping on her weapons and pulling on the camouflaged head cover that was part of her body armour.

"Here, put this on too," John said holding out what looked like a black respirator mask with a broad elastic strap.

"What is it?"

"A voice modulator. It will change the frequency of your voice so they won't recognise it again if you're forced to speak. It's also good against tear gas and pepper spray."

She knew that the medical nanites in her body would neutralise such chemical irritants within moments, but even a distraction lasting a few seconds could be fatal. The version of the soft flexible head piece they were wearing had built in eye protectors that made them look slightly like bug eyed aliens although they were optically transparent. "You've been thinking about this encounter," she said as they darted across the field towards the road. She heard the access ramp of the Vampire close behind them. Besides the remote control, she could open it again with a voice recognition system which was tuned to ultrasonic frequencies that no ordinary human could produce.

Suddenly their super sensitive hearing picked up the sound of massed gunfire. "We're late to the party. Come on!" John said as he broke into an all-out run. To a normal observer he would have disappeared in a blurred streak of movement.

***

It appeared that Alpha Five had not been exaggerating or mistaken, Commander Blair reflected bitterly as he ducked down behind the counter to reload. Their bullets had absolutely no effect on the … hell, by every definition they were werewolves. A scream, and then another made him pop up, rifle ready for action again, useless as it might be. He watched in helpless horror as the creatures charged right into the gunfire and pounced upon his men, ripping them apart like chickens thrown into a giant mincing machine. The remaining men broke and tried to run, but the creatures moved with unbelievable speed and caught up with them with insulting ease, batting their prey aside, their clawed fists striking with the power of sledge hammers. Blair winced at the sound of breaking, shattering bone. He saw that Sergeant Murphy was still on his feet although his armour vest was ripped and hanging loosely from one side of his body. Blair vaulted over the counter and moved towards the werewolves with steady strides, firing single aimed shots in synchronisation with the Sergeant as he went.

The werewolf Murphy was shooting at spun around on all fours like a giant spider and roared in defiant anger. He hopelessly continued to fire as the creature sprang, and from the corner of his eye he saw the other creature leap towards the Commander. "Where the fuck is CO19 when you need them," he spat.

Suddenly the glass walls of the reception area shattered in a double crack and both werewolves were swatted aside by a burst of strangely muffled gunfire coming from outside the building. For a moment Commander Blair thought that CO19 snipers had come to the rescue, but one look at the terrible wounds inflicted by the bullets told him that no sniper rifle in

111

existence, not even a .50 calibre, could have fired those shots. He was about to turn towards the outside to see who his rescuers were, and then he froze. The werewolves' bodies were changing, twisting and reforming into what he realised were human bodies. Of course, he thought hysterically, isn't that what werewolves were supposed to do when they were killed?

"They're not dead."

Blair spun towards the shattered glass walls and squinted into the bright sunshine. He brought up his weapon again when he saw the silver bodies, bulging eyes, and strange weaponry. He felt light headed with shock. First werewolves, and now … aliens?

"We're human, and friends," John said in an amused tone, clearly guessing the Commander's thoughts. "Since we just saved your lives, that ought to be proof of that."

"Sir?" Sergeant Murphy said.

Blair realised that what he was seeing was two people in some kind of advanced body armour and masks. In full kit, his own men looked just as strange and alien. "Unless you have official identification, I must ask you to put down your weapons and surrender yourselves."

John glanced at Tara. "That's official gratitude for you." Then he turned back to the Commander. "I'm afraid that we can't do that, and we will defend ourselves if you attempt to fire."

Commander Blair studied the strange and huge muzzled weapons and the confident manner in which they carried them. Then he recalled the damage those guns had done to the werewolves when their own supposedly modern weapons had had as little effect as water pistols apart from tearing up the hospital's walls and furnishings. He sighed. "I suppose those suits would protect you from these," he said, tapping his rifle with a finger.

John nodded. "I'm afraid so. We really are here to help. We're friends."

"Then why the masks?" Sergeant Murphy asked suspiciously. "And where did you get those guns? I don't recall anything like them being licensed to the public. Are you some kind of secret military unit?"

"We're a private security team, and our equipment and weapons are all prototypes. Our employers are aware of the ... problem, and have been studying ways to help the authorities."

"Then as my Sergeant said, why the secrecy? Why not just come forward and offer to help?"

John pointed at the downed werewolves. "Would you have believed us if we had come to you just yesterday and told you we know we are facing werewolves?"

Blair opened his mouth, and then sighed as he closed it again and nodded. "You have a point. I'm still not sure that I'm not hallucinating, affected by some kind of drug."

"Do you feel drugged Sergeant?" Tara said, and was surprised at how different her voice sounded. Even her accent was subtly changed.

Sergeant Murphy grinned. "No ma'am." The tight fitting suit made it easy to see that the speaker addressing him was female, and a very shapely one too.

"Commander, I hope you will take my word when I say that those two are still not dead. They will heal if given enough time and will revert to their werewolf form. I suggest at least three pairs of steel hand cuffs on wrists and ankles, and preferably a steel cage with really stout bars."

"They can't be killed?" Blair asked disbelievingly.

"They can, but you won't like it," John replied.

"Try me."

"You have to behead them."

"Are you mad? We're the police. We can't..."

113

John held out his palm in a pacifying gesture. "I know that. And your doctors and experts won't find any drugs or viruses. They might find some unusual DNA changes, but that won't explain their condition. Just remember when the time comes that I warned you and what I said. Beheading. An anti-tank rocket also might do it, but it's unlikely that you could hit one and a near miss would just piss them off." He pulled an untraceable satellite phone from his belt and placed it on a counter. "When you are ready to listen, you can reach us with this. Until then, just remember what you saw today and imagine similar creatures popping up in increasing numbers all over the country. Good luck. We'll be going now." He started to walk backwards until he was back outside the building. "Oh, and there aren't any more of them in the immediate vicinity. Not at the moment anyway."

"Wait! You can't just..." Then he was suddenly talking to empty air. "Damn."

"So sir, what do we do with these two bastards?" Sergeant Murphy asked, kicking one of the naked corpses.

"Make sure they're dead, and..."

"Sir?"

"Handcuff them anyway."

"Yes sir!" Sergeant Murphy replied. He had no trouble with being extra careful. Not after what these two had done.

Blair went around checking on his men, but all of them were either dead or looked to be that way soon. He didn't call for assistance since they were already in a hospital. Instead he stood up and shouted. "It's all right. It's safe to come out now. The situation is under control. I have men who need help here. Are there any doctors or nurses around?"

***

"You didn't warn him about the possibility of his own men turning," Tara said as they neared the Vampire.

"Do you honestly think he would have listened? That would have just confirmed in his mind that I – and you – were crazies. I'm afraid he'll have to learn the hard way."

"So what do we do now?"

"We'll find somewhere nearby to land and wait. I suspect that we'll be needed back at the hospital within a few hours unless they move all the bodies elsewhere, which seems unlikely except for the two werewolves. The DOD or MI5 or some other super-secret group might want to have a closer look at them."

"I suppose your right. The staff at the government research facilities are paid to take risks, unlike the people in the hospital, and we can't protect everyone even if they'd let us," Tara said grimly.

***

Commander Blair watched grimly as the hospital staff efficiently moved around collecting the dead and wounded. There where over a dozen fatalities, and four critically injured, including two police officers, one from Alpha team and one from Beta. He tried to compose a report as he watched, wondering what he could say that wouldn't get him sent for psychiatric evaluation, along with the Sergeant.

The Sergeant was boiling mad at the deaths of his men and even more angry when the government continued to deny the existence of werewolves on the TV in the waiting area of Reception. "But sir, we've got to say something, warn everybody." He waved his hand at his blood drenched surroundings and shook his fist.

Blair closed his eyes in exhaled in a long sigh. "Orders are that nobody is to use the "W" word.

Officially they don't exist."

"But what about..."

"What about what, Sergeant? All we have are two dead naked men, killed by people we can't identify with weapons we've never seen before. If I kick up a fuss, either I'll be reassigned, sent to a mental hospital, or ordered to hunt down the threat of armed vigilantes running around with guns and discharging them in a public place, something which I admit I'm not keen to do." He tapped the pocket of his coat. "The best I can do at the moment is forget to mention this," he said, meaning the satellite phone. "But you will be debriefed too, numerous times. The Metropolitan Police has not suffered casualties on this scale since World War Two and the Battle of Britain."

"I'll not say a word, Commander. You can count on me. I have the feeling we may need their help sooner rather than later."

"I certainly hope not Sergeant, but I fear you're correct. But for now, you and I have to head back to London to explain this … fiasco. I suspect that after we report what really happened, taking care to refer to our attackers as UPs, we shall be told what our final report should say and will be ordered to toe the official line or else."

"But sir, the original sighting was of three of the things, not two. What about the third one?"

"They managed to disappear in the middle of Oxford Street, so how much success do you think the local lads will have out here? I would guess that it too has changed back into a man or a woman. And even if they found the person what would they charge that person with? Changing into a werewolf without a permit? We already know the DNA can't be matched to any human, and if someone was brave and stubborn enough to testify in court that they saw a werewolf change into a human the judge would probably have the witness locked up for contempt of court."

"So we just hope for the best?" Sergeant Murphy said angrily.

"And hope that our unknown allies will step in if the hospital is threatened again."

"They must have been monitoring our radio. Perhaps you could use the radio to suggest that the local lads concentrate on patrolling Guildford. After all, we have to use our resources to protect as many people as possible," he said gravely.

Commander Blair smiled. "An excellent idea, Sergeant."

***

John listened to the Commander's radio conversation with the local Police and grinned. "He's sending us a message that we won't run into many of his men or CO19 at the hospital. This Blair is a clever one."

Tara tilted her seat back and closed her eyes. "So now we wait."

"If we're unlucky, we won't be waiting very long. I just hope that not too many of the victims turn. Especially the policemen. They were brave men and it would be unpleasant to have to kill them a second time. And fortunately no children were attacked." If the wounded recovered on their own, the alien nanites would not be driven by their emergency protocol to revive their new hosts and would remain undetected and inactive in their bodies. They would only intervene if the situation was critical and the host actually reached the point of death. Of course that didn't mean they wouldn't change some time in the future. From his observations, most of the infected who died of old age did not turn. He wasn't sure why this was.

"You sound very confident that we can take on a horde of the creatures and prevail," Tara said with her eyes still shut.

"They will be newly converted and confused. Only a few will be a serious threat to us."

"Those like Viktor. Those who keep their minds," Tara said.

"Yes indeed. Those are the dangerous ones," John replied, wondering what Viktor and his followers were up to at that moment.

Chapter Eight

A message had reached Viktor through a chain of street gang members. The leaders of some of London's biggest and most powerful gangs wanted to meet with him to discuss terms and to stop his wholesale slaughter of their members.

"It's a trap of course," Jenny said.

Viktor laughed cheerfully. "Of course it is. I've been waiting for this. The biggest, baddest of the gang leaders have come together to rid themselves of a common threat. They'll be armed to the teeth and ready to pounce upon us in large numbers."

"So what do we do?"

"Oblige them of course. How else could I ever get all the people I want to kill neatly gathered in one secluded place?"

Jenny giggled and hugged him from behind, resting her head upon his shoulder. "I love the way you think."

"Go and tell the rest of the pack. We hunt tonight. Dinner is on me."

***

The selected meeting place was an abandoned factory that criminals always seemed so good at finding. Viktor guess that many a drug deal and arms purchase had been carried out here. But tonight's event would be a little different. He and the members of the pack that were in London arrived at the factory in two cars. None of them were armed. Unlike the police, the news that Victor and his crew were different and extremely deadly had spread through the gangs like wildfire. Some believed, some didn't. But he knew the gang leaders couldn't afford to look afraid. They would be forced to show that they were not helpless or their little gang kingdoms would crumble and they would be driven out or killed by their own subordinates. They would all be here, carrying the best weapons they could lay their hands upon. Shotguns, pistols, and probably some AK47s, Mac10s and other automatic weapons. They would lure him into the middle of the huge, rotting, junk filled building and then gun him and his people down. Or at least they would try. He could have changed out here in the darkness and then led his pack in to slaughter the would-be ambushers, but he needed to appear a man of his word if he wanted to take over all the gangs and their members. He would not be the one to strike first. Of course, he would make sure to be the one to strike the last blow. The thought made him grin.

Just as Viktor had predicted, each of the gang leaders and their bodyguards were positioned in separate areas around the perimeter of the huge empty space. They had set up a table and chairs in the middle of the floor under a fluorescent light fixture, with a few of the lower ranking members seated there to act as Judas goats.

Viktor could smell the fear rolling off of the men seated under the light, as well as the scent of the men all around him. The masses of rusting iron and steel scattered about the factory floor should have masked the scent of any firearms they were carrying, but many of the guns had been fired and not well cleaned or cleaned at all, and he suppressed a chuckle when he caught the scent of burnt gunpowder. He wondered if the gang leaders were ruthless enough to gun down their own men, but he guessed not. Loyalty, or apparent loyalty was important in street gangs and a leader who needlessly allowed his followers to be killed would not last long. He wondered how close they would let him and Jenny get before they ran. He had chosen to come in with only Jenny. The survivors, if any, would remember that. The rest of his pack mates were moving silently around and onto the exterior of the factory, picking entrance points. Once in werewolf form, window glass, bars and locks would mean nothing to them.

The moment they stepped into the lighted area surrounding the long table, the young men at the table jumped up from their seats and ran away into the relative darkness. One, more daring than the others, stopped to give them the finger. This made Jenny giggle. "That one is mine," she said softly.

"As you say, my dear," Viktor replied. He held out his arms to either side, looked around and shouted, "Well? We're here as you asked. Since you invited me here, aren't you going to say something – or are you all too afraid?"

"Fuck you!" a voice shouted from the shadows. "You've been killing our mates, ripping them up like they was trash. Now you're gonna pay!"

"How very brave, threatening me from hiding. Is that what your mother taught you?" Viktor said mockingly, deliberately taunting. "Come on then, show me how tough you are. Or are you too afraid to face me like a man. Have you wet yourself? Is that why you're hiding?"

As Viktor had expected, this was too much for the street tough to bear and he stepped out of the darkness, a pistol in his hand, a Beretta 9mm. "Fuck you. Fuck you and your bitch," the man shouted, waving his gun at Viktor as if it were a wand. Viktor put his hands on his hips. "Perhaps I should let Jenny here take care of you. You don't look to be worth my time."

With a snarl of rage, the gang leader shouted, "Kill them, kill the mother-fuckers!" and fired wildly at his verbal tormentor.

A bullet hit Viktor's arm, and although his flesh almost immediately began to heal behind the track of the projectile, it still hurt. It was also enough to trigger his change, even if he had not willed it. The transformation came easily and he felt the sweet pain of twisting, reshaping bone and sinew.

The gang leader saw the bullet hit. He grinned and shifted his aim to Jenny. He had never shot a girl before and it excited him. He noted that she stood calmly with her arms at her side even as he prepared to fire, and a corner of his mind wondered if she was so scared and shocked that she couldn't move, or if she was just stupid. Then the gun exploded in flame and bucked in his hand. "Yeah!" he cried at his shot hit the pretty woman right in the chest. It felt good, and he prepared to fire again. He stared over the sights, trying to decide where to put his next bullet, shifting from one foot to the other in excitement. More bullets were flying, none of them hitting the woman, one or two coming perilously close to him. He turned his head to shout at the shit-head who had almost shot him, just in time to see a huge set of fang filled jaws close around his forearm and the huge hairy form behind them. Flesh tore and bone crunched and he screamed shrilly in agony, the gun falling from his hand which was dangling from his arm by a few shreds of tissue.

The shot hitting her chest was burning, blinding agony, but Jenny welcomed it. It made her change faster and the pain quickly faded as the change came over her. She felt strong and good, and she loved it and she was almost grateful to the lab coated bastard Jap scientist who had made her this way. But most of all she loved Viktor for showing her that she could have a new life with him, a new life in which she never had to feel afraid or weak again.

Viktor placed a clawed paw between the gang leader's shoulders and shoved him towards Jenny, who had just completed her transformation. He saw her grin at him, her slavering jaws opening wide.

The crippled gang leader mewled in shock when he saw what the girl had turned into, and he felt a warm wetness running down his legs. "No! Stay away from me you freak..." His words were abruptly cut off when one set of clawed fingers closed around his throat and a second over his crotch, the steel hard claws ripping through his jeans and closing over his genitals. He desperately beat at her wolf-like head as she lifted him up off of the filthy concrete floor and began to pull.

Even as he ran, Viktor howled a signal to his waiting pack. Loud cracks and crashes sounded all around the building and the cries of alarm from the suddenly ambushed ambushers made him bark in amusement. He was still Viktor, but he also knew he was a werewolf and that he was on the hunt. His nose led him to a man cowering behind a rectangle of rusty oil drums. He vaulted over the metal shield and landed upon the startled man's back. His victim's shotgun went off, the heavy lead pellets knocking another gunman from the top of a large empty crate standing on its side like a magician's cabinet. Screams came from all directions, mixed with staccato bursts of gunfire and bowel shaking roars and snarls. Viktor sniffed the air as he snapped the man's neck with such force that the flesh of his neck tore. "Women!" The confident gang leaders had brought some of their women along with them to witness their prowess. Even better. He could have some fun while attending to business. Abandoning his dead victim, Viktor bounded up onto the pallet of oil drums and looked around, searching with all of his senses. There! That one was a woman, young and shapely but hard looking, her hair cut short and features almost masculine. She would do for a start. He howled again and barked, warning the others off from his newly selected prey. He leaped in her direction, and to his surprise she produced a small pistol and emptied its magazine in his direction. He shrugged off the impacts and pain, continuing his charge as if nothing had touched him. He reared up in front of her, and allowed her to hit

123

his ribs with the butt of her pistol. He appreciated her fierceness, especially in his werewolf form and although she had struck hard, he had barely felt the impact. But when she drew her hand back for a second try his paw darted out and closed around her elbow. In his human form that would not have been a good move, but he wanted her to feel his strength and to realise her own helplessness. His fingers and claws closed tighter and she gasped in pain, and then again in shock when he lifted her to her toes by that grip, almost dislocating her shoulder, her arm forced into a rigid straightness by his strength. He lowered his muzzle until it almost touched her nose and then he squeezed harder, and harder, until at last she surrendered her grip on the chrome plated pistol which fell to the floor with a metallic rattle. This one did not go off on impact, not that he really cared. His other paw came down upon her lower, unstretched shoulder and again his claws pressed through her jacket and T-shirt and lightly pierced her skin, immobilising her.

She was unable to struggle or kick without risking tearing her ligaments and she stared in frozen terror into his gleaming black eyes. It was obvious that this was not just a simple animal. She could see the intelligence in his eyes and even in his inhuman expression. Finally, as if it hurt her as much as his claws, she said, "Please don't kill me." She closed her eyes when his jaws opened wide and she felt the dripping fangs touch her throat, his hot breath bathing her skin. When she didn't die she opened her eyes again and gasped when an irresistible pressure upon her shoulder forced her to her knees.

Victor pointed at the spot in front of her and growled menacingly. When she said "I understand. I won't move" he nodded in satisfaction and then whirled around to throw himself at another gang member who was still defiantly shooting at his pack.

The kneeling girl winced and covered her eyes when she saw Viktor drive his claws into the man's chest. There was a sickening crunch of bone and raw meat and his paw emerged again, holding a still beating heart. He licked it and howled.

Then it was all over. There was silence in the huge echoing building save for low rumbling growls, sobbing moans of pain, the drip and trickle of blood, and the sound of the werewolves gorging upon fresh meat. A few of the fighters had managed to throw themselves out of windows or open doors, but most of the gang members who had gathered here for the ambush were dead. Viktor changed back to his human form and smiled in satisfaction act the carnage that surrounded him. "A nice little object lesson. You fuck with us and you get eaten." The pack were under instructions to ensure none of the dead were in any condition to reanimate.

The pack howled and roared, Jenny amongst the loudest.

Viktor returned to the kneeling woman. "I'm glad to see you decided to be sensible. Now stand up and strip. Everything including those nice boots."

The woman looked around her and shuddered. She thought of herself as tough and a fighter, but nothing on Earth would make her disobey Viktor at that moment. Without a sound, she undressed until she stood in bare feet.

"Now don't move. Stay very, very still, and you won't be harmed – much," Victor said before willing the change to come upon him again. When he was in werewolf form he reached out his index finger and drew a "V" on the woman's belly with his claw.

The woman hissed and stiffened, fighting the urge to run as the claw cut the bloody shape in her flesh.

Viktor licked his claw and grinned a great lupine grin at her. Then he shook and shuddered his way back into human form. When he was able to speak properly again he said, "There. My mark should convince them you were really here. Go and tell them. All of them. I

125

shall call another meeting sometime soon, and they will all send representatives empowered to speak for each of their gangs, or what's left of them. If anyone brings a weapon or tries to attack any of us, we will kill all of you as well as your families, just like this. Is that understood?"

She nodded convulsively, light headed at the thought that he was going to let her go. She even forgot about her nakedness or the fact that her feet were being cut by the broken shards of glass and metal on the floor. "I understand," she said hastily. When Victor pointed at the door she turned and sprinted for the exit as if all the demons in Hell were after her.

Viktor dusted his hands. "Well, that takes care of that. So unless any of you are still feeling peckish we can go home and celebrate with a drink and some of your so English fish and chips. After that, we can make some plans to pay a visit to some real villains and not these children."

Chapter Nine

It was inevitable that the events at the hospital would be picked up by the new services. It didn't matter what rubbish they reported or how censored it was. For the next few hours at least there was live coverage of the scene of the crime, and all Tara had to do to keep an eye on the situation was to turn on the TV in the Vampire. She checked the time display in her internal HUD. "It's about time, if anything is going to happen."

John nodded, peering at the screen over her shoulder. "It's not a science, but you're right. They've had just about time to complete emergency resuscitation and conversion for those who weren't missing large chunks of their anatomy."

They continued to watch in silence and Tara didn't comment when John's hand rested on her shoulder. She wasn't so self-centred as to believe that every touch by a man indicated a sexual advance, but she couldn't help but notice how strong his hand felt either. She mentally snorted. He was a vampire. *The* vampire according to folklore and literature. Of course his hand would he strong. Which led her to wonder about the rest of his body.

"What's that?" John said, pointing at the screen.

A female reporter who happened to be interviewing some of the nurses inside the hospital was saying, "And there seems to be some kind of disturbance in that ward. Isn't that the ward room where the surviving policemen were placed?" That wasn't hard to tell because there were a number of uniformed officers standing in front of the door, and who were now staring towards the doorway with concern on their faces. The reporter waved at her cameraman. "Come on, lets go over and see what's happening." She came to a skidding halt when the policemen started to hastily back away, shouting into their radios and waving their arms excitedly. "Something's happening. We'll try to get you a better – what the *beep*..."

The body of an eviscerated doctor came flying out of the room to hit the wall on the opposite side of the hall with a sickening splat and the screaming began.

"Oh my God! Oh my... that's just..." the reporter stumbled to a halt, lost for words. "What's that coming out of the..." The camera caught the reporter drop her microphone, turn back towards the lens, her face bloodless and mouth open in soundless panic. The image rocked wildly when she pushed her way past the cameraman and ran away down the corridor.

The cameraman regained his balance just in time to see what appeared to be a werewolf in a hospital gown punch his fist into another police constable's chest. He shouted "Fuck this!" dropped the camera and joined the reporter in panicked flight, his footsteps captured by the dropped microphone as they faded into the distance.

Lying on its side, the camera continued to transmit, capturing a pair of clawed feet stalking across the floor, then blood splashed the lens and a nurse's body fell right in front of it, half of her face missing, her remaining eye staring right into the camera. At this point the signal suddenly cut off and the transmission returned to the main studio and the horrified faces of the news team.

Tara dashed down the ramp and followed John as he ran towards the hospital. The ancient vampire seemed to flow over the ground like a moon cast shadow, silent and fast as death and Tara was amazed that she struggled to keep up. To any observers they would have looked like ghosts flitting across the land at impossible speed, an illusion, a trick of the eye.

"Sabres only unless we're clear of the people. Remember there could be a patient behind every wall and curtain. If we kill even one of them by accident we become criminals," John shouted over his shoulder to

Tara. "The authorities are under too much pressure and the police too frightened. They won't discriminate between the werewolves and us."

"I understand," Tara shouted back against the rushing torrent of air blowing against her face as she ran. Without her vampire's sonar and night vision, their run would have been impossible in the darkness, but all her senses, vision, hearing, even smell, were combined into a synthesised vision by the alien nanites and the vampire race's inherent capabilities.

They reached the main hospital building in less than two minutes and John lead her straight up the wall, claws digging into brick, plaster, and concrete.

Tara realised the wisdom of his choice. The interior of the building must be jammed with frightened and confused staff and patients trying to respond or flee, depending on whether they had seen the werewolf as yet. She wagered that more of the creatures were rising up even as they climbed and they were in for a running battle through the network of hallways and rooms that made up the hospital complex. It didn't matter if the werewolves escaped into the area surrounding the hospital. Their first priority was to prevent them from harming the hundreds of people inside. If no one intervened it could be a slaughter. The police were swamped by hundreds of calls from frightened people seeing werewolves in every shadow in Guildford and they would be a while in coming, and when they did they would be no more effective than they were previously. Heavy weapons like .50 calibre machine guns, anti-tank missiles, and grenades could hurt the werewolves, but they couldn't be employed so long as the hospital was full of people.

John found a window that opened into an unoccupied room, and he pried the double glazing out of its mounting with a clawed finger, dropping the panes of glass to the ground below. Then he disappeared into the building like flowing smoke.

Tara followed with almost as much grace and speed, feeling her body flex and flow through the tight opening in ways that would have shocked a human observer. Looking around it appeared that they were in a single in-patient room that was undergoing renovation. There was a larger and more complex looking than normal bed and a large TV mounted on the wall across from it. There were also ladders, plastic sheets and buckets of paint and various tools lying around. But from the sounds of pandemonium coming through the door they were on the right floor. She sniffed and actually detected the scent of werewolf, so the creature or creatures were not far away.

"Don't draw your sabre until we have announced ourselves. We will look frightening enough without waving swords around," John said softly as his gloved hand reached for the door. He turned to look at Tara and when she nodded, he slowly opened the door and peered out. There was a nurses' station just metres away, lined with drug and filing cabinets, as well as monitor screens of various kinds. The entire area was jammed with frightened people. A glance at the direction signs mounted upon the wall revealed that at least one werewolf had to be between these people and both the stairs and lifts. John let the door swing open and stepped out boldly out of the room. Staff, mobile patients, and visitors were all shouting and crying and otherwise making noise in a confused jam of people. "Attention! Your attention please!" he shouted in his battlefield voice.

The shout was loud enough and backed up with such an authoritative tone of command that it brought a relative silence to the crowd, most of whom turned to look for the speaker.

"I and my partner are here to help and to deal with..."

"It's a monster!"

"No, a werewolf!"

"It can't be a werewolf you silly cow!"

"Enough!" John roared. "We will deal with whatever it is. But first I need all of you to move back. Get into the rooms to either side if you can and lock or barricade the door. Stay inside until someone comes to tell you it's safe." His suit looked sufficiently like a uniform when the camouflage system was turned off for him to present a recognisable figure of authority.

"What if nobody..."

"Do as I say. Someone will come, I promise you. Now get moving and make way for me and my partner so that we can get over there and protect you."

Some of the nurses and doctors recovered sufficiently from their shock and terror to begin ushering the others into rooms. One of more senior looking doctors came up to John. "Can you really stop those things? The other constable's were completely useless..."

John smoothly drew his sabre from over his shoulder and nodded firmly. "We are a special team. We're trained and equipped for such situations. Now see to your patients and staff. Keep them as safe as you can."

The confident tone and authoritative manner convinced the doctor and those around him, all of whom were desperate for someone to take charge and offer hope anyway. He turned away and commenced ordering the nurses around even though they were already doing everything they could to guide the rest, those who were not hysterical anyway.

While John was establishing their authority, Tara pushed herself through the crowd who were all pushing madly to go in the opposite direction. But even her superhuman strength couldn't force a way through the crush, not without hurting anyone, so she climbed up on the desktop of the nurses' station and threw herself up and over the crowd, bounced off of a wall and landed behind the bulk of the crowd. What she saw made her swear. "John, I can see two of them. Join me when you can." She knew she should have waited, but that would have meant at least one or two more people getting hurt or killed. Amazingly, one police constable was still on his feet and trying to hold off the werewolf facing him, striking and blocking frantically with two collapsible truncheons, all the while backing up and away from the creature. But she could see that he would soon run out of space to avoid the werewolf's claws. She drew her sabre and dashed forward.

The werewolf's claws ripped the truncheon from the officer's hand, and he grunted in pain when a finger broke. He raised his forearm to protect his face, knowing that it was useless. He had hit the thing as hard has he could, hard enough to have seriously injured most men, but the truncheon just seemed to bounce off the monster's body. But suddenly a slim silver clad form dashed in from behind him and blocked the descending paw with, of all things, a thick bladed sword of some kind. To his surprise, the werewolf's arm recoiled when it touched the edge of the blade, and for the first time, he saw the creature – who until recently had been a fellow police constable – bleed. He had actually witnessed the change in the critically injured man begin, and he had run out of the room shouting for a doctor instead of pressing the call button, which action had saved his life. The others who had remained in or near the room had quite literally been ripped apart. Nurses and a doctor had come running, only to have a second monster jump out from another intensive care ward room a few doors down. He remembered that the room had contained a patient who had been injured and nearly killed by the first attack.

Tara flipped the edge of the sabre around and slashed the werewolf across the chest, and then slammed a claw tipped palm strike into its lower ribs, sending the creature stumbling backwards, roaring in pain.

The policeman gaped as he took a step back. His rescuer, clearly a woman, had moved with incredible speed, and the force of her blow had sounded like a sledgehammer hitting a punch bag. To his amazement, the werewolf actually staggered backwards and for the first time seemed to be actually hurt, even though it had shrugged off his hardest kicks and punches. He had a black belt in Karate, and he knew how hard he could hit, but this woman made him seem like a kindergarten student. "Who are you?" He asked, gasping when for the first time he actually felt all of his wounds and injuries.

Tara snapped, "Reinforcements. Special Action Team Vampire. Now move back and protect the others. My partner will be coming up to support me in a moment."

The constable jumped to the conclusion that she was some kind of special services operative, something like the SAS, just as Tara had intended, and he nodded. He knew when to take orders. He turned around to move towards the struggling crowd trapped in the dead end hallway and saw a second silver clad figure leap over the heads of the civilians and run towards him in a blur of speed.

John patted the confused police constable on the shoulder. "Stout fellow. Well done. Now leave this to us." He saw Tara engaged with one werewolf, and headed towards the second one.

Unlike her first encounters with Viktor, Tara was more aware of her capabilities, and John had been training her hard. She was fitter, stronger, and much faster. She had seen her palm strike leave a dent in a three centimetre thick sheet of steel and her claws tear open a car door like a can opener. Now she faced the new born werewolf with confidence, especially with the silver inlaid sabre in her hand. She had felt a rib break when she struck, but she could see the werewolf and ex-

133

policeman visibly healing and recovering from its injury even as it straightened up. Only the cut caused by the sabre was still bleeding. In the past she had known that she was faster than a werewolf, but John had taught her to use her speed as a weapon. From a standing start, she dashed forward, slapped the werewolf hard on the muzzle, raking her own claws through its flesh and then stepped back out of range before the werewolf could retaliate.

Enraged, the werewolf instinctively dropped on all fours and charged forward, jaws open wide and intent on bringing her down by biting her leg.

While a four legged charge was faster and harder to avoid by an ordinary person, as anyone who has ever been attacked by a large dog can attest, it also limited the creature's natural weaponry to its jaws and fangs. Tara took advantage of this to spring up and over the werewolf, tucking her legs into her chest and performing a mid-air somersault with the sabre held protectively over her shins. She landed on the ground and spun around just as the werewolf crashed into the wall. Although the impact didn't hurt the creature, for a second it was stationary and facing away from her. She extended her sabre as she spun, the sword slashing through the air like a helicopter blade or the blade of a blender, catching the backs of the werewolf's thighs just as it reared up to turn around. Her blade cut deep, slicing flesh and severing tendons.

The werewolf roared in agony as it toppled over on its side. With its legs nearly useless and slow to heal because of the silver in the blade that had slashed it, the creature used its front paws to drag its body around in preparation for another attack.

Tara glanced at the pale and shocked police constable who was watching the fight. "I have to kill it. You understand that," she said to him, remembering that the werewolf used to be a policeman too.

The constable glanced around at the dead and bleeding civilians and the terrified huddle behind him, and then nodded grimly. "Do it."

In the time taken to say those words, the werewolf had almost reached her and raised one set of claws to slash. Tara skipped to the opposite side, half turned and using both hands, brought the sabre down at a slight diagonal with all her strength and speed. The werewolf's head and one paw flew free of its body and the tip of her sabre cut a furrow in the hospital's synthetic flooring.

The watching police constable winced as blood shot out from the creature's severed neck in a thick jet, and then gasped in horror when both the head and body began to turn back into human form.

***

Knowing that he was facing a newly created werewolf, John drove in aggressively. He was vastly more experienced with a sabre and his blade was a whirlwind of steel and silver in front of him, cutting and stabbing at the werewolf from all directions and blocking each of its attacks.

Within seconds the creature was covered with deep bleeding wounds and was backing away from its attacker despite its instinct to always fiercely attack an opponent, as it quickly weakened from damage and loss of blood. Desperately it grabbed at the vampire's blade, and then howled in agony when a twist of John's wrist severed three of its fingers.

Moments later the werewolf was down, its head rolling across the polished floor, and John whirled to see if Tara needed his assistance. Then he turned his head from side to side, listening for signs of another werewolf attack. He caught the faint but familiar sound of an inhuman growl. "Tara! Come on, there are more of them that way," he shouted, pointing down the hall and deeper

135

into the hospital complex.

Tara flicked the blood off of her sabre, sheathed it and trotted over towards John.

When the police constable came up to them, obviously curious as to the identity of his unexpected rescuers, John pre-empted his questions with orders. "Excellent work constable. You did well against those things. Now you need to stop these people from trying to leave. There are more werewolves in the building and they could run right into them. Make sure that this area is clear and lock or barricade all the doors leading into it. If there are any more survivors from the earlier attack, I suggest you find a way to lock them in their rooms as well, although if they haven't changed by now it's likely that they won't, unless they become critically ill again. Can you do that?"

Taken aback by John's confident manner and commanding tone the constable nodded. "Yes sir. I understand. But..."

"No time for chat now, there are more of those things for us to take care of. I'm leaving these people in your care."

Just as John had expected, the reminder of his responsibility to protect the public took the police constable's mind off of his questions.

"Yes ... yes of course sir. I'll keep them safe."

John nodded briskly and said, "Good man." He didn't pat the man on the shoulder because a senior officer would not have done so. He spun on his heel and marched away followed by an amused Tara.

"Good man?" Tara whispered, suppressing a chuckle. "I was waiting for you to twirl your moustache."

"It's what he expected to hear, and the familiar is comforting in a situation like this."

"A rat fuck?" Tara said, teasing him.

John laughed at that. "I know more crude words

136

and obscenities than you will ever hear. But there's a proper time for that," he said, his march changing to an all-out run once they were out of sight of the constable.

Tara moved forward to stand level with him as they approached the next section of the Intensive Care ward. "You mean like now?" she said, all playfulness wiped from her voice.

John glared at the five werewolves tearing at their victims, a couple whom seemed to be still alive. Almost all the staff and patients were down or had fled, but there had to be more who were helplessly trapped in their beds. His rifle seemed to magically appear in his hands and the odd hollow sound of the rail gun firing thumped in the wide hallway all in a single motion and the head of one of the werewolves exploded, hit by a modified version of a Glaser Safety Slug, a hollow bullet filled with silver bird-shot and capped with a polymer ball, but much larger than the normal versions and capable of much higher speeds than in a normal gun because the acceleration was gradual instead of from an explosion, which would have shattered the fragile bullet in the barrel. These bullets were designed not to penetrate dry wall or to ricochet if they missed their target, but imparted tremendous amounts of kinetic energy and hydrostatic shock when they hit.

"Nice! I thought you said no guns?" Tara said, drawing her sabre.

"These shells are experimental and I only have a few of them. They've never been tested in combat and might have exploded in your barrel or fallen apart mid-flight," John replied, his sabre replacing the rifle in his hand in another blur of motion. "Thought this would be a good time to try one."

"I agree," Tara said feelingly as she charged forwards. With two opponents each, speed and agility would be even more important than ever if she was to win and not get hurt or worse in the process. She took on the nearest two leaving the more experienced John to get past them and attack the two on the farther side. Her sabre lashed out at the closest as she tried to keep it between her and the second werewolf, but it didn't cooperate and moved around to stand shoulder to shoulder with its fellow. The corridor was wide, but not so wide that she could manoeuvre around them. Tara dodged a set of jaws snapping at her upper arm, while blocking the claws that tried to disembowel her. Fast as she was, it was impossible for her at least, to hold off four arms, two legs, and two sets of jaws all at once. If one of them managed to grab one of her arms in their jaws she would be in serious trouble even if the teeth didn't penetrate the super tough fabric. She knew there was a nurse's station just a short way behind her with the hall widening into an alcove to her right, so she allowed their attacks to drive her back, but she didn't let them get past her. If they managed to bracket her she would be in even more trouble. Her sonar and her HUD told her where she was in relation to the counter and as soon as she was parallel to it, she allowed a blow from the left hand werewolf to help her spring to her right in a side somersault, her alien instincts allowing her to land firmly on the counter top while slashing at her opponents as she flew through the air. As soon as she landed she kicked a monitor screen into the face of the right side werewolf.

The creature swatted at the flying monitor, but it was still plugged in and when its claws drove through the electronic device, the werewolf was jolted by a powerful electric shock, stunning it momentarily.

The other werewolf slashed at her shins with its claws, and though her boots resisted penetration and shielded her from the impact, it swept her of her feet and she fell sideways towards the counter, the corner of another monitor striking her temple. Ignoring the pain and blurring of her vision, she kicked out and caught the werewolf on the snout. The speed and impact of her kick and the armoured toe of her boot sent the creature stumbling backwards, allowing her to jump back onto her feet. Blinking away the blood that ran into her eye from her split temple, she bent her knees and sprang at the other werewolf who was still trying to shake the sparking, smoking monitor off of its arm. Her sabre sliced down, driven by the entire weight of her body and the acceleration of her fall, the silver impregnated edge slicing through the werewolf's elbow. The creature's bones were iron hard, and the blow jolted her wrists and arms, but she managed to retain her grip on the weapon. Although she would have liked to stay and finish off the crippled monster, the werewolf that she had kicked had recovered and was throwing itself towards her, arms and claws raised high in preparation to rake them down her face and body. Now it was her turn to go low and she dived forward in a tight roll. She came out of the roll with her sabre held above her head with both hands and its edge facing upwards at a shallow angle that caught the werewolf's belly just as it passed over her, slicing it open and drenching her in blood. However a kicking rear paw caught her joined arms and the impact sent her sprawling to crash against the base of the counter, the sabre flying out of her hands. Instinct and vampire sonar made her immediately roll in the opposite direction, barely avoiding a clawed kick from the one armed werewolf which instead hit the side of the counter, shattering the fibreglass and fibreboard, and sending medical items and stationery stored below the counter flying like shrapnel to embed themselves in the wall behind.

Tara pushed herself to her feet, her forearms and fingers still tingling from the impact of the werewolf's passing kick. She glanced longingly at her sabre, but it was too far away. The werewolf, still on its feet was too close for her to turn her back. Instead she drew fighting knife, which was also coated in silver. Even

139

though the other one was down, its belly sliced open and slow to heal because of the silver in her sabre, it still could be dangerous if she got too close and allowed it to get its jaws or claws around her ankle.

Despite the silver, Tara' standing opponent's stump of an arm had already stopped bleeding and the werewolf showed no hesitation or signs of slowing down as it stalked towards her, fangs bared in a furious snarl. Knife held low and point forwards, she allowed her opponent to come towards her, separating it from its downed companion. When the werewolf clawed at her, attempting to pull her towards its jaws, she cut backhanded at its paw, drawing a yowl of pain from the monster when the blade sliced its knuckles. She cut low when it drew its hand back in pain, aiming for the femoral artery in its thigh. Her knife sliced deep, but it seemed that the werewolf's arteries were placed differently and she didn't get the huge gush of blood she had hoped for, and she was forced back by the creature's slash at her face.

Angry and frustrated, the werewolf threw itself forward, ignoring the threat of her knife and determined to get its jaws around her throat.

But this move finally gave Tara the opening she needed, and instead of dodging, she went forward, moving with blinding speed. Her shoulder slammed into the right side of the monster's chest, her speed compensating for her lighter weight. Both bodies came to a sudden halt, and before the werewolf could bite off her face she drove the knife straight up under its lower jaw and into its brain. Tara pushed herself free when the werewolf stiffened as if it had been given another huge electric shock and toppled to the floor. But neither creature was dead and so she bent her legs and sprang into the air and across the hallway to where her sabre lay. She snatched it up and ran back towards her opponents, and moments later both werewolf heads sprang free of their bodies. She whirled around to see if John required any help, just in time to see him cut the last of his opponents in half at the waist with a single incredibly fast and powerful stroke of his sabre and then behead the toppling torso before it could touch the floor.

John flicked a lock of hair out of his eyes and smiled at her. "Not bad," he said, nodding at her beheaded opponents, who were changing back into human form. "But a little sloppy. You need more practise with the sabre. If there had been one more of them you would have been in trouble."

Tara started to protest, and then noticed how his two werewolves had literally been cut to pieces. She gulped and just nodded back. He was right. If there had been more of them or if they had been more in control, like Viktor's people, she might have been the one lying dead. She just nodded back. "More practise. Right."

"Come on. We have to see if there are any more of them," he said, cleaning and sheathing his sabre.

Tara noticed that the blood was running off of his suit in neat droplets without leaving a mark. She looked down at herself and realised that she was equally clean, despite the shower of gore she had been subjected to. Apparently the suits were like Teflon, at least when it came to blood.

***

There were in fact two more werewolves, but they were still in the mortuary when John entered, and the only human present was the night attendant, who was already dead. Undisturbed by screaming crowds the two werewolves were busy eating, and they only sprang erect when two more humans entered.

However John's amplified senses had told him to expect the empty building, and both he and Tara fired almost simultaneously, the huge silver slugs ripping the

141

creatures' heads off before punching hand sized holes in the brick wall behind them.

Tara checked her HUD and no warning of further werewolves appeared on her display. "I think we're clear."

John said, "It's possible one or more patients might turn if they die later, but we can't stay around to find out. Everybody will just have to take their chances. I hear sirens approaching, so the CO19 chaps have finally arrived."

"Which means it's time for us to go?"

"Before the dawn," John replied in an exaggerated Romanian accent as he activated the camouflage system of his suit. "Perhaps I should add black silk capes to the suits."

"Don't you dare!" Tara rolled her eyes and activated her own camouflage. She wouldn't put it past him to turn up at their next outing in an evening suit and top hat just to tease her. She sprinted along beside him as they flitted away through the grounds and back to the Vampire. As they ran she had the uneasy feeling that he was holding himself back to match her pace.

Chapter Ten

It was another abandoned factory, and once more a long table sat under flickering fluorescent lights, although the rest of the building was better lit than before, a fact that made Viktor smile. It was a small but significant demonstration of how well he had terrorised the street gangs of London that they were afraid of the dark. He sat at the head of the table, fingers steepled in front of him. This time the leaders of the gangs, many of them newly appointed, sat with him. None carried weapons, and all looked distinctly uneasy, even though only Viktor and Jenny were in attendance. "Thank you for attending this meeting, gentlemen … and ladies," he said, smiling at the tough looking dyed and tattooed women.

"So what do you want? We don't have lots of money to give you," said one of the bolder, or stupider, gang leaders.

Viktor leaned forward, hands flat on the table, his smile feral. "You may be surprised, but I want very little from all of you." Their disbelief was written plain upon their faces. "Honestly! What do I want? I'll tell you. First, you, all of you, leave my people alone. Not because they can't take care of themselves..." he paused to see if anyone was stupid enough to challenge his statement, " – but because I want them to move about freely in every area of the city without drawing attention. Having body parts and blood flying everywhere does tend to upset the neighbours." He had to hide a smile when more than one face winced at this. "Win – win, right? Right??" he asked with more emphasis when no one spoke up.

"Yeah."

"Uh huh."

"Good with me."

Viktor rubbed his hands briskly. "Excellent. So

that's number one taken care of." He made a ticking motion in the air. "Second, you shall supply all help and cooperation if any of my people call upon you for it. Borrow your car or bike, your girlfriend, your gun, whatever." There were several winces when he mentioned cars and bikes. Not so many at the mention of girlfriends or guns. He raised his eyebrows, tilted his head and waited.

Once more there was a chorus of agreement.

"Very wise of you, I'm sure. And the last. This one will be easy. I want each gang to list down on paper, your mob connections, contacts, drug and gun suppliers, and any other mob related interactions you might have." He deliberately paused for a second and added, "That means all of them. If I find that anyone held back in the slightest, I shall not be pleased … and the entire gang and their families will cease to exist. And that is a promise. Cross my heart." He allowed the claws to form at the end of his fingers and he carved an "X" into the hard wood of the table top deep enough for a pencil to fall into.

Faces turned pale all around the table. They were trapped between their fear of Viktor, and the more long established fear of the organised criminals at the top of the food chain.

A voice said, "You're asking us to snitch on some really bad people. That's suicide." There was a subdued but significant rumbling of agreement at this.

Viktor had expected this reaction. "Those people are going to soon have something more important to worry about than you. You, on the other hand, are going to have some pretty immediate problems if you don't give me what I want. Perhaps my earlier object lessons were too subtle?" His claws dug into the table top and the wood crumbled beneath his hand when he made a fist.

There was a deathly silence in the room as

144

everyone stared in horrified fascination at the hand sized hole in the table.

"Be my friend, or be my enemy. Choose. Now!" He slammed his fist down hard and a crack ran down the length of the table.

One gang leader held up his hand. "Um, have you got a pen and paper?"

But another stood up, knocking his chair back and onto the floor. "No! You don't know who you're dealing with. I..." His voice was suddenly cut off when Jenny, changed into full werewolf form, sprang onto the top of the table and walked slowly towards him on all fours, growling menacingly.

"Perhaps you would prefer to reconsider your decision? I like to think I can be reasonable."

The man was shaking violently and seemed torn between fleeing madly and begging for mercy. He nodded convulsively, eyes locked upon Jenny's slavering jaws. "I … ahem, I've um, changed m-my mind." When Jenny backed away slightly and pointed at the chair with her nose, the man scrambled to right his chair and sit down.

Someone had found the note pads and pens that Victor had left on the floor by the table, and everyone began busily scribbling. Viktor watched them write and then said, "Remember – the truth, the whole truth, bla, bla, blah. Mistakes will earn you detention," he said, chuckling.

***

When all the gangs had submitted their homework, Viktor dismissed them with a wave of his hand.

"At least one of them is going to run to the mobsters with a warning; play both sides," Jenny said.

"Exactly what I would expect," Viktor replied.

"You want the mobsters to be warned?" Jenny asked in surprise. As a prostitute she had more than one run in with the mob, both as distant employers and as clients, and had learned to be very wary of them.

"Indeed I do. Hopefully this will reduce the amount of time and ... object lessons required to convince them that cooperation is the only sensible course."

Jenny pouted. "I was hoping to do a little hunting. There are a few mob bosses that I'd like to have a chat with."

"Oh I'm sure that some degree of persuasion will inevitably be required, so don't fret my dear."

Jenny stroked his arm possessively. "That was an impressive display of control back there," she said, nodding at the hole in the table. "I couldn't have limited my change to just my hand like that." Viktor's smile made her shiver in delicious fear.

"It's control that makes us different from those animals running around the streets right now. Besides, as a test pilot I have a great deal of experience in learning to control new capabilities, and make no mistake Jenny, I intend to remain in control come what may." He held out his arm to the attractive young woman. "Come. It's time to head uptown."

***

Even though Viktor had told the gangs that he wasn't interested in their money, his campaign of terror had allowed him and his followers to pick up ample amounts of money from the occasional drug deal and weapons sale that had been rudely interrupted by a visit by one or more werewolves. That plus several ATMs pulled from the wall and smashed open gave him a sizeable war chest. The next day he led the pack into the centre of London on a shopping spree. He also picked a luxury hotel to serve as his base of operations, booking a suite for Jenny and himself, and several more for the rest of the pack.

Seated in his newly upgraded accommodations, Viktor studied the lists the gangs had provided. Several names immediately stood out as a result of appearing upon the most of the lists. He circled the names with a red ball pen and tapped them. "This time we start at the top. These men will not give up no matter how many of their minions we kill. They may not be the very highest on the ladder, but we'll hear from the true bosses once we start poking their nests at that level."

Jenny looked around. "They're likely to retaliate. People could get hurt."

"Do you care?" Viktor asked, his voice toneless.

She laughed. "About these people? Fuck no. But it would make us unpopular to say the least."

"That's why I chose this hotel. If they bomb or shoot it up, the police will descent upon them en mass as terrorists, so they'll have to be more discreet."

"Hit men?" Jenny asked. When Viktor nodded she licked her lips. "I've never tried a hit man, or woman."

Viktor gave Jenny a hug. "That's why I love you, Jenny. You're such a beast." He pointed at the lists again. "We'll spend the next few days locating each of these men..." He checked the list again. "– and woman, and learning their habits. Then we'll pick the right places to make our um, offer to work together. We'll need some maps, cameras, and one or two notebook computers."

"You order some room service, while I get the pack working on the rest," Jenny said, kissing him on the lips.

***

"That's her. That's the girl who goes around with Viktor," the gang leader said, pointing out of the car at the hotel entrance.

"Your lot let a pretty little thing like that make you piss yourselves?" the driver of the car said in disgust.

"She's a monster I tell you. She's got fangs and claws and stuff," the gang leader protested.

"She's got a nice arse is what she's got," the other man said. He pressed a speed dial number on his cell phone. "That's the one we want. The one in the sports gear. Yep, that's the one. Pick her up. The boss wants to talk to her." The man turned to the younger man. "You better not be wasting our time, or you'll wish your monsters had got you. If it hadn't been for all the dead bodies and the other gangs supporting your story..."

"You'll find out," the gang leader said, torn between terror and confidence.

***

Jenny spotted the van and car following her almost immediately. She had always been street smart, and her new predator's senses made the threat almost childishly easy to see and hear. She touched her earpiece. "Viktor, I have company. Should I turn around?"

Back in the hotel Viktor tapped his chin. "No, but stay in the crowds for the moment and wait for me. I'm coming to join you." Even though the random werewolf attacks had terrorised the cities, the death and destruction hadn't been on a sufficient scale to interrupt the day to day functioning of the city, and the streets were crowded with people, although the number of tourists amongst them were fewer than normal. The opposition had responded faster than he had expected, and he suspected that all kinds of people, including policemen had been ordered or paid to watch out for him. But he was not dismayed or upset. Moving swiftly but not in such a way as to attract attention from the hotel staff or patrons, he exited the hotel, a cap and dark glasses serving as a simple disguise, and soon caught up with Jenny. He too quickly spotted the van and car and he moved up to them from the back, moving with the flow of pedestrian traffic. He had his cell phone in his hand and wandered along apparently busy sending text messages, but actually watching the suspect vehicles and talking to Jenny. "All right. I'm in position. Stroll out and look tempting." He heard her giggle.

"Don't I always?" she said.

Viktor watched and followed as the crowd thinned and Jenny strolled along, apparently admiring the scenery and window shopping. She even stopped in a store and came out with a plastic shopping bag in her hand. He grinned when he spotted the sliding side door of the van open just a hand's width. "Get ready Jenny, here they come." Jenny let herself wander closer to the van.

The van door was thrown open and two men jumped out, grabbed Jenny by the arms and threw her into the dark interior of the van. Then the door slammed shut.

It was all very slick and efficient. Viktor admired professionalism. He moved out onto the road, as if intent on crossing the street behind the car, still tapping industriously at the screen of his cell phone.

"What the hell are you tossers playing at?" the driver of the car shouted at his phone when the van failed to move off. When there was no response he cursed under his breath and pulled the lever to open the car door. With his eyes still on the van, he opened the door and placed a foot upon the tarmac of the road. But when he turned to check the road behind him he found his view blocked by the body of a man. Before he could protest or even react, the door slammed back against his leg, crushing it between the door and the chassis of the car. There was a sickening crunch of shattering bone, and the man went pale with agony. He tried to scream but a hand came through the side window, smashing the glass as easily as if it was the fake sugar glass traditionally used in Hollywood and struck him in the throat. It didn't quite crush his larynx, but it was more than sufficient to render him incapable of speech.

Viktor pulled the door ajar and got into the driver's seat, easily pushing the groaning man aside to squash him between his own body and the horrified gang leader who sat frozen in terror. He closed the door and put his arm around the choking man, his hand landing upon the gang leader's shoulder. "Hello again. Remember me? Sit very still unless you enjoy the sight of your own intestines."

The gang leader nodded convulsively and sat absolutely still except for the shaking of his hands which were clasped in his lap. He couldn't lift his head and just stared at his hands as if not seeing what was about to happen would protect him.

The mobster tried to reach for his gun but Victor gripped his wrist and twisted, hard.

The man made choking, gurgling cries of agony when the bones in his wrist broke, with a sound like twigs snapping inside a burlap bag.

Viktor plucked the pistol from the man's waist and let it drop to the floor of the car between his feet. "That was naughty. Fortunately for you, I have a forgiving nature." His enhanced vision spotted a rocking motion of the van in front of them.

Then the van's side door slid open again, and Jenny stepped out, wearing the raincoat with a cheerful white pattern with splashes of scarlet that she had recently purchased. She stopped to close the door and nodded to Viktor before heading back towards the hotel.

Viktor sniffed the groaning man he still held in his grip. "Russian?"

The man hesitated and bit back a scream when Viktor squeezed his broken wrist. "Da. Yes, yes. I am

150

Russian."

"Let me guess, your boss is Dmitry, Dmitry Vasnetsov. Am I correct?"

"Yes. Dmitry Vasnetsov, he is my boss," the man replied sullenly. "I swear! On grave of my grandmother, I swear!" he cried frantically, sweat dripping down his face when Viktor's grip increased to bone crushing pressure again.

"Very good. See how easy that was? Now I want you to get out of this car and get into the van. Jenny has left a gift for Mr Vasnetsov in there. You will drive the van to where your boss customarily spends his time and show him Jenny's little gift. Tell him I desire a meeting to discuss business. Remind him that your people laid hands upon mine first and without provocation."

"I'm not sure I can drive van with broken hand," the man said.

"I suggest you find a way, before Jenny decides that you would serve better as part of her gift," Viktor said genially. He opened the door and stepped out of the car, inviting the man to follow with a wave of his hand, and watched as the man staggered and hobbled towards the van, his broken wrist pressed against his chest. He smiled when the man climbed into the van and he heard a sound of absolute horror and disgust emit from the vehicle. Moments later the man's head stuck out of the driver side window and he vomited noisily onto the tarmac. Viktor slipped back into the car and saw that the gang leader, who could be accused of being loyal or treacherous depending upon the point of view, had wisely not moved in his set. He nodded at the van. "I see our friend has examined Jenny's present."

The young man made a whimpering sound and didn't look up.

Viktor shook his head and tsked. "I'm very disappointed. I thought we had an understanding, you and I. You do as I say, and your internal organs remain in your interior."

The gang leader whimpered and slowly moved his head from side to side, his shoulders quaking in terror.

"What am I to do with you? I'd like to just let you go with a stern reprimand. I really would, but I'm pretty sure that your compatriots would see that as a sign of weakness. But ripping your spine out would be untidy, to say the least. Ah, I know!"

The man began to rock back and forth in near hysteria. He gurgled and wet himself when Viktor fully transformed and a werewolf's paw closed about his throat.

A minute later Viktor stepped out of the car, once more in human form. He slammed the door, strolled down the road to the nearest waste basket and casually tossed something in before walking briskly towards the hotel.

It was about ten minutes before a police constable frowned and bent over to peer into the illegally parked car. "Bloody 'eck!" the constable shouted as he took a step back, fumbling for his radio.

Inside the car, the gang leader desperately tried not to bleed to death from the gaping wound caused by the forcible removal of his tongue.

***

The Russian mafia struck back early the very next day.

Jenny and the others had gone about their tasks unmolested and then had room service bring dinner to their rooms according to Viktor's orders. He wasn't afraid of his people getting hurt, but rather that an attack might take place in a bar or restaurant, or some other public place, which would attract the attention of the police or whoever had been given the thankless task of stopping the werewolf attacks. For the moment he wanted the

152

fight to be limited to the mobsters and his pack. Fortunately, the criminals shared this desire to keep their turf dispute private. "Don't let their lack of response fool you. They are definitely preparing what they think will be payback. Stay alert and stay together," Viktor told the pack. None of them were carrying guns. He wanted to be sure that they would look like innocent travellers if the mob resorted to using their contacts inside the police.

Jenny rolled out of bed naked, walked out of the bedroom, pulled back the curtains and stretched, lifting her arms high, arching her body, and coming up on her toes. She knew that Viktor was watching and she liked it. Although she had once been a prostitute, but she did not hate the clients who had allowed her to make a living when no other means would, and she was truly devoted to Viktor, both as a leader and as a man. She knew she was pretty and that she had a good body, and she was pleased that she could give him pleasure by such a simple action. She wasn't trying to seduce him or to buy his affection with sex. Victor could be cold and ruthless, and she knew that he was also too clever and calculating to be manipulated by a good pair of breasts or shapely buttocks. But he valued loyalty and she liked and trusted him for that, because he was loyal too. He did not sacrifice his followers on a whim or abandon them because it would be inconvenient to do otherwise. She was street wise, and understood that if sacrificing one of them, including her, would save the rest of the pack, Victor wouldn't hesitate a moment. But that only made her admire him more. There was no room for softness on the street. They were all monsters now, feared and hated by the normals. They would only survive if they stayed together and helped each other. It wasn't much different than in a street gang, except that Viktor was cold, brilliant, and far more ambitious. She was his woman. His eyes and hands might wander, but at the end it would be her standing by his side and watching his back. The

153

bed creaked and she turned with a smile when Viktor crawled lithely out of bed to join her in front of the window.

***

The targets were in four rooms, with the man Viktor and the woman in the far suite on the left of the corridor. One team moved up to each door, each with one member dressed in hotel livery and pushing a serving trolley. The front desk showed that each room had pre-ordered breakfast to be delivered by room service at 8.30 a.m. The leader of the strike team, all of them ex-Russian military, checked his watch. He was taking no chances. This Viktor person and supposedly the woman, had proved themselves to be dangerous and capable. He had sent a sniper team up to the roof of the building facing the hotel. The position gave them a clear view of the couple's room.

"I have a clear shot at both of them" the sniper reported.

"Roger that. You have green light to proceed. You are weapons free," the leader said in a near whisper into his throat microphone.

The sniper checked the figures from the ballistic calculator and let the cross hairs gently settle on the first target. "Preparing to fire in five..."

The team leader held up his fingers and folded them down as he counted.

The sniper exhaled half way, stopped breathing, and fell into the rhythm of his heartbeat so that the tiny up and down motion caused by his pulse was accounted for. His trigger finger caressed the trigger, the pressure smoothly growing –

***

The armour piercing bullet shattered the window and punched into the side of Jenny's chest moments after they had pulled apart from a kiss. A normal person wouldn't have heard the sound of the shot from across the street and through the window. Viktor did, but even he couldn't move fast enough to avoid the second shot that followed a second and a half later to slam into his chest. He fell sideways, Jenny still in his arms, the surprised expression on her face changing into one of pain.

The door to the hotel room opened a moment later, the leading man dropping the duplicate master key-card and raising his AK-47 assault rifle even as he stepped into the room and to the side so that the rest of the team could follow.

The team leader stormed into the room right behind the lead man and saw his targets on the floor, both naked. He grinned and dropped into a half crouch as his finger tightened on the trigger. He wanted to keep the angle of his shots as shallow as possible so that he wouldn't perforate any people in the room downstairs. He sensed the rest of the team dropping to one knee for the same reason even as the first round exploded from his rifle. Normally he and his men would never be deployed in the middle of London. His employer liked to keep a discreet profile. But the events of the previous day had enraged Dmitry and such an open and blatant challenge and the terrible deaths of his men couldn't be ignored, not if he wanted to keep his position at the top of the organisation. The AK-47 bucked in his hands as he fired in full-automatic mode, spraying bullets at both Viktor and Jenny, filling the room with the smell of burnt propellant and floating wisps of smoke. Brass cartridges flew through the air like hail, covering the carpet with a scattering of gold. The bullet strikes were unmistakable due to the couple's nude state, and he knew that no one could survive such wounds, even if they were still breathing at the moment. He heard similar gunfire in the other rooms, and signalled for his men to prepare to withdraw. The police would be quick to respond to an apparent terrorist attack on such a prestigious location. He stepped forward, and changed to semi-automatic in order to finish his victims off with aimed shots to the head.

As soon as the muzzle came within reach, Viktor lifted his head and reached out to grip the hot barrel pushing it aside even as he began to transform. "That wasn't very nice," he said, the last word slurring into an angry growl.

The leader of the Russian assassination team stared in sick amazement as he watched their wounds heal right before his eyes and fur sprout from their skin. He tried to bring the gun to bear, but it seemed as if it was set in concrete and totally immobile. He let go of the AK-47 and reached for his pistol as Viktor reared up off of the ground. But a clawed paw slammed down upon the back of his hand, shoving the pistol back into the holster.

In barely recognisable English Viktor growled, "My turn." His other arm shot out to grab the Russian mercenary by the throat.

The mercenary was tough and well trained. He slammed his joined forearms against Viktor's arm to loosen his grip and then gripped the hairy paw at this throat to bend the hand back against the wrist in a break lock. His eyes widened in shock when he was unable to move Victor's grip in the slightest even with a two to one advantage, and his face turned red when he was lifted off of his feet by the grip around his throat.

The other Russians tried to get a clear shot at Viktor but their leader's struggling body blocked their line of sight. One remembered Jenny and turned his AK-47 towards her, but groaned in fear when he saw that the bullet riddled woman's body wasn't there any more. He had seen the news reports about furry creatures rampaging throughout London, but he had just laughed, confident of his toughness and his guns. Suddenly he wasn't so confident any more. He scanned the room with his eyes, trying to locate the woman. Perhaps she had crawled – then a deep rumbling growl to his rear made him freeze and he nearly pissed in sheer terror as he crouched and spun around, his assault rifle at hip level, stock pressed tightly against his side. "Fuck!" he screamed when he caught sight of the werewolf standing just an arm's length away from him. His finger crushed the trigger and the assault rifle hammered, bright flares of light reflecting from the werewolf's belly. Bizarrely he noticed that the creature had shapely breasts as he emptied the magazine into its body with no noticeable effect. Before he could do anything else, the werewolf's paw shot out and grabbed his hand, the one that was supporting the weapon's wooden fore-stock, and crushed it immovably against the steel and reddish brown wood of the gun. He felt his knuckle bones pop and crack, but before he could cry out in pain the werewolf twisted the AK-47 upside down and then ripped it away from him, breaking the leather sling as if it was spaghetti. Unfortunately for him, the sudden movement also ripped his hand off at the wrist and snapped the trigger finger of his right hand, which was caught in the guard. He fell to his knees, screaming in agony.

Viktor bent his elbow and turned the wildly struggling leader so that he was facing his men and with his back pressed tightly against Viktor's chest.

The ex-Spetsnatz commando tried to drive his elbow into Viktor's ribs, but with his feet barely touching the floor and most of his weight supported by his neck he couldn't exert the necessary force. Besides which, the monster's body felt as hard as iron when his blows did land. He watched in helpless horror as Jenny used the AK-47 like a club to hit the head of one of the two

157

remaining mercenaries, making his head explode like a dropped watermelon.

The remaining member of the team spun and fired at Jenny, but his bullets missed, piercing the wall and entering the next room.

Taking the opportunity, Viktor stepped forward, still holding the leader in his grip like a rag doll, and thrust the claws of his left paw forward, piercing the mercenary's side like the blade of a shovel or pitch-fork and driving upwards to impale the man's heart.

A gush of blood shot out of the fatally injured man's mouth and Jenny nimbly dodged that too and then grinned at Viktor, her tongue lolling out playfully.

Viktor squeezed a little tighter and the leader's face turned purple. In human form he might have considered letting the man go to send another message and to spread fear, but the werewolf part of him had a much simpler philosophy. A threat to the pack could not be allowed to exist. But neither was he needlessly cruel. His grip tightened until his claws pierced the man's skin, and then continued squeezing until he felt the man's throat collapse under his fingers. He felt the prey kick and convulse, and then go limp. He tossed the corpse casually aside and headed for the door.

The shooting in all the other rooms had ceased as well, and Viktor stopped in at each to ensure that his pack members were all right. One of his male followers was lying on the floor, his head surrounded by a pool of blood.

His partner, a middle aged woman who used to be a Yoga instructor, said, "Ben was hit by three shots to the head before he could change. He's alive, but his head is taking a while to heal. I dealt with the bastards though."

The room resembled a slaughterhouse, with pieces of meat and internal organs everywhere. Viktor knelt to check on the downed man and saw that his head was intact and the wounds were healing as he watched. When the man's eyes focused, Viktor smiled at him. "How do you feel?"

The man grimaced, worked his jaw and blinked a few times. "I … I'll be fine. My fault. I was too slow and over-confident."

"You'll know better next time," Viktor said with a smile. He stood up and gripped the woman by her shoulder. "You did well. I'm proud of you."

The woman actually blushed, as if he had complimented her features or figure. "Thanks, Viktor. We need to look after each other."

He nodded. "Exactly right. No one is like us, no one cares about us. The pack looks after its own. Always. Remember that. Now pack up your things and prepare to leave. The police and Counter Terrorism lot will be here soon, so we need to be gone." None of the other pack members had been badly hurt and there were no survivors of the Russian hit team. He had picked this hotel because they did not have security cameras in the corridors or lifts since its clientèle placed a premium upon their privacy. They slipped down the stairs and exited through a side entrance. He had paid in advance for the rooms and the damage was not his fault. He had also rented a short stay apartment in Soho as a backup location. He had picked that area for the busy streets and large number of foreign tourists so that he and his people wouldn't stand out because of their luggage or strange hours. That was where they headed now, splitting up into pairs and travelling by underground and changing clothes and bags purchased from convenient departmental stores. The dead Russian mobsters had not been carrying any identification, but they did each have a wad of cash on them. They also had car keys, but Viktor knew better than to steal something that could so easily be spotted or traced. The apartment also put them conveniently close to Dmitry Vasnetsov. They had tried to kill his people. He owed Dmitry a return visit. It was only the polite thing to do, after all.

***

"Damn it Blair, you're making me look like a fool. I supported your appointment, and a week later things are looking worse than ever. The Force is being made to look bad. We can't even stop and catch a bunch of wild animals. Did you see that editorial this morning suggesting that we hand the job over to the RSPCA?"

The Deputy Commissioner was practically foaming at the mouth and if the situation hadn't been so grim Colin would have laughed. "Animals sir? I've lost over a dozen men to these so called animals and I still don't have permission to even tell my people how truly dangerous these things are."

"And that's another thing. The casualties. We haven't suffered such losses since the peak of the fighting in Afghanistan. Serious questions are being raised about your competence."

Colin frowned. "Do they understand, do you understand, what we are facing?"

"Don't be impertinent," the Deputy Commissioner snapped. "I've read your reports."

Colin shook his head angrily. "I'm under orders not be "alarmist". You might as well be reading Little Red Riding Hood! Haven't you being studying the supporting information? The photos and videos, the victim statements?"

"You know very well I don't have the time for that. That's what executive summaries are for."

Colin sighed. "Sir, you can reprimand me. You can replace me if you like. But I ask that you give me ten minutes to show you something you might not be aware of first."

The Deputy Commissioner glanced at his watch and then nodded. "Ten minutes."

Colin lifted the screen of his notebook computer. "First, some security camera footage that has been confirmed as real and unedited by our tech boys." He pushed the computer in front of his superior and handed him a pair of earphones. "This room isn't soundproof." When the DC was ready he clicked the "play" button with the mouse-pad.

The DC watched in silence, his face going pale as the minutes dragged on. He pulled the earphones out. "What is this rubbish? Some kind of joke? By God Blair, I'll have your..."

Colin slapped a pile of documents down beside the computer. "Signed and sworn statements from the IT chaps, members of my field teams, and civilian witnesses. This is no joke sir. I only wish it was."

"But … but … that's impossible. Our own men. Victims rising from the dead. W-werewolves?" The DC could hardly bring himself to say the word. "There has to be some other explanation. A disease, mass hallucinations..." He stopped when he saw Colin slowly shaking his head.

"I've seen them myself. They're real, sir. As real as you or I."

"But you stopped them. The ones at the hospital? You're here and unhurt..."

"Sir, we had help. They had weapons and skills that I've never seen before. They said they're a private contractor. I could..."

The DC held up a hand. "I can't present this stuff to the Commissioner or the chaps from MI5 or Home Office. Downing Street would have my head if I tried. The government would be a laughing stock. No, the Prime Minister has decided this is another of those situations where ignorance is bliss, sort of like that Area 51 thing the Yanks have. Weather balloons, freak lightning, pranks on the Internet, and all that." He stared at the statements and impossible, gory photographs spread out in front of him. "No. You do whatever you need to, and I'll support you as much as I can. I'll have a quiet word with my Lords and Masters, and Home Office will work out some kind of cover story. Perhaps some new, very virulent strain of Rabies. Just get me results, and I'll hold everybody off, including the press. If you need to work with these private contractors, do it quietly. Scientific and medical advisers, that sort of thing. Developing a vaccine. Remember I told you not to talk about infections and plagues? Well that's beginning to look like a better alternative than the truth, whatever that may be. But God help you if a single word about werewolves or holy water and suchlike is attributed to you. Then you'll be the one thrown to the wolves. Understand?"

This was pretty much what Colin had expected, so he nodded. The DC was a good man and was giving him all the assistance he could – and the rope he needed to hang himself if he screwed the situation up. He stood up at attention. "I understand sir, and I'll do my best."

"You're best better be good enough, or we're all royally screwed," the DC said, shaking Colin's hand.

Colin watched as the Deputy Commissioner walked out of his office looking confident. He had studied the report of what had happened after he had left the hospital. Those unknown "experts" had saved a lot of lives. In the meantime more outbreaks had occurred in London and elsewhere. He prayed that whoever they were, their names didn't start with "Super" or "Captain". He wasn't sure his sanity could stand working with a bunch of comic book superheroes. "At least we don't have vampires and zombies," Colin said to himself with a chuckle as he stared thoughtfully at the unmarked and unbranded satellite phone. The tech people told him that it was connected to a commercial satellite network, heavily encrypted, and impossible to trace since some of the satellites were Russian and Chinese and their owners were not willing to cooperate with Scotland Yard or MI6. He could try the Americans, but he knew the DC and even the Prime Minister would have a heart attack if he consulted the Yanks without their permission. So far, this was a British problem, and no one wanted to go running to the Yanks for help. God only knew what kind of access or favours the Yanks would want in return.

***

Dan Jackson looked up from his own room service meal, a rib eye steak with brandy mushroom sauce, at the knock on his door. "Come in," he said, putting his knife down to check that his pistol was near to hand under a folded newspaper. His eyes narrowed as he watched the man approach. He could tell that the man bore news. "Well? Have you found her?"

"We're getting close, Mr Jackson. We had no luck tracing Tara Harker or her father, or her helper. But, we also had a team searching for the missing members of the staff and security team at the Werner Biotechnologies distribution facility since we know that something happened there other than a werewolf attack. Our contacts in the British Secret Service finally came through. One of their facial recognition computers spotted a Ms Karen Duncan, British, female, and member of the facility's security team. She disappeared right after the attack."

"So did a great many of the other staff," Dan said, annoyed to have his lunch interrupted by such insignificant news.

"But not like her. The others still left traces. Sightings by friends and neighbours, credit card activity, cell phone calls and so on. But she disappeared off the face of the Earth, just like Tara Harker and the rest of our targets."

This sounded more promising and Dan put his

knife and fork down. "And you've found her current location?"

"We've had a sighting. A street security camera caught an image of her in Bristol."

Dan frowned, turned to his notebook and typed in a search. He scanned the results. "Ah, Bristol is home to a major aviation industry activity. That makes sense if Harker wanted to continue working on his new aircraft without standing out like a sore thumb. Send a team out there. Observation only. I'll have their balls if they spook her. Got it? Then get out."

The man stiffened and nodded. "Yes sir. Observe only. The team will get their asses moving right away."

"Good, good." Dan's appetite suddenly returned and he set about carving up his steak, transferred his fork to his right hand, and began eating. He would compose a report for Mr Werner right after he finished his meal. It would be good to have something positive to report to his boss, which he needed badly if he didn't want to be suddenly retired by his replacement and a bullet in the back of his skull.

***

John was away in London, seeing to business and meeting up with some of his more secretive contacts in the Government and military. Tara and the others, including Duncan, were having a late breakfast. "I just wish I could get out more and do some ordinary things like checking out the latest stuff in the stores. I could use some new shoes. High-tech combat boots are fine, but a girl's got to strut her stuff once in a while."

"Shoe shopping spree – yeah!" Emily agreed enthusiastically.

Rowland looked puzzled. "Every time were out of the lab and workshops, you can't wait to get na..."

"Rowland! Hush! You'll embarrass Tara," Emily

said. "You don't understand women at all, do you? If it wasn't for Tara I wouldn't believe you were ever married."

Rowland frowned in thought. "Theresa wasn't one for frivolous things. Sensible brown shoes was more her style."

Emily covered her mouth and giggled when Tara rolled her eyes and shook her head. Then she kissed Rowland on the cheek. "Never mind, I love you anyway." The scientist and engineer appeared to be the stereotypical absent minded professor, but Emily had discovered that in large part that was a façade that he employed to hide from people who found his thoughts hard to understand, and the streak of ruthlessness that Tara had inherited. She also knew from Tara that Rowland had been devoted to his deceased wife.

Duncan swallowed some scrambled eggs and said, "But you can always go out incognito. With your abilities, you'd hardly be noticed by most people."

Tara sighed. "But the whole point of shopping is to be noticed, isn't it. Besides there are the security CCTV cameras. We know Werner has very influential friends in the security services and the face recognition systems aren't so easy to fool or avoid."

Duncan nodded. "CCTV can be a real pain in the..." She abruptly stopped talking and clenched her fist, pounding it slowly against the table. "Damn! I'd forgotten all about the CCTV. If they're looking for you, they'll also be looking for anyone who might have last had contact with you and John."

Tara put down her fork. "And that includes you," she said slowly.

"I've been traipsing all around town ordering equipment and hiring people for the new Vampire security team, and I didn't make any attempt to hide my face from the cameras. Bloody hell, I'm sorry Tara. I've been a fool."

"Don't be silly. You are ex-military and a security guard for Werner Biotechnologies, not a spook or criminal. That sort of thinking was never part of your job description." She picked up her cell phone and sent an encrypted text message to John. "I'm asking John to find out if anyone has been asking GCHQ or Police Intelligence about you."

"If they have, they might already be here or on their way," Rowland said thoughtfully as he sipped his tea.

Duncan was already on her radio, putting the facility's security on high alert.

Rowland smiled at Emily as he mopped up his egg with a piece of toast. "This looks like an excellent opportunity to test the Children of the Night."

Tara watched in puzzlement as Emily grinned and nodded. "Children of the Night? Weren't they wolves?"

Rowland looked smug. "Emily and I have been working on Artificial Intelligence based on nanite clusters, and we've had some success in duplicating the instincts and behaviour pattern of a mosquito. Then we installed it on a small drone equipped with Infra-Red, sonic, air pressure and scent detectors and a digital camera. When they detect human bodies in their assigned zones they hover and follow them, transmitting sound, video, and military GPS coordinates back to the lab. But even better, they are built to operate in a swarm, and the information is collated and integrated in our computers, giving a three dimensional map of any intruder's movements."

"Ah! I get it. Children of the Night." Tara shuddered. "I hate mosquitoes. But your system sounds intriguing. Security cameras and alarms that actively seek out intruders."

"Exactly! Each drone can only stay in the air for about twenty minutes with the transmitters and sensors at full power. Longer, if only the Passive Infra-Red is on until a potential target is spotted. But they recharge in five minutes and the swarm works as an integrated whole, so we can keep sending freshly charged ones out and the tracking computers are smart enough to anticipate target movements and so produce good guesses as to where they are headed. Better still, we have a mobile version that fits a swarm, charger, and notebook computer in a backpack or briefcase. Each drone is the size of a USB flash drive and hard to spot in the air. They also have a mosquito's threat avoidance instincts, so they're hard to swat too." Emily sounded like a proud mother.

"We're also working on a version that packs a sting. Tranquilliser or Taser dart," Rowland said.

"Or a fatal overdose of Etorphine, that's elephant tranquilliser to you, if they deserve it," Emily said, putting her hand on top of Rowland's. "A two to four milligram dose would knock down a Black Rhino and almost instantly paralyse and seconds later kill a human. So a drone armed with an Etorphine injector would be extremely deadly."

Tara's eyes widened at the thought of insect-like drones attacking in a swarm. She also saw the genuine anger in Emily's eyes at the thought of anyone trying to hurt her father, and it warmed her heart. She and Rowland were close, but there were things that a daughter couldn't give a father, even a grown up daughter. Her sense of smell was thousands of times more sensitive than it used to be, and she could smell the sex pheromones on both of their bodies. They had been busy before coming down to breakfast, and she had to hide a smile.

"We'll get the swarm in the air right after breakfast," Rowland said, buttering a slice of toast. "I've set the Children's central computer to relay the composite real time image to your HUD. So long as you're within range of the facility's Wi-Fi network, you

167

should be able to both receive the images and direct the Children of the Night just as you would the Vampire."

Tara tilted her head bemusedly. "You're really getting into this vampire thing, aren't you? I would have thought you'd be more upset."

Rowland studied the tines of his fork. "No matter what the ultimate consequences, the alien nanites saved your life and are helping to keep you alive, keep all of us alive. I can't be upset about that. Plus I have John's example. Hundreds of years and he hasn't demonstrated any ill effects, and he doesn't even have the neural interface bio-implant that you have to help him control and communicate with the thing." He stuck the fork into a juicy piece of sausage and smiled. "Besides, how many proud fathers can claim to have a vampire for a daughter?"

Tara felt a sudden warmth. "Are you proud of me father? You've never said it before."

Rowland looked contrite. "If I haven't then I should have. And yes I am. Very proud." He didn't mention the little twinge of pain he felt each time he looked at her and saw her mother's smile.

***

Dan Jackson studied the images on the screen of his notebook PC and smiled. "Yes. That's Tara Harker and her father Rowland Harker. I've been staring at their file photos often enough to recognise them in my sleep. Do we know who owns the house and the rest of the facility?" he said into his cell phone.

"No sir. Only layer over layer of corporate shell companies and trusts. Officially the house is listed as Transient Staff Accommodation."

Dan's fingers tapped the frame of the notebook. "Keep digging. Not knowing who we're dealing with makes me nervous. And it would be ridiculous if it turned out that we've stumbled upon an American covert operation, or corporation. At this moment it could be the Chinese for all we know. Your orders are still to observe and report only. No direct contact until I give the word. We've found their lair, now all we need to do is wait for everybody to come back and we'll have them. Those fucking werewolves may be bulletproof, but these guys aren't."

***

John dialled Tara's phone, and when she picked up he said, "You were right. Someone's been running a facial search for Duncan. My intelligence contacts just confirmed it. I think you should expect an attack. Perhaps I should..."

"No. It's more important that you establish contact with that Police Commander and his people. Without his support and at least unofficial approval, our hands are tied," Tara replied. "Duncan and I can handle security at this end. Plus my father has just given me a new toy." She told him about the Children of the Night.

John frowned, but he knew she was right. "Just remember. These people aren't bulletproof, and if they come after you, you have every right to defend yourself."

"I intend to," Tara said grimly.

"We all do," Duncan said, leaning towards the phone.

"Just be careful. Whoever is coming won't be amateurs. They know about Duncan and it's obvious from the outside that the facility has formidable security, so they'll be coming in hard," John said. He smiled when the satellite phone buzzed. "Speak of the Devil, I think our dashing young Commander is on the line. I'll talk to you later. Oh, remember to switch out from the silver bullets. They're expensive," he said lightly, although his

169

face was completely serious. He had seen too many friends and lovers die over his long life, and he didn't want to lose this unusual group prematurely. Even vampires died, and the female companions in Stoker's novel had been based upon real vampire women that he, Vlad had known. Like most, they had been good people who had been driven slightly mad by their vampiric transformations. Even the alien nanites couldn't help if its hosts thought the Devil had taken their soul.

John mentally shook himself free of maudlin thoughts and picked up the encrypted satellite phone. "Hello?"

Commander Blair's brisk tones said, "We need to meet. People are dying, and I can't stop it."

"And your superiors?" John asked suspiciously.

"They've agreed to turn a blind eye – for now."

"Just until the first time we screw up?" John said cynically.

Blair sighed. If he wanted this man's help he had to be truthful. He suspected that this mysterious vigilante was already more than familiar with the treachery of politics. "I'm afraid so, although I shouldn't be saying that. But you already knew it. My head will probably roll right along with yours, if that's any consolation."

John chuckled. "I expected as much. Hence the necessity for all this cloak and dagger stuff."

"Ah! Plausible deniability works both ways. What I don't know I won't be obliged to tell," Blair replied.

"And can't be responsible for," John added, dangling the carrot.

Blair laughed. "You've definitely dealt with government organisations before, haven't you?" His face turned serious. "I've been going over the reports of your actions in the hospital after I left, plus I saw your people in action myself. I have to ask – you seem to know a lot more about these … things than we do. Please tell me you're not responsible for them."

"That's the one thing I can assure you of. We had no part in creating or unleashing these things. But we've been tracking and studying them for a while now."

"Then why on God's Earth didn't you tell someone? We might have saved lives if only we had known more!" Blair cried angrily. He saw faces in the outer office turn towards him and he waved them away.

"Yes, mister copper, we believe there are werewolves who are going to go on a killing spree. We can't prove it and we can't tell you why they are going to do it, but we have a team of trained security experts who can advise you on them. Would you like to work with us?" John said, in a lightly mocking tone. "I don't know about you, but I try to avoid being locked in padded cells."

For a moment Blair was driven to protest, but then his shoulders slumped and he sighed. "And that's exactly what would have happened. Or if they believed you, they would have arrested the lot of you and confiscated your research, "for reasons of national security", the mocking quote clear in his voice.

"Do you really want to know the truth?" John asked.

The Commander didn't hesitate. "Yes."

"Go alone to these coordinates in two hours. Stand at the side of the field and wait to be contacted. Bring the satellite phone. If we see anyone else, or if you carry a tracker, we will know and you will never hear from us again. And people will continue to die."

Blair wrote down the coordinates. "I'll be there." He put down the satellite phone when the line went dead and took the coordinates to his computer. The on-line map went to a derelict football club's grounds in East London.

***

Two hours later Blair stood at the edge of the abandoned football pitch. The gate to the grounds had been padlocked, but someone had picked the lock and left it hooked to the chain. He opened the rusting gate, drove his car into the grounds, and closed the gate behind him. He drove down the road and parked behind a building and out of sight of the main road. It wouldn't do his reputation any good if someone stole his car. Standing at the agreed meeting spot he looked around at the mouldering buildings and the unkept field. The dead surroundings and echoing silence gave him a chill. If whoever he was supposed to meet was indeed in league with the werewolves, he was a dead man. He frowned. Despite the emptiness, he had the feeling that there was something or someone there. He jumped when a man's voice, the same voice as had been on the satellite phone, spoke just beside him.

"It's strange how quickly nature reclaims the works of men, isn't it."

Blair spun around and for a moment his eyes wouldn't focus upon the man standing within arm's reach of him. "Bloody heck! How did you do that?" This time, the man had a face. His training took over and he scanned the man's face like a computer, memorising the distinctive features, noting the firm gaze and confident expression and the way he held his body. This was a man used to command and used to getting his own way. Blair recognised a predator when he saw one. He didn't however, assume that the man was a threat or not to be trusted. He simply would be very careful not to get on this man's bad side unless he was forced to. But he also realised that showing his face was intended as a sign of trust. Or that he, Blair, wouldn't survive this meeting, but that didn't make sense.

"Come this way. I've taken the liberty of arranging a comfortable spot for us to converse." John led the way off of the field. Before he had approached Blair he had physically searched the area. When he approached the Police officer, equipment in John's pocket scanned him for transmitters and even passive electronics. The satellite phone also contained a second set of scanners that would have detected any equipment being tested and placed upon Blair's clothing or body. A van owned and driven by his employees scanned the air with anti-aircraft radar to detect any drones circling the area, and sensitive detectors scanned other vehicles in the surrounding roads as the van circled the football grounds. John was a certain as he could be that Blair was not bugged or carrying a recording device of any kind and that he had come alone.

Blair stared at the man's back speculatively. It was obvious that this man was not simply a security consultant, a fancy title for a mercenary. He had the air of someone who knew wealth and power, but who also got his hands dirty when necessary. He wasn't a giant, but gave off an air of great strength, the way really good martial artists did. "You haven't told me your name," he said.

"There is still a chance someone is listening, and not just your people. Let's wait until we get to my um, transport, and then I'll answer your questions," John said, smiling over his shoulder and pointing at a side entrance which pierced the rusting perimeter fence.

When they went through the gate, Blair was surprised to see what looked like a conventional air conditioned tour coach with curtained windows. "You do tours too?"

John chuckled. "Super high tech mobile command centres bristling with antennae tend to attract unwanted attention, not the least from your people. But a coach full of tourists is almost invisible despite its size." He pressed the button on his keychain and a small hatch swung open to reveal a keypad and retinal scanner. John typed in a password and let the device scan his eyes, both of them. There was a "ding", the panel swung shut, and the conventional looking door hissed open and the first step lowered. A partition next to the door concealed the interior of the bus from the gaze of passers-by. The driver was also hidden by another partition. He waved his hand. "Please."

Blair hesitated for second. Once he was inside that thing, he was committed and completely at this man's mercy. He had no idea how many others were inside, or whether they were armed. But he had come this far, and he really had no other options if he wanted to learn more. Once inside he realised that the exterior of the coach was a fake. None of the windows opened into the smooth walled interior. The inside looked more like a modern submarine. There were swivel seats, several control stations, a row of tall steel cabinets, and doors that led to partitioned-off rooms, one of which, according to the sign on the door, was a shower and lavatory. There was even a mini-kitchen with microwave, refrigerator, and tea and coffee makers. "All the comforts of home. Your organisation is a lot more generous than the Home Office. This thing must have cost a bomb."

"It has its advantages. A tour coach can circle the streets for hours without raising eyebrows, and groups of strangely dressed people can board or disembark without alarming anyone. Cosplay and Sci-Fi conventions provide a very useful cover." John nodded at a chair. "Take a seat. The bus is going to move off in a moment."

Commander Blair picked a seat and said, "You people are serious about what you're doing." He smiled in realisation. "Ah! That's what this dog and pony show is about."

John brought over a tray bearing a tea set and futuristic looking insulated tea pot. He set it down on a table and seated himself across from the police officer. "Help yourself. Yes, in a way. I want you to understand that we have significant resources behind us and that we're not simply a group of vigilantes with superhero delusions." He held out his hand. "My name is John, John Seward."

Blair shook the man's hand and then frowned. "That name sounds familiar for some reason."

"I'm quite well known in some circles," John replied easily.

"No, it's not that. It's something else, something I've read ... ah!" He smiled. "Dracula. The book, I mean."

John chuckled. "I get that a lot. But it's my real name, not a literary alias. As I'm sure you'll verify as soon as you're back at the station."

Blair raised an eyebrow. "Will I be returning to the station?"

"You're my guest. No harm shall come to you so long as you are under my roof," John said.

Blair was surprised by the ritualistic tone of the man's words. It sounded like something a feudal lord or clan chieftain might say. Then his eyes went to the tray. Food and drink. He realised that it *was* a ritual, that the man was offering his hospitality and protection so long as he was under his roof. He didn't know whether to be disturbed or relieved. "Uh, thank you." He cleared his throat and said, "You requested this meeting, so you obviously have something to propose."

John leaned forward. "First of all, I would like your honest understanding of what is happening here in London and all over the country."

Blair glanced around. "If this is some kind of ploy to get leverage over me by having me make embarrassing statements, my superiors have already made it clear that they will disavow my actions the moment it looks like it will be an embarrassment to them or the Metropolitan Police."

"That suggests that they expect something worth

disavowing," John said gently. "And you have my word that we are not being recorded in any way. Even the driver can't hear us."

The policeman smiled. "Did you ever see that old American TV series 'Mission Impossible' or the films based upon it?" When John nodded he said, "Well that's me and my team. My superiors know something terrible is happening, but suspect that the actual cause will be unpalatable to our political lords and masters, and probably to a large section of the public as well. Sometimes, people just don't want to know."

"And you, Commander Blair. Do you want to know?"

Blair sighed. "If it will help to stop whatever is happening and whoever or whatever is responsible."

"And if I said that werewolves are real?"

The Commander shook his head. "I don't know what they are, but I've seen them kill. They're not human and they're not just animals. Bullets don't even slow them down. And … and I saw them change back after they died. I can't believe in the supernatural, but I can't deny they fit all the requirements to be werewolves." He sighed again. "But I can't put that in my reports, not the official ones anyway, even if the news agencies and bloggers have been throwing the "W" word around for a while now."

"I don't care about your reports Commander, but will you work with us? Give us access to ongoing attacks, hold back CO19 and CTC, keep the SAS from shooting at us when we turn up. Block investigations into who we are and where we come from."

"If you know how to stop them, why don't you just tell me and I can have our people do it. Why the secrecy?" Blair asked suspiciously.

"No secrecy. The werewolves are allergic to silver. By itself, silver won't kill them, but it slows their healing and recovery. In order to kill them, you have to behead the bodies once they are down. Can you authorise silver bullets and give orders for your men to behead prisoners?" John asked, even though he knew the answer.

"Bloody hell! Of course not. They'd have me in a straight-jacket and padded room before I could put my cap on. Are you serious?"

"Deadly serious. And there's one more thing."

"Why do I get the feeling I'll like this even less? Go on then."

"Their bite is infectious. Anyone who is critically injured by a bite might turn. The only way to prevent it is to behead the victims or the corpses. Although less likely, those who are bitten without fatal injuries might still turn if they suffer a life threatening injury later on. Dying of old age won't do it."

"It's a disease?" Blair asked in horror.

"Not as such. Think of it as a toxin that needs to be injected into the victim."

"How do you know all of this? You couldn't have had the time to study these … these things in any detail." Then he lowered his face into his hands and groaned. "Don't tell me. They've always been here. But if that's true, why have they suddenly become active after so long?"

"I can't tell you how long they've been around, but from our investigations, it seems we have a new Patient Zero. Because we took this outbreak seriously much earlier, we have detected a pattern of infection." He reached behind himself to pick up a plastic folder. Inside were charts showing the pattern of attacks and how they had initially spread out from a single point in London and then suddenly spread.

Blair studied the charts, then frowned and tapped at them with a fingertip. "Wait a minute, if these are right, the waves of incidents outside of London each happened at approximately the same time! Are you suggesting that they were deliberate and coordinated?"

"I'm not suggesting anything. I've given you the facts, which you can verify if you can find people open minded enough not to self-censor the questions or results," John replied cautiously.

"But these figures also suggest that there was one or just a few initially infected. If we were to treat this as a disease, then it suggests that there is a Patient Zero, an original source." Blair eyed John with renewed suspicion. "Your people must have come to the same conclusion. Do you know who it was?"

John had discussed this point with Tara and her father. If Viktor's name was brought up, it would bring the Harkers into the investigation and unwanted scrutiny along with it. But Rowland had pointed out that even if they denied knowing Patient Zero, as Blair had called him, they would most likely come across Viktor's name sooner or later and inevitably link him to Harker Industries. That might ultimately destroy any trust and rapport they develop with Commander Blair and his superiors. John agreed, but since the Harkers would be the ones on the firing line, he needed their approval.

Blair was quick to notice John's hesitation. "What's the matter? Is there something you don't want me to know?"

John shook his head. "I do have a name, but no proof, only hearsay. You understand that I am reluctant to point the authorities at someone without any physical evidence to support the accusation. Nor do I wish to be accused of trying to mislead you if it turns out we were wrong."

"Fair enough. But if you have a name, I need to have it if we are to work together," Blair insisted. However his tension visibly eased. John's explanation made sense.

"The name Viktor Tiranul has been mentioned," John said, obviously reluctant.

"Tiranul? That doesn't sound British."

John smiled. "You're not going to like this."

Blair's sighs were getting progressively louder. "I don't like anything to do with this case. Tell me."

"My confidential sources tell me he's Romanian."

Blair wrote the name down in his notebook and added "Romanian". Then realisation struck him. "Romania? As in Transylvania?"

John grinned. "How did you guess?"

"This is insane. Next you'll be telling me that your information came from a man named Van Helsing."

"You're a fan of Bram Stoker?" John asked in an amused tone. "Anyway, you can see why we were hesitant to approach the authorities."

"To be honest, up to a few days ago I wouldn't have agreed to meet you. But my superiors are getting desperate and have authorised me to investigate um, unorthodox leads, with strict orders to be discreet in what I report and with the clear understanding that my arse is on the line if it all goes pear shaped." He nodded ruefully. "Yes I can see why you hesitated. Werewolves, silver, beheading, Transylvania? This is like something out of an old time horror film." He rubbed his chin. "The beheading is the sticky part. I can't see how I'm going to explain that one away."

John nodded. "I was afraid of that. I suppose we shall have to give your people a greater incentive to work with us."

"How?"

John produced a rectangular ABS plastic box. He undid the catch, opened the lid and showed the contents to Blair. "Standard large animal tranquilliser darts, CO_2 powered injectors, loaded with a proprietary sedative formula, produced by a reputable pharmaceutical company on an experimental basis. Not approved for human use or commercial sale. They will bring down a werewolf, but only for a short time, ten minutes or so maximum. Please sign this liability waver."

"Ah, I see. The contents are a proprietary formula, so I don't need to know what's in it, or why it works on the … things. Very clever."

John closed the case and handed the box over to Blair after he had signed the waiver. "Take my advice and lock your prisoner or prisoners in a very strong cell indeed. And when they turn back into human form, be very careful not to get them worked up or hurt."

"I understand. Like that comic book character, the scientist who turns green."

"Make no mistake. These creatures are not dumb animals. The might not act or speak like a human, but do not underestimate their intelligence. They are as smart, or smarter than us even in their um, hirsute form. Contact me again when you're ready to work with us. Now drink your tea, and I'll have the driver drop you off near to your office."

Blair tapped the satellite phone and nodded. "Thank you for your help, no matter how this turns out."

"I just hope for all our sakes that your superiors don't hesitate too long," John said grimly as he turned to speak into the intercom that connected him to the driver.

***

Tara was startled when her HUD suddenly appeared in the air in front of her eyes. A red icon flashed and the words "Suspicious activity detected near the perimeter" followed by an aerial outline map of the facility grounds and moving red icons indicating the location of the suspected intruders. She realised that the computer was smart enough to tell the difference between hikers or animals, and a deliberate scouting action or direct attack. Her radio bud crackled.

"Tara, we see it too. Duncan's electronic map on her tablet has been updated as well and a warning transmission sent to her. The security guards have been put on alert."

Duncan's icon appeared on Tara's HUD. The security specialist said, "Roger that, Emily. Take no action until I give the word. We want to be sure of what we're facing before responding. For all we know they might be planning a helicopter drop to bypass the fence and guards, or long range sniping. I wouldn't put it past Werner to use RPGs or something."

"RPGs?" Emily asked.

"Rocket Propelled Grenades. Despite the name, they are actually missiles like the Russian RPG-30, the more advanced ones like the Brimstone used by UK forces include guidance systems," Duncan replied briskly.

"Do you think they would actually employ something like that against us?" Rowland asked, shocked at the thought.

"Werner are an arms manufacturer. I know they have ready access to all kinds of military weapons and gear, even in Britain. Theoretically only for export of course, but that wouldn't stop them from using them if they thought it necessary. But I doubt they'll go for anything as drastic as that. Not yet anyway. They have no idea what John and I are. As far as they are concerned, we are just inconvenient witnesses to their acquisition of the alien technology," Tara said. "They might resort to IED's or even more sophisticated explosive weapons like Claymore mines outside of the compound though. Duncan, you and your people need to be particularly careful."

In her HUD Tara could see that the possible scouts were getting closer to the perimeter fence and from their icons, were hunched down and moving in little darts from cover to cover. More and more details developed on her display as the insect-like drones made pass after pass around the perimeter and the area where the activity had been detected. The security system detected a movement further out and directed some drones towards that direction. Her radio clicked and an icon indicated that it was John calling her.

"I'm on my way back, but it will be several hours, depending upon the traffic," John said in Tara's ear. "I can see the security display. It looks like they are going for a direct breach of the fence."

"Don't worry John. We'll take care of this. How did your meeting go?" Tara replied.

John summarised his meeting with Blair for her. "Basically he seems open to what we're saying and proposing, but he's just a cog and he needs to get his superiors on our side as well, even if it is only covertly. I've given him the tranquilliser darts."

Tara grimaced. "I hate that we had to do that. You know that despite your warnings, something bad is going to happen." She stopped speaking when the security system sounded a silent alarm, silent in the sense that the alert klaxon only sounded in their ear pieces. "Perimeter fence breached at these coordinates" appeared on her HUD and a section of the fence strobed red. The fence was not electrified, but each wire was part of a sensor grid like the nerves of the skin and reported both pressure and damage. Concealed security cameras activated and a window formed in her HUD showing the black clad man cutting a hole in the wire large enough for armed men to pass through. She swore when the security system reported breaches in the fence at three more places. They were attacking in force and from several directions. "Father, is the Vampire's hangar secure?"

"Don't worry Tara. The building is locked up tight and the security doors have deployed. Even with explosives or anti-tank weapons they would have a tough time getting in. Emily and I are in the bunker along with all the other hangar staff. It's you, Duncan and her people that need to be careful. I see lots of automatic and even heavy weapons. It looks like a full on military assault. I have all the cameras and audio recorders working and the evidence of the attack is being copied in real time to a remote backup site so that it won't be lost even if they manage to destroy the entire facility."

"That's great. I'm heading out now to join Duncan and the other guards." Unlike most private security staff, all of the guards Duncan had selected and hired were ex-special forces or other elite military units with actual combat experience and good records. But because they were in the UK and not the US, they could not be armed with assault rifles or submachine guns or even pistols. Instead, John had his workshops design a CO_2 powered auto-cocking, magazine fed crossbow for the guards. Silver coated hunting tips were available in the event they were faced with werewolves, and for normal humans, conventional broad head arrows but with a tiny high-pressure injector built into the tip that shot a droplet of Etorphine bonded to skin penetrating nanites. The high pressure spray combined with the arrow's impact would drive the liquid through body armour and normal clothing. This special adaptation of the drug was very fast acting and almost immediately fatal to a human. Since one of John's oldest companies specialised in pharmaceuticals and biotechnology, it was easy for him to gain access to the drug and Rowland had worked with him on the nano dermal injectors. The crossbows were not as powerful as a modern assault rifle, but they did not require a permit, were nearly silent when fired, and could be re-cocked in less than two seconds. A single charge of gas allowed the crossbow to be fired eighty times in a row. The folding blades of the arrow-heads cut through body armour like paper, although stab vests provided better but not complete protection.

Tara herself was armed with her high-tech mass

183

driver rifle. At full power, an armour piercing bullet fired by the weapon would pass completely through a man wearing the highest level of body armour with ceramic trauma plate inserts. On the other hand a slug or shot shell would impart such force upon impact that even if the vest held, the force would smash the victim's bones and flesh like the impact of a high speed car, but without the dangerous penetration. But she didn't intend to use it unless she was forced to because doing so might reveal its existence to Werner. Instead the plan was for Duncan and the guards to hold the attackers off, and she would go from group to group of the enemy taking out any of them that avoided the arrows. She would only use her rifle if the enemy broke through the defences and threatened the house or factory facilities, or to save her own life. Other than that, she would rely upon her suit and her super-human toughness to protect her from the attacker's weapons. She studied the three dimensional map in the middle of her HUD mentally rotating it one way and then another to get an idea of the terrain immediately around each breach and the way the enemy were positioning themselves. John had been working hard with her to impart a basic feeling for close combat tactics and the use of cover and terrain. It helped that the alien system in her body was a military one and seemed to adapt easily to the information requirements of combat, storing and integrating them. For instance, when she focused upon a single opponent, the HUD provided a constantly updated projection of that person or vehicle's course and possible objectives, as well as any information regarding the person's size, weapons and protective gear that they possessed. It felt almost like a First Person Shooter computer game. Although it appeared that the enemy was attacking simultaneously on all fronts, their synchronisation was not perfect and the distances from the breach to the nearest defender's position were not equal either, so she was quickly able to determine which group would be a threat soonest. In this case it was the group assaulting the left side entrance to the complex.

The defenders were split by Duncan into four groups, three covering the primary entrances and one the rear. The back of the complex was a large open space, incorporating the runway, air tower and various parking pad and work areas for test aircraft. In order to assault the rear the enemy would have to cross almost a kilometre of flat cover-less space and would be easily spotted from the control tower. So far, all the breaches had been in the front and sides of the complex.

Duncan didn't have enough men to form a solid perimeter, and without automatic weapons, she couldn't afford to split her men up into mobile two man teams. Instead she had arranged with John to install concrete bunkers that were disguised as planters and borders to protect landscaped areas from vehicles. The huge hangar front entrance which allowed large lorries and trailers to drive in from the main road were reinforced with Kevlar panels and saw resistant steel rods, as well as huge steel bollards that were lifted by hydraulic rams up from the ground behind the gate to prevent a vehicle from ramming its way through. Because of this, she placed her men to defend the less solid entrances to the office building and the attached accommodation wing. The landscaping was carefully designed to provide clear fields of fire and little cover for intruders, with no large trees and bushes. She had thought this strange for a modern industrial building complex, until she realised that John still saw every piece of property as a place to be defended like a castle or fortress and was willing to spend what was necessary to provide the needed defensive features. There were even strategically placed fountains that were actually deep water filled moats or tank traps. All his companies were structured to give him total control, so there were not meddlesome directors or

185

managers to question his odd follies. She smiled as she studied the ant-like icons moving across the screen of her military grade tablet. She also had another surprise waiting for the intruders.

***

Tara ran, bent low and almost appearing to glide over the ground, her electronic camouflage making her a moving blur in the air. Though not as fast as John and still in human form, she was moving faster than any living creature on Earth. Using the HUD as a guide, she avoided the enemy's scouts who had been the first to come through the broken fence. She wanted to come up behind the main body, trapping them between herself and the guard force and hopefully allowing her to pick off the rearmost ones without alerting the others that something was wrong. The fact that they were attacking during working hours meant they were going after the people and not just the facility or to steal industrial secrets. Everyone in the complex was at risk. The last time Werner had attacked they had burned John's household staff alive. Tara was determined that they were not going to succeed this time. She reached the fence and moved sideways until she found the rip in the wire. Turning back towards the buildings, she quickly spotted each of the invaders even without the aid of the HUD. Her fangs and claws extended as she headed for the back of the nearest man. They were attacking in four man teams, leapfrogging forwards in two pairs. Suddenly, just as the leading man rose to dash forward, an arrow hissed out from the direction of the main entrance and punched into the man's chest. He stiffened convulsively and then went completely limp when the Etorphine entered his bloodstream.

"Whatever they're wearing, the arrows are penetrating well," Tara whispered into her microphone.

"Thanks for the info," Duncan's voice replied.

Then Tara caught up with the last man. All three of the survivors had dropped to the ground and were firing back blindly, laying down suppressive fire in lieu of actual cover as they crawled forward. One of the effects of her vampirism was that she was able to move just as quickly on all fours as she could running, although it was more tiring. Moving low and fast she darted across the remaining distance and leapt onto the man's back. Kneeling upon his back she pulled his head back and her claws ripped out his throat with a single savage motion before she twisted his head around until she felt the spine snap and tear. A huge gout of blood soaked the grass below him as his body jerked in its death spasms, but she was already gone, bounding towards the next man.

***

Duncan knelt on one knee behind the reinforced concrete and calmly snapped off an arrow even as she directed the fire of her men using the high resolution display of the ruggedised tablet in front of her. She cursed as she saw her arrow miss, ducked down and shuffled to the side as a hail of bullets hit the concrete and passed through the air where she had been, sending up a cloud of concrete dust and a stinging spray of fragments. Her crossbow had reloaded by the time she raised it to her shoulder again. She found a moving body in her telescopic sight which automatically compensated for the target's motion once she touched the trigger. Holding her breath, she squeezed. The crossbow thumped just as one of her guards screamed in agony when a bullet shattered his cheekbone. She grinned savagely when her arrow struck home and the man flopped down on his face. With the arrows they were using, there were no flesh wounds. The Etorphine was like an insane dose of Morphine and much faster acting. At a safe dose it would bring an elephant crashing down in seconds. The massive overdose the arrow delivered shut down the victim's bodily functions as if a switch had been thrown. She ducked down behind cover when bullets from two submachine guns converged on her position. That was the greatest risk. If the enemy could keep them down behind shelter long enough and often enough, they would be able to advance right up to the positions of the defenders, and their crossbows would be no match for full automatic weapons at close range. She rolled back to her original position, popped up and fired another arrow. A bullet went by her head, close enough for her to hear the hum of displaced air over the rattle of gunfire. The battle seemed oddly one sided, since the guard's crossbows were almost silent compared to the roar of the attacker's gunfire. So far, three of the Werner mercenaries were down and only one of her men, but they were getting steadily closer and her casualties would rapidly mount despite their advantage of bullet proof cover since, she didn't have enough archers to lay down a suppressive rain of arrows as they had done in medieval battlefields.

***

Tara managed to kill the second last man just as quickly and silently as the first, but the remaining man glanced over his shoulder and spotted her just as she was finishing her target off. She was forced to dive and roll as her sonar detected his submachine gun swinging around towards her. "Incoming" flashed on her HUD and a red circle highlighted her enemy's weapon. She had already moved two metres to the side when the bullets punched into where she had been just a moment earlier. Moving even faster than a werewolf, she transitioned from a sideways roll to a forward motion without visibly slowing down. Her opponent panicked and held down his trigger, forgetting all fire discipline. The gun muzzle blazed, shooting out a jet of flame as a stream of bullets tracked her motion.

But the man had already been firing at the guards and then at Tara, and his thirty round magazine emptied in less than two seconds. The mercenary's eyes widened in his green and black camouflage painted face as he desperately ejected the empty magazine and flipped it around to fit the second magazine that had been taped upside-down to the first into the receiver of his weapon. He gasped in shock when a swipe of Tara's claws ripped the weapon from his grip, the force of her blow slamming the sling against his shoulders, sending him sprawling onto his back.

Tara threw herself on top of the man, her knee driving into his lower belly, winding him with the force of a battering ram. The man's torso arched upward in an agonised contraction of his abdominal muscles and she rammed her claw tipped fingers into his chest just below his sternum, plunging her entire hand into the cavity of his chest like the blade of a spear. She didn't bother with anything flashy like ripping his heart out since there was no one nearby to be horrified. Instead she consulted her HUD and headed for the next group that presented the greatest threat to the defenders.

***

Three more of Duncan's men were dead or badly injured, and the bullets were coming closer and more often, making it difficult for the defenders to pop up to fire. The concrete mouldings had decorative shapes that served as effective crenellations, but peering through the gaps still limited the archer's angle of view and fire. On the other hand, the guards were taking aimed shots instead of hammering off three round bursts in the

189

general direction of the enemy, so when they did fire, more often than not they hit their target. Then abruptly the fire from the middle of the three remaining groups of attackers faltered when they realised that someone was attacking them from the rear and flank and that one entire team had been wiped out. The suppressive fire from the middle faded away as they turned to fire in Tara's direction. The teams at either side also paused, confused by what was happening to their sides. Duncan grinned when she realised that the enemy squad to her left was taking friendly fire from their compatriots who were shooting at Tara and missing. "All teams concentrate your fire on the left and right flanks of the enemy. Let Tara handle the centre team," Duncan said into her microphone. With the momentary lull in the enemy's fire her men and two women, were able to re-position themselves to best effect. She glanced at her watch and was surprised to see that over an hour had passed since the first of the enemy scouts had been detected.

Then Duncan's eyes were drawn to the tablet's screen by a flashing icon. She touched the "Threat" icon and the screen changed to an image created from a combination of surveillance camera feeds and data from the drone swarms. "Oh shit!" she said when she saw the moving image of a Werner mercenary carrying an RPG launcher and another man with a canvas satchel containing two reloads coming up behind. "Warning, incoming RPG watch for contrail and prepare to take cover." The disguised bunkers could withstand even an RPG round, but the blast and shrapnel could still injure or kill anyone who was partially exposed, as well as stunning the others. She realised that only Tara would have a chance of stopping the RPGs from being launched. "Unit One, target the enemy forces in the centre. Send as many arrows as you can their way. We need to support Tara with covering fire."

Tara had received the same warning, which had appeared on her HUD. She had almost reached the next team, weaving and dodging her way through a storm of bullets, but the RPG was a greater threat. She went into a skidding turn, and ran towards the breach where the RPG launcher team was passing through. But even as she ran towards them, she saw the mercenary raise the RPG to his shoulder, aim, and fire. She dived to the side, almost flying through the air and away from the path of the rocket, which struck the ground where she had been a second ago. The blast still caught her in mid-air, flinging her forward. But even under such extreme circumstances, the vampire part of her was at home gliding through the air and her body automatically made the best of the height and velocity, and she found herself shooting towards the RPG operator like one of Duncan's arrows. A spot on her back and lower thigh throbbed painfully from being struck by shrapnel, but the suit had held and her HUD told her she wasn't bleeding. A small sliver of metal had sliced the side of her face, but the bleeding had stopped almost instantly and was already healing. She saw the surprised expression on the man's face as he struggled to reload his weapon with his partner's aid just before she slammed into him.

The flying mass of Tara's inhumanly solid body slammed into the RPG operator. The body of the launcher was driven back into his face and blood sprayed as the wood and metal shaft shattered his teeth and jaw, and he was thrown backwards, arms windmilling as he fell.

The other man held up the canvas bag containing a reload rocket to shield his face, but he screamed in agony when Tara's razor sharp claws raked down the length of his forearm as she flew past, ripping his flesh down to the bone from wrist to elbow.

Tara landed rolling and sprang to her feet. She spun to face her opponents both of whom were clutching themselves and moaning in pain. She wasn't in a merciful mood right then and moved in to finish them off. But before she could strike, the "Incoming" alert flashed on her HUD. She looked over her shoulder just in time to see a second team with an RPG launcher fire a rocket at her in a whoosh of flame.

***

Rowland cried out in horror when he saw Tara disappear in a blinding blast of fire and smoke. He slammed his fist against the stainless steel topped table. "Tara! Are you all right. Tara, answer me," he shouted into the microphone frantic with concern for his daughter. The death of Tara's mother had almost destroyed him, and he couldn't bear the thought of Tara dying like that. It was bad enough when he had to let her climb into experimental and possibly deadly aircraft, but he knew she would never forgive him if he tried to stop her. This was different. He was a gentle and peace loving man, but right now his rage could have wiped out an army.

Emily gripped his shoulder. "She could be too busy trying to stay alive, or she could be injured and hiding. She doesn't need you shouting in her ear." She knew they could have checked on Tara's vitals by activating the flight bio-monitor system, but because the drone system was experimental, they couldn't run both at the same time.

Rowland nodded. "You're right but I have to do something..." His knuckles whitened as he gripped the edge of the table. Then his agile and inventive mind started working again. "The drone attack sequence!"

"But the Etorphine injectors haven't been installed

yet," Emily protested.

"Yes, but the mosquito based attack pattern is already in place. Each drone is about half a kilogram and diving downwards from twenty metres or more they can move as fast as an arrow. Just a small change in the parameters and..."

Emily nodded eagerly. "Set their injection point a centimetre beyond the surface of the skin..." she said, her fingers already busy on the computer keyboard. "There! We can't use them all up or we'll lose our monitoring system ...."

"But there are only ten of the enemy left. We activate the target acquisition system like so..." His finger punched a button and red danger warnings flashed on the control screen.

"And we manually select a target, like him..." Emily said, her fingers moving the targeting selector to the second RPG operator, who had entered the combat zone and fired too quickly for the drones to mark his presence and warn Tara, "select a CTN drone..."

Rowland scanned the list of active drones and found the ones highlighted in flashing blue indicating they were close to the selected target. "And..." His finger tapped the keyboard.

***

The RPG operator's narrowed eyes scanned the scene in front of him, searching for a trace of his target. Even an RPG explosion would leave some trace of human victims, some blood or a limb. He spotted a trail of blood and he raised the reloaded RPG launcher as he followed the blood trail. He spotted an indistinct blur on the ground and he looked at it through the targeting scope. Before his eyes could focus he heard a high pitched whistling sound above him and he looked up. The drone smashed into his face like a flying golf ball.

193

He dropped the RPG launcher and clutched at his face, shouting in pain and falling to his knees.

His reloader looked past his injured partner, but the indistinct target, if it had been there at all, was gone.

***

"Got him, the sonofabitch!" Rowland shouted in glee, pumping his fist in the air. The main screen showed Tara's icon moving and he sighed in relief when he heard his daughter's voice come in over the speakers.

"I'm still alive, father. A bit battered, but alive. Don't worry about me. See if you can help Duncan and her people with the drones."

Shaking with relief, Rowland grinned at Emily. "Yes, yes Tara, I'll do that. Be careful."

Emily turned back to the targeting screen. "The other attackers are moving around and a bit harder to target, but we should be able to ... there!" The system indicated a target lock on one of the mercenaries.

"On it!" Rowland snapped as he selected a drone. "Take that, you sodding bastard!"

***

Tara had been less than forthcoming in her conversation with her father. The blast of the RPG had broken her leg and dislocated her shoulder. The suit had held up incredibly well, protecting her from puncture wounds and cuts except for the side of her face because she hadn't been wearing the skin tight hood. Other than the initial surge of agony, she wasn't in much pain because the alien medical nanites were blocking it as well as dealing with the internal bleeding and severed arteries caused by the broken bone. She had been stunned for a moment and that was when the RPG operator had spotted her. But when the man had been painfully distracted by the dive bombing drone, she had managed to crawl and wriggle away into cover, and with the suit's camouflage capability, she was close to being invisible if she didn't move too quickly. She had been grateful for the pain killing capabilities of the nanites when she had fixed her dislocated shoulder with a simultaneous blow of her hand and by ramming her body against the ground. Without the nanites the pain of moving her broken leg like that would have had her screaming in agony, but all she felt was a dull ache. She managed to lift her head and shoulders using an irregularity in the ground, and with both hands she had pushed the ends of her broken femur back into rough alignment. The nanites could have taken care of it by themselves, but it would have taken much longer. Now all she needed was time for her vampire metabolism and the nanites to heal her injuries and get her back on her feet. Her canines itched and she felt a surge in her desire for blood as her body consumed its reserves in order to power the healing. But worst of all, she was out of the fight for the moment, and her absence could prove critical.

***

With the disruption caused by Tara's flank attack, her foiling of the first RPG attack and the advent of the dive bombing drones, Duncan had been feeling hopeful that they could drive off the attackers. Her men had broken the momentum of the enemy's advance and had them pinned down. Every time a mercenary lifted his head to fire, two or more arrows would send him diving back down for cover. She even had two of her men firing upwards so that their arrows arched up and then fell almost vertically down to threaten the mercenaries' backs.

Then suddenly everything went to hell when the

second RPG team gave up searching for Tara and climbed through the fence. While there were no thick trees to hide behind, there were some small decorative trees just inside the fence line which provided some shade for the perimeter patrols and just looked pretty. The RPG team took shelter beneath one of these trees and its leaves and branches were thick enough to disrupt the vertical drone attacks long enough for the operator to aim and fire his weapon.

Several of the guards spotted the flare and smoke of the missile launch and shouts of "RPG!" and "Take cover!" rang out in the relative silence. The rocket seemed to be heading directly in her direction and Duncan threw herself flat behind the bunker, eyes closed with her hands over her ears and her mouth open. The missile whooshed over her head and slammed into the building behind her. The concrete and brick was too thick for the RPG to penetrate, so most of the blast was deflected back towards the hiding guards. The concussion made Duncan's head ring and concrete shards hammered at her body. Despite the fact that her head was spinning she tried to climb upright, shouting "Get up! Get up! Keep firing!"

But the defenders diving for cover gave the Werner attackers the opportunity they needed and they took advantage of the lack of deadly arrows coming their way to get up. Their submachine guns hammered, sending a deadly sleet of bullets towards the stunned guards and they began to advance again, one man moving as another gave him cover with his fire.

A bullet clipped Duncan's neck and she felt blood soak her collar, followed a moment later by stabbing pain that made her teeth ache. She prayed that it had not severed an artery or vein as she desperately fired back, ignoring the bullets that buzzed past all around her. The guards to either side of her were down, one gruesomely dead and the other clutching a wounded shoulder. She knew that they were only moments away from being overrun, and she felt a moment of bleak amusement that it was her former employer who had proven to be the most determined to get her killed.

The leading mercenaries were just mctres away from the bunkers when a horrible sobbing scream rang out behind them. The sound was of a man in unbearable agony and the entire battlefield froze as everyone turned to look. What they saw made several of the hardened mercenaries blanch in fear and gasps came from all quarters and from both sides.

"Leave my land or die like these curs!" Dracula roared in a voice that rang across the entire field and struck the attackers like a physical blow. Impossibly, he held the shaft of the RPG launcher upraised vertically in his fist, and impaled upon the other end was the mercenary who had operated it. The man's arms were obviously and hideously broken and the thick body of the RPG launcher had obviously been driven deep into his body upwards from between his legs, which dangled on either side of the ancient vampire's fist. Worst of all, the man was still alive, screaming and crying pitifully in mortal agony. Dracula's other fist was tangled in the hair of the missile operator's partner, holding up the man's severed head. A second later he flung the bleeding head like a catapult throwing a boulder at a castle wall and the head smashed into a mercenary with such force that the snapping of his ribs could be heard by everyone around him. "Throw down your weapons and flee or upon my word you shall all die like this!" Dracula roared, shaking the impaled man like a doll on a stick.

One mercenary vomited, and then threw down his submachine gun. "Fuck this. I wasn't paid to fight monsters." With that he started to run for one of the breaches in the fence, ignoring everything but the fastest way away from the nightmare behind him. Suddenly the others broke like a pane of shattering glass. Weapons

197

thudded onto the grass and the air was filled with the sound of boots pounding the grass as the mercenaries fled for their lives.

Dracula stood for a moment longer with the still screaming man held in the air, then he grimaced in disgust and flung the man towards one of the solid steel columns that supported the fence. The man's body struck the immovable pillar with a sickening crunch. Blood and flesh sprayed the backs of the fleeing mercenaries, whipping them on to run even faster, mad with fear. Then, as if a magician had thrown a cloak over him, Dracula was gone and John Seward stood in his place, looking slightly sad as he took in the sight of death and destruction.

Tara limped up behind him. "I never thought of Dracula as the cavalry coming to save the day."

John shook his head. "I was too late. If I had not done something drastic, Duncan and her guards would have been overrun and killed in moments. I do not enjoy doing … that." His eyes indicated the pulped remains of the RPG operator.

Tara placed her hand upon his shoulder. "I understand, and so will the others. If I could I would have torn all of them apart with my bare hands as well as my teeth. We protect our own, no matter the cost. I understand that now."

John sighed. "I fear not all of the guards and staff will feel that way. Those who wish to leave I shall pay off handsomely in exchange for their oaths to remain silent about what they saw today. But I fear that I, we, have shown our hand and Werner will now know that more than werewolves stalk the land, although it is unlikely that they will think of vampires. Not right away, at least."

She nodded. "You're right. They, Werner, won't give up. He'll hit back, and he'll want at least one of us for dissection in his laboratories. We can't stay here,"

Tara said.

"Werner will need time to recover and make plans. We will be safe here for a little longer. After that, well, I have made plans for this day." He smiled at her. "And now you need to assure your father of your well-being. No doubt he is frantic with worry about you."

Tara looked down at her still healing leg. "That RPG nearly got me. I was over-confident. You were right. There is much more I need to learn. Like how you got here so soon."

"Later. As you say, there remains much for you to learn." He held out his hand to her. "Come, let us find out the butcher's bill and help those who need healing. A lord looks to the welfare of his followers first, if he expects to survive very long and to retain their loyalty. Oh, and I forgot to mention, that Renfield has fully recovered and shall be joining us again soon."

"Marvellous. One cannot do without one's butler for long, can we?" she said with a grin. She liked Renfield who had been badly beaten by Werner's goons and had been left for dead. But Dracula's faithful attendant who was the latest in the long familial string of Renfields, had survived the burning of John's mansion and had been recovering in hospital.

"No indeed. My suits are in a terrible state of disorder, and my tea supply is running short. It will be good to have him back," John said, every inch the Victorian gentleman.

"Do you think he would mind helping me dust my model aeroplanes?"

John laughed. "I've had much stranger interests than model aircraft over the years, and Renfield has managed to cope with them splendidly. I'm not sure what he'll make of your um, eccentric colour schemes though. He's quite traditional in some things."

Tara made a dismissive motion with her hand. "Military markings are so drab. My creative side needs to find some expression, and it's better than spraying graffiti on walls." She rubbed her hands. "Once father stops mucking around with the Vampire's exterior I can design a proper default design for it. I only have to do an electronic image and upload it. Come to think if it, I could do a variety of themes for all situations and tastes." Her face turned serious as she looked around at the carnage and she lightly touched the back of John's hand. "I have to tell you that I've still been wondering if you are a monster, and if I'm turning into one. But today has made me realise that you don't need fangs and claws to be a monster." She looked up at his face to see if her words had offended him.

"I've never found a satisfactory answer to that question. To many I, and you, will always be monsters. All I can tell you is to look into the eyes of the ones who love you. So long as you can meet their gaze without shame and they can meet yours without fear, then no matter how you look or what you have done, you are no monster." He touched her cheek, his fingers feather light. "Just remember, whatever you did today, you did not for gold or power, but to protect those who look to you for protection and safety."

Tara felt a rush of relief when she saw Duncan wave to her, and her father and Emily come out of the hangar. She nodded and waved back at them. "We need to do something about Werner. They're not going to give up."

John's expression hardened. "I intend to send him a message. If he is wise he will heed it, otherwise he will learn why the Turks pissed themselves at the very mention of Dracula."

Chapter Eleven

Commander Blair had called a meeting with experts from Animal Control and in consultation with them requisitioned tranquilliser guns that matched the darts that John Seward had given him. He had looked up the man's name in the Police intelligence databases as well as on Google, and as far as anyone knew, Seward had a clean record and was a respected industrialist who the Government and MOD often consulted with over matters of science and especially defence technology. He represented the contents of the darts as an experimental drug that had been offered for the use of the Police under conditions of strict confidentiality and with the understanding that no attempt would be made to analyse the contents. At a briefing of the SO15 officers who were to be issued the darts, Blair said, "The makers believe that this drug will be effective in taking down these creatures, but they are not sure for how long. We have seen how strong these creatures are, so we shall take no chances. Officially we are dealing with dangerous animals, so standard guidelines regarding the use of restraints do not apply. Use of leg restraints are approved. Since they are known to use the claws upon their hands as weapons, their arms are to be secured behind their backs. Once placed in a cell, the restraints may be removed if the prisoner is still fully sedated. Officers are not to open the cell doors or enter the cells alone under any circumstances. The use of pepper sprays and Tasers are approved." He leaned forward over the podium. "Be careful. You've all seen what they can do, and the condition of their victims. Don't take any risks. If the drug doesn't work, do *not* attempt to apprehend." He scanned their faces for any signs of bravado or aggression, and nodded in approval at what he saw. The fact that they finally had a weapon that might give them a chance to take down these things improved their morale immensely. Now all they could do was to wait for another attack.

***

Blair didn't have to wait long. Seven hours after the briefing an emergency alert came in. A werewolf attack was happening right in the middle of London, in Piccadilly Circus. Everyone had been issued full tactical gear except that they wore stab resistant vests instead of body armour. The location of the attack couldn't be random. Seward had been right. This was a deliberate hostile action, a terrorist attack. If Seward was also right about all of this being just a diversion, he shuddered to think what the actual intention was of the persons behind this. He was still waiting for the results of the information request on Viktor Tiranul. Since the man wasn't British and had no criminal record, it was taking time to get the information from the Romanian authorities, who were justifiably suspicious about his request regarding one of their citizens when he couldn't produce any evidence or basis for his interest. He was bound by his orders and common sense not to mention the werewolf attacks, so he had to allow his request to pass through normal channels. He grabbed his helmet and ran for the car park. Instead of his car, he headed for the tactical command vehicle that he had requisitioned. Everyone else in the command team was already aboard and he had to grab the back of a seat to prevent himself from falling over when the van lurched into motion. Every man available was scrambling to respond. There were always news cameras on or near Piccadilly and this attack, as well as the response, would be seen all over the world. There would be no denying what happened this time. If he failed to stop the creatures this time he might as well hand in his resignation on the spot. The interior of the vehicle smelled of stale coffee and bacon for some reason and it made him feel queasy.

One of the communications officers tapped his arm. "Sir, you need to see this." He pointed to a monitor that was showing a live BBC news transmission and switched the audio from his headphones to the loudspeakers.

"… anonymous tip-off, our news team was on the spot here in Piccadilly Circus the moment the creatures that some people have been calling werewolves made a sudden appearance. People are fleeing in all directions, running right into the heavy traffic as well as towards Regent Street and Shaftesbury Avenue." The cameraman zoomed in on the creature who had climbed the statue of Anteros like a miniature King Kong.

Blair groaned. The close up shot clearly revealed the wolf-like countenance and upright bipedal body. No one could mistake it for an animal unless some mad biologist had somehow blended a wolf with an ape. The traffic around the Circus had totally jammed up, with drivers abandoning their vehicles in the middle of the road. Fortunately Blair had anticipated this and the strike unit was rapidly approaching the scene in a military helicopter, a spanking new Agusta Westland Wildcat. The team comprised six armed officers and a battlefield medic, the last because every previous event had resulted in disastrous casualties. Fortunately the circus was sufficiently wide enough for the helicopter to come down low, allowing the men to rappel down on ropes dropped from the aircraft.

"Command One, this is Strike Leader. We are approaching the target. Will deploy on the traffic island in front of County Mark House, over."

Blair took the proffered microphone. "Roger Strike Leader. Tranquillisers only. Repeat Tranquillisers only. There are too many bystanders. Acknowledge."

"This is Strike Leader. Acknowledged Command One, tranquillisers only." The man's voice was calm and professional, even though his orders might get him and his men killed if the untested tranquilliser darts didn't work, or even if they were slow to work. It was the middle of the afternoon and despite the pandemonium, there were dozens of people still running about or worse, just standing and gaping or taking photographs with their cell phones. There was no time to deploy snipers and besides they had proved ineffective at previous attacks. Blasting away with submachine guns would only put civilians at risk.

Blair was able to watch his men slide down the ropes from the helicopter on the news broadcast as well as feeds from security cameras. He could even see the long barrelled air rifles slung on their backs. None of them carried a submachine gun or rifle, although each man had a Glock 17 automatic pistol holstered on his hip. He hoped to hell that they wouldn't need them, especially since they had been as useful as water pistols against the werewolves so far. Fortunately for them the traffic immediately around the statue was completely immobile so the police team was able to advance towards the two rampaging werewolves without risking being run over. Now that they were on the ground he was not going to commit the sin of trying to micro-manage a tactical situation from a distance. All he could do was watch, unless he decided to order the team to withdraw entirely. As he stared numbly at the screen, he swore under his breath. The monsters were actually herding the people towards the statue and the circular basin beneath it. One or the other of the creatures would dart out and chase down their victims, hurling them back to the statue. There were already more than twenty men, women, and children of both sexes huddled at the base of Anteros, many with bruises and more serious injuries such as broken bones. It was like watching sheep dogs at work. For a frozen moment everyone just watched in horrified fascination.

Then one of the werewolves climbed to the very top of the statue, hanging out to one side by one hand as it roared in defiance. Then it dropped down onto the groaning huddled captives, pulled a teen-aged boy from amongst them, and almost casually ripped one of his arms off and bit into it as if it was a chicken wing.

This horror seemed to trigger everybody into action. The other werewolf pounced and tore into a middle aged woman with fangs and claws, spraying the statue with a glistening red coat of gore. The remaining people in the square made a mad dash to escape, and the police strike team attacked.

The news broadcast had cut off when the blood started flowing, and Blair watched the feed from a security camera as his men opened fire. He watched intently, fists clenched, waiting to see if the darts would have any effect. The first couple of darts missed, one hit a bleeding human victim who's eyes rolled back in his head and tumbled backwards. Then the darts started hitting the werewolves. Blair punched the wall of the van when the first werewolf to be hit brushed the dart off of its hide as if were an irritating insect, and the other did the same. It appeared as if he had failed and all the victims huddled at the base of the statue were doomed. He rubbed his eyes tiredly.

"Sir! Look!"

Blair's gaze returned to the screen. One of the werewolves was clawing at the air and shaking its head. Then suddenly it was down. Moments later the other one followed. Blair realised that he had been holding his breath. He inhaled, and then shouted "Striker One. Get in there. Secure them. Wrap them in bloody chains from head to toe if you have to. Then get the medics in." He clicked to the local police channel. "Get crowd control in there. Don't let the injured leave the scene. We still don't know if…" Then he realised that transcripts of his words might be reviewed later. "We don't know how badly they are hurt. At the minimum they'll need rabies and tetanus shots." He watched in satisfaction as the creatures were bundled up and carted away in prisoner transport vans while the rescue teams moved in and crime scene tape was used to cordon off all of Piccadilly Circus. "They worked, by God. The bloody darts worked!" he crowed jubilantly.

The men in the van started cheering and clapping each other on the back. Finally they were able to strike back, and for the first time they had prisoners.

"Maybe now we can figure out what these fucking things are and where they came from," Blair said to no one in particular. Unlike the others he was painfully aware that despite their success, what most of the world would see was a massacre in one of the most famous symbols of London. There were bodies scattered all over the large open area, many gruesomely disfigured or ripped open. It was as if someone had dropped a bomb on the Circus. But all he knew was that he needed to get in touch with Seward. They were going to need more of that tranquilliser, lots of it, whatever the cost. He turned to the driver. "They'll be taking the prisoners to West End Central Station. Get us there. Now. We'll go in through the Burlington Street entrance. I don't want our faces on telly and the evening newspapers."

***

Blair peered through the peep hole in the cell door and watched in fascination as the werewolf struggled against the handcuffs and shackles that held its ankles. Despite the thick steel door, he started backwards when the handcuffs snapped with a metallic crack, followed seconds later by the leg irons. He stared in disbelief at the freed werewolf. What he had just seen should have been impossible. With its hands behind its back the werewolf shouldn't have had enough leverage to break

206

the solid link cuffs, but he could clearly see them on the thing's wrists like some kind of insane bangles, the metal at the joint twisted and broken. It was not even bleeding. He jumped back when the werewolf sniffed, swivelled its head towards the door, and suddenly sprang, hitting the locked door with sufficient impact to make dust fall from the door frame. "Those doors are to stay shut no matter what. Is that understood?" he said to the watching police constables. He had just received notice that experts from the Defence Science and Technology Laboratory (Dstl) out of Porton Down were on their way to study his prisoners. It was roughly a two hour drive, but the scientists needed time to organise and equip a team so it would be at least four hours before they would arrive.

***

The second werewolf soon joined its companion in pounding against the cell door, and after shouting at the inmates failed to produce silence, the guards soon learned to ignore the noise, although they couldn't resist the occasional nervous glance at the vibrating, shuddering doors. But after about two hours the noise in both cells died down, and the duty officers sighed in relief, and then went back to their regular duties.

It was four and a half hours before the experts from Porton Down arrived. Blair greeted them as they entered the station to a chorus of shouted questions from the gathered press and curious passers-by. Although he was not particularly biased, he was still surprised to discover the medical team was comprised of three people, led by a good looking black haired woman wearing expensive looking glasses and power suit. He had been expecting a bunch of mad scientist types in lab coats, although he realised that was silly. The only sign of their occupation were the large wheeled suitcase-like

207

containers covered with biohazard stickers that they pulled and pushed along.

"I'm Professor Jamieson, head of the Xenobiology Department, Porton Down and these are my field team. These are my credentials. Please note that in the event of a biological emergency I have overriding authority over the police and military. As of now, a medical/biological emergency has not officially been declared, but I am quite prepared to do so at any moment if I deem it necessary. We have some concerns that these unidentified life forms are some kind of genetically modified species, and that what we are seeing is a biological attack or field test of a bio-weapon." She shook Blair's hand briskly and pushed her spectacles up on her nose. "No time to waste, show me what you have."

Her steamroller personality made Blair smile. He liked confidence and competence. "Of course, Professor Jamieson. Come right this way."

The scientist nodded to her team and then to Blair. "Lead the way, Commander."

Blair set off towards the holding area and nodded to the desk sergeant. "These people are to have our full cooperation and access to the prisoners."

"Yes sir. This way sir, ma'am," he said, checking that the cell key chain was on his belt and then leading then down the fluorescent lit corridor. Although he already knew, he consulted a clip board before saying, "The special detainees are in cells seven and eight. As per your orders, no one has been inside the cells since they were put there. There was a lot of noise and fuss at first, but then they quietened down." He stopped in front of the holding cell marked seven and peered through the view port. What he saw made his eyes widen, but he didn't comment. He would let the experts deal with it. He stepped back and waited for instructions.

Professor Jamieson stepped up to the cell door,

slipping on a pair of rubber surgical gloves. She held out her hand for an alcohol wipe, which she used to sterilise the area around the view port.

Blair watched as her assistants unpacked biohazard suits complete with N95 filtered breathing systems attached to the belt and linked by a pleated tube running to the faceplate. "Are those really necessary? My men and I have already been in unprotected contact with them," he asked uneasily.

She gave him a thin lipped smile. "Don't worry, Commander. There is no indication of any kind of virulent infective agent. We're just being careful and avoiding further cross contamination in order not to complicate our work. Then she turned to peer through the view port.

Blair saw her body stiffen and he frowned in alarm. "Is something wrong, Professor?"

The woman turned back towards him, anger on her face. "There is a naked young woman in the cell, and from the blood on the walls and her bruises, she has been badly mistreated. What is the meaning of this, Commander?"

Blair looked at the Sergeant who held up his clipboard.

"The cells have not been opened since the prisoners were brought in sir."

"Then how do you explain the naked woman in there?" Professor Jamieson snapped. "Open the cell at once. She might require medical attention. We may have to run a rape kit on her and call in the IPCC." Her anger made the Sergeant jump and hasten to unlock the cell.

"Professor, what about your suit?" one of the assistants asked.

"Don't be ridiculous. There has obviously been some kind of administrative screw up here, and I don't intend to let it be covered up." With that she pulled the door open and strode over to the slim naked figure lying on the floor. Broken shackles and handcuff parts lay scattered across the cell. She snapped her fingers. "Medical kit." When her assistant handed the red cross marked case, she knelt down beside the nude woman and began a gentle examination after clipping a digital voice recorder to her lapel. "The subject seems to be in a state of extreme shock. I am administering 5mg Midazolam, a mild sedative via an intramuscular injection." Turning to Blair she said, "Summon an ambulance. Tell them on my authority to bring a rape kit. I don't have one with me, since I had not anticipated the need for one." She pointed at her assistants. "Lift her onto the bed." She stopped the Sergeant when he moved to help. "You people have done quite enough to her already. Please don't touch her."

The sergeant started to protest and then saw Blair shake his head and subsided.

Professor Jamieson stood up. "What about the other prisoner? Show me immediately," she snapped.

The sergeant shrugged and went to the adjoining cell and peered through the port. He sighed morosely at what he saw and unlocked the heavy metal door.

Professor Jamieson didn't miss his expression and marched angrily into the second cell, where there was another naked girl in the same state as the first. "This is insane. Did you people really think you could get away with this?"

Blair didn't reply. He knew that all witnesses and security camera records would support the police account, but he also knew there were many in the public who would be eager to accept another lurid story of police misconduct. But he was more concerned that the Professor didn't seem interested in examining the prisoners in relation to the werewolf attacks as he watched her inject the second girl. Then suddenly he realised that according to Seward, the tranquilliser would have no effect. In fact it might..." He turned towards cell seven.

"Where do you think you're going, Commander? I'm not allowing any of you to get near either victim before we have had a chance to perform full examinations and to document their injuries," Professor Jamieson barked as she stripped off her gloves.

Biting back an angry retort, Blair said, "Despite what you imagine happened, I am concerned about the two prisoners. I have reason to believe that they might react badly to your sedatives. Please check on the other girl again, for her sake if not for mine."

The Professor sensed the sincerity in Blair's eyes and tone. She realised that as Commander, he might not have known what had happened in the cells either. Although that would still make him negligent, it didn't make him guilty of actual abuse. "Very well. Although the sedative I gave her is safe, there is no harm in being careful." She brushed past Blair and nodded at the sergeant. "Open it."

The sergeant waited for Blair to nod, and then unlocked the door, stepping back to allow the Professor access.

The door opened and Blair frowned when he heard a rumbling sound, which he realised was a growl. "Wait! Professor, don't go..." Before Blair could finish his warning, the Professor staggered back out of the cell, and slowly turned towards him. "Oh shit," he groaned. The front of her elegant suit had been ripped open as if by five razors and blood was rapidly soaking the fabric.

The Professor opened her mouth as if to speak, but then a gout of blood poured out from between her lips, and then she slumped down to her knees and onto her face.

"Close the door!" Blair shouted at the sergeant waving his arms in a closing motion as he bent down to pull the Professor clear.

The sergeant reacted with admirable speed, but the heavy door stopped short of closing, blocked by the front

211

of the Professor's shoe.

Blair yanked at her limp body with a strength born of desperation, but it was too late. A furry arm struck the door, denting the hard metal, throwing the portal wide open and clipping the sergeant on the forehead in passing. Blair watched helplessly as the furry arm darted out again, grabbed the front of the sergeant's stab vest and pulled him into the cell. Behind him, Blair heard a growl from the second cell. He was unarmed, without even a telescopic baton. He knew that to stay here was to die. "Run!" he shouted, grabbing the arms of one of Professor Jamieson's assistants and the other police constable present and pulling them in the direction of the exit from the detention area. As they ran Blair heard screams coming from cell eight and realised that the second of the Professor's assistants wasn't with them. "Clear the way! Move!" he shouted at the curious faces crowding the doorway leading to the detention area. He dashed through as they scattered and he skidded to a halt and gripped the door, waiting for the sergeant to get clear. He slammed the heavy door shut and nodded when the sergeant locked it. But the door was made of wood, unlike the doors to the cells. "Sound the fire alarm. Evacuate the building," he shouted. "Where's the Strike Team?" he asked the confused cluster of policemen around him.

"Er, they were allowed to go home sir," one of the officers replied. "On your orders they're on twenty-four hour call, so they went home to catch some sleep." The man brightened. "But Strike One is still around I think. He was doing the post action reports."

Blair realised that with all the confusion, it might not be possible to reach the strike team leader with the Airwave. He pulled out his cell phone. He had made sure to have the numbers of all members of the SO15 team as a backup. He found the right number and waited impatiently as the phone rang. There was a loud jarring impact against the door to the detention area and the sound of splintering wood and he knew that he was running out of time. "Everybody move. Get out of here, now!" He held the phone to his ear as he ran, heading for the main entrance. This was not the time to worry about the press.

"This is Strike One, commander. Do you have orders for me?"

"The tranquilliser darts. Where are they now?"

There was an ominous hesitation. "Um, there aren't any more darts left, sir. We used them all up at today's action. The darts aren't like bullets sir. Most of them missed."

The darts were Blair's last hope of stopping the werewolves once they broke free of the detention area, and his shoulders sagged. Then he remembered the satellite phone, which was still at his desk. If he could get Seward's people here quickly enough they could still stop the werewolves before they went on a rampage in the middle of London. The Oxford Street and Piccadilly Circus attacks had been bad enough. Having werewolves escape from police custody and slaughter more civilians would be a political and public relations disaster. Heads would roll, probably including his own. His own career wasn't all that important to him given everything else that was happening, but if he failed and was removed the head-in-the-sand crowd would win until it was too late. Many were not evil, but like Professor Jamieson, they were short sighted and had other priorities that seemed more important to them, even though the werewolf threat could doom everybody. No one even noticed when he turned around and headed for the stairs to get back to his office. He could hear the pounding on the door, and he knew that it wouldn't hold for very much longer. He suppressed his fear and sprinted up stairs and down corridors, cursing the layout of the building and the pieces of furniture that seemed determined to collide with him. All the while his ears searched for the sound of a growl, a roar, or that of claws clicking against the floor and walls.

The door to his office slammed against the partition so hard that it seemed as if the glass would shatter, but he ignored it and the whirlwind of paper as he searched his desk for the satellite phone. It was not until he flicked a folder off of the desk, sending it tumbling through the air like a multi-winged butterfly that he found it. He stiffened when he heard the faint sound of wood smashing and being thrown aside so hard that the entire building rumbled from the impact. They were free! He began to run, even as his fingers worked the buttons on the slim electronic device. Pain flared in his thighs when he slammed into the edge of a workstation, unable to turn a corner sharply enough, sending the computer and keyboard tumbling off of the desk top, the mouse flailing like an absurd tail. Then the phone's screen flashed indicating a connection. "West End Central Police Station. Two werewolves. They're free. No more tranquillisers. Can you help?"

"On our way," Seward's voice said from the tiny speaker.

Panting painfully, he paused to catch his breath. He was still on the third floor and he had to get to the stairs. The lifts were too risky. He could just imagine the lift stopping and the doors opening to reveal a pair of waiting werewolves. He had no idea if they were intelligent enough to operate the call buttons and wait for the lift, but he wasn't going to take the chance. He weaved his way through the maze of desks and whiteboards and was heading for the nearest exit when a sound made him freeze. Above the shrill and annoying sound of the fire alarm he heard the sound of movement, of something heavy being pushed aside with great force. They had found him. He turned to run in the opposite direction. There was another exit at the other end of the building. Perhaps he could reach it before the werewolves reached him. Then the automatic door smoothly rolled open to reveal a werewolf standing in the doorway in front of him and he almost tripped over a chair. They had split up to trap him. The monster in front of him seemed to be grinning as it slowly stalked towards him. A sound made him glance over his shoulder and he felt a cold chill at the sight of the other creature. He was trapped. He could try for a window, but he knew they would be upon him before he could get one open or smash the tough glass. There were no weapons in sight, not that anything other than an axe or mace would have helped him anyway. Unlike in the films, there was no conveniently placed fire axe on the wall for the hero to use. His lips quirked at the thought of him playing the leading role. The way it looked, it was going to be a very short part indeed. He picked up an old battered wooden stool that someone had brought in to serve as a makeshift ladder and hefted it like a club. A good blow to the head could give him the time to dodge around one of them and make a run for it. He ran forwards rather than waiting to be bracketed between the two creatures, yelling an incoherent war cry as he charged. With both hands he swung the improvised club at the werewolf's head. But the werewolf barely moved except to raise a forearm to meet the blow. The solid seasoned wood splintered into fragments, the stool shattering when it hit the creature's arm, the vibration numbing his hands and making him drop his improvised weapon.

The werewolf roared and was answered by its companion. It seemed in no hurry to finish Blair off, advancing slowly, claws held out low to either side of its body. It sniffed the air and then licked its lips with a long, very wolf-like tongue as it looked straight into the police officer's eyes.

Blair dodged to the side, heading for the rear wall

so that he would have something at his back and could face his enemies when they inevitably came. The light from the window behind him made every detail of the nearest werewolf startlingly sharp and clear, and he could see the intelligence in its eyes and the very un-wolf-like movement of the muscles of its face which rippled in a series of unreadable expressions. He snatched up a metal paperweight and prepared for his last stand. He intended to throw the heavy metal object like a shot putt, hoping to strike the thing in the face. He knew that they could be hurt, if only momentarily. Then as he pulled his hand back, the window behind him shattered into thousands of glittering fragments, some of which hit the back of his head, and something flew over his shoulder to strike the werewolf in the chest and bury itself deep. He recognised the shape as a throwing star, similar to many he had taken from street toughs and even football fans. But for some reason this one actually seemed to hurt the werewolf and he watched in fascination as it staggered back and clawed at its chest, howling in pain. He gasped when something yanked at the back of his shirt and jacket collars, pulling him off of his feet and dragging him backwards with irresistible force.

"I suggest you don't stay for the rest of the show," Seward's voice said from outside of the building.

The grey façade of the building housing the West End nick was flat and lacked any ledges or balconies, nor were there any convenient drain pipes or ivy covered trellises and Blair blanched in fright when he was pulled right through the window into the open air. With nothing beneath his feet but empty space he looked up and to the side only to grunt in shock when he saw that his rescuer was clinging to the wall, unsupported by rappelling rope or any other climbing gear. He looked at the broken window as if to confirm that he was really outside the building and he caught a blurred movement as

216

something dived into the building.

Seward would have preferred to be the one to go up against the werewolves, but he had been coincidentally closer to Blair and there had been no time for anything else. Using one hand and both claw tipped feet he began to climb towards the roof with the police commander dangling from his hand like a knapsack.

His rescuer's face was obscured by a tight fitting mask, but he recognised the voice and general build of the man who was carrying him in one hand as casually as a bag of washing. He held completely still, afraid that the slightest motion might unbalance Seward and send them both tumbling to their deaths. "How..."

"The satellite phone has a GPS tracker that only transmits when it is switched on, so your tech people couldn't detect any signal. When we saw the capture on the news I hoped for the best, but guessed that things wouldn't go well so we were waiting nearby. When the fire alarm went off and people began running from the building it wasn't hard to guess that it had all gone pear shaped."

"We? There's another one of you?" Blair said looking around.

"You probably saw her going in the window."

"I saw … something. Her? You let a woman go in there alone to face two werewolves?"

John chuckled as they neared the edge of the roof. "She needs the practise. And I wouldn't use that tone when speaking of her where she can hear you."

There was a sound, a hollow thump and crack that made Blair start. He felt a seam in his jacket ripping and he paled. But before he could say anything, he felt himself being mortifyingly lifted up with impossible strength and tossed over the edge of the building and onto the flat roof. He landed on his hands and knees, bruising his shins against the ledge as he went over, and when he managed to straighten up he found Seward standing beside him.

"Are you all right? Did the werewolf bite you anywhere?"

Blair shook his head. "No, thank god. Would I have … turned if I had been bitten?"

"Unlikely, but their bite can be nasty. Paralysing toxin in the saliva." Seward stepped back to the edge. "I'd be grateful if you waited here for a moment while I check on my friend."

Blair nodded, but Seward had already disappeared over the side. He sat down tiredly, ignoring the dust and dirt that coated his trousers and hem of his jacket. "Paralysing toxin. Terrific. Just what I needed to hear." His mind buzzed with questions even as his body still quivered from the rush of adrenaline that had flooded his body. He saw that his hands were shaking.

***

Tara had fired as soon as she landed on the floor inside the building, the shotgun round blasting a load of silver pellets into the nearer werewolf's head, blowing part of its skull away. She knew that even this horrific wound would not result in a certain kill, but the creature would definitely be down at least for the rest of the battle. She swivelled the muzzle around, searching for the second werewolf, only to find that it was nowhere in sight. Her nanite enhanced senses indicated that it was still in the room and gave her a general direction but unlike another vampire, she couldn't pinpoint its location precisely. She realised that the second werewolf must have ducked behind or under a desk. Using her sonar she scanned the room for the slightest trace of movement and soon had the creature roughly located at one side of the large, furniture filled room. A telephone rang, making her jump, and the werewolf chose that moment to strike.

Rather than leaping over the tables and chairs, the werewolf rose up and hurled itself forward, turning a heavy desk onto its side and driving it at Tara like a massive shield.

Focused upon the moving desk, Tara was slow in reacting when the werewolf suddenly leapfrogged over the still sliding desk and flung itself at her. She fired, but the pellets passed beneath its belly and smashed a "U" shaped hole in the top edge of the desk. She managed to bring the mass driver rifle up in front of her and jammed the steel and carbon fibre body of the weapon between the werewolf's jaws. But its teeth closed on the rifle and when its paws slammed into her chest like a pile driver, she was catapulted backwards and down the length of the room, and the rifle was ripped from her grip.

The werewolf threw the rifle aside with a toss of its head and charged at its downed prey.

Tara winced and gasped in pain when the edge of a desk crashed into her back. If she had been fully human the impact would have snapped her spine. Ignoring the pain, she drew up her knees as she threw herself backwards on and over the desk, putting it between herself and the charging werewolf, and then rapidly backing up as she drew her sword, relying upon her sonar to avoid furniture behind her.

Encouraged by its initial success in putting Tara on the defensive, the werewolf bounded over the table, its deadly claws reaching out for the kill.

But the table had given Tara the time and space to recover her balance. She had been practising hard with John with a focus upon countering the werewolves' natural attack patterns. Most of the werewolves they encountered would be newly turned, and would be relying on almost pure instinct and were unlikely to display any sophisticated fighting forms. She timed her move precisely and just before the claws slashed down the front of her body she sprang into the air, her vampire physiology allowing her at attain a height that would turn an Olympic athlete green with envy. She flipped upside-down at the peak of her jump and came down again with her sabre in front of her, gripped tightly in both hands. Driven by the weight of her entire body and acceleration of the fall, the point of her silver coated sabre plunged into the werewolf's back and spine with a terrible crunch. Without waiting to see the results of her strike, Tara used her arms to push her into a flip and roll, tearing the sabre out of the creature's body and her feet landing on the floor just behind the werewolf's hind claws. She whirled around, the sabre a deadly spinning propeller, but the werewolf was still down, its spine severed and only slowly healing due to the silver. When the monster pushed its head and shoulders up on its arms, Tara took a gliding step forward and to the side, the edge of her sabre sinking into the werewolf's thickly muscled neck and going almost all the way through. She pulled her sabre free and sprang back to avoid the creatures wild convulsions and the huge gouts of blood that shot from the stump of its neck. She didn't turn when she heard the sound of clapping from the shattered window, her senses searching her environment for further threats. It was entirely possible that the werewolf she had shot in the head had survived and had healed enough to attack her again.

"Nicely done! But that last cut should have gone all the way through, you know," John's voice said from the window. "The other one's dead. I checked while you were busy with your acrobatics. Now it's time for us to leave. Besides, there's someone on the roof who is waiting to talk to us. At least I hope so. That improvised rescue might have frightened him off."

Tara cleaned her blade and studied the almost beheaded werewolf with a frown. He was right. Her technique still needed improving. Then the werewolf started to change back into a pretty teen-aged girl and she gritted her teeth in anger at Viktor's tactics which had just forced her to kill two innocent young women. Turning on her heel she headed towards the window.

***

Commander Blair's mind was filled with a blizzard of disparate thoughts and questions. He could still see Professor Jamieson's terrified face although he knew there was nothing he could have done to prevent her death other than physically grabbing her. But her response was a perfect illustration of what he faced and what John Seward had warned him against. Even scientists would refuse to consider the possibility of werewolves unless they saw one in person. And even then, there was the humanitarian aspect to be considered. These were not merely monsters, but innocent victims as well. In a sense they were sick. But it was a sickness that could literally rip a medical team to shreds despite every precaution. They, he, needed to know more, and the only person who seemed to have any answers was John Seward. Then he remembered the impossible rescue and climb up the vertical wall while holding him with one hand. Perhaps the question should be, what was John Seward. He didn't have the shape of a werewolf, so it was unlikely that he was some kind of werewolf 2.0 and unlike the werewolves that were formerly in the holding cells, Seward seemed to have his unusual strength even in human form. He absolutely refused to consider a real life Spider Man. Blair told himself that the moment he seriously started considering that possibility was when he would know that he had truly lost his mind. Besides, Seward hadn't shot any webs out of his wrists. This thought made him grin. A movement at the edge of the roof made him tense, and then he saw both Seward and another similarly dressed or costumed figure climb onto the roof. Then he saw something he had missed so far.

"You've got … um, you're a woman!" he said accusingly.

Tara looked down at her breasts, their shapes clearly visible through the tightly fitting suit. "How very observant of you. It must be all that police training," she said dryly.

Blair blushed. "I'm sorry. I'm usually a lot more politically correct, but sensitivity training seems to have gone out of the window today along with the rest of me." He watched the pair walk towards him and thoughts of superheroes came back again. They looked improbably fit and lithe and somehow alert to their surroundings to a degree no human could achieve. He nodded at Seward. "Thank you for saving my life. I don't want you to think that I'm ungrateful. And speaking of werewolves … are they..."

Tara nodded. "Both of them are dead. Which may present a problem."

Blair sighed. "Don't tell me, they're both cute naked girls again, but dead."

"Won't the security videos back up your account?" Tara asked.

He shrugged. "That's assuming the videos don't mysteriously get deleted or disappear. You'd be amazed how far people will go not to face the truth. Or in this case, to protect public order." He realised that he was sounding bitter and cynical. "Don't get me wrong, my superiors will want to do everything possible to fight this menace, so long as a politician doesn't have to stand up in public and use the "W" word."

"You realise that they'll be playing right into the hands of the Internet sceptics, who in this case will most likely be absolutely right," she replied.

Blair nodded. "I know. But the majority of the Great British Public still accept what the mainstream press tell them, especially if we throw enough talking heads at them. The fact is, if the PM stood up and said there were werewolves in Britain, the people in the street would go mad. There would be monster hunters popping out of the woodwork and innocent people getting killed because they looked or acted differently. I wouldn't be surprised of someone managed to turn it into a racial or religious thing as well. Some people will take any excuse to be bastards. I know who John is, what about you? Is your identity a deep dark secret? Sorry, but policemen are incurably nosy."

Tara pulled her hood back from her face, letting it roll up around her neck. "My name is Tara Harker. You'll probably come across my name if you investigate Viktor Tiranul. He was employed by my father's company and was my co-pilot in a recent series of test flights we performed in Romania."

"You're a test pilot? Then how did you come to be here … hunting werewolves like this?

Tara took a deep breath and exhaled loudly. "Because Viktor tried to kill me and steal my father's aircraft."

"And you can prove this?" Blair said, his fingers itching for a notebook and pen.

She nodded. "We have the black box recordings, plus a live, real-time biometric feed of both myself and Viktor, and any doctor who sees the recording of my body functions will tell you that I suffered a sudden and serious injury in mid-air consistent with a gunshot wound."

Nodding slowly Blair said, "How does this supposed crime tie in with an outbreak of lycanthropy?"

"When my father and the SAR team flew out in a helicopter to rescue me, Viktor attacked us."

"With his gun?"

"With his fangs and claws," Tara said calmly, leaving out the discovery of the alien spaceship or the fact that her life was saved not by the SAR team but by an infusion of alien medical nanites. Or that it had turned her into a vampire.

223

The policeman's eyebrows lifted. "He was a..." Blair rubbed his eyes tiredly. "Until recently I would have thought you were um … mistaken. But now if I said you were mad, I'd be sitting in the padded cell next to you."

She smiled. "It's not an easy thing to accept. If it makes you feel better, my father believes that there is some kind of scientific cause for the phenomena. No curses or magic required. Somehow, in between the crash and the rescue, Viktor was changed. At first I thought I was being pursued by some kind of animal, a rabid wolf or something. But just as I was boarding the helicopter, he attacked, throwing himself at the helicopter and hanging on to the door. Several of the crew including myself clearly saw that he was still wearing shreds of his flight suit and that it was no ordinary animal. The helicopter lifted off, and one of the SAR team attempted to shoot Viktor who was trying to bite and claw me. But as you've discovered, bullets didn't stop him and the poor crewman was thrown to his death. But the effort ripped the door from its track and it, along with Viktor, fell to the ground."

"How do you know he wasn't killed by the fall?"

Tara's face turned grim as she recalled the events of that day. "I know because I saw him again when a team of mercenary soldiers in helicopters of their own attacked our airstrip and gunned down the security guards we had hired to protect the experimental aircraft from theft or industrial espionage. They also killed some of the engineers and mechanics. My father and I fled into the forest, but not before both of us clearly saw Viktor Tiranul in his human form accompanying the raiders. We managed to lose them in the woods, but we heard him roaring and tearing up the forest behind us."

Blair was about to ask whether they had reported this incident, and then realised what a stupid question that was. He could well imagine walking into a

224

Romanian police station and claiming that a werewolf and a group of armed mercenaries had attacked them, and the probable response they would have received. Very much like the official response he was getting from his superiors right now. He pointed downwards and looked at Seward. "Before I forget, I saw you chuck a throwing star at the werewolf attacking me, and I could see that it was hurt, even though bullets are bloody useless. Silver?"

John chuckled and nodded. "Perhaps after this you can get approval for silver weapons."

Blair groaned. "Not a chance. No one is going to sign the approval. It would leak out to the press in hours, and then we'd be in for it, right and proper. I can see the headlines now. 'Desperate Police Resort To Silver Bullets. Will Holy Water be next?' But we still have your tranquilliser darts. But I feel obliged to warn you that the Government are likely to demand that you donate the formula to the authorities in the interests of National Security." When John didn't say anything, Blair had an epiphany. "You *want* then to steal it from you, because then they'll take it seriously! But what about the silver?"

"The formula my labs worked out do contain an advanced animal tranquilliser using silver nano-materials as a sterilising agent and preservative," John said. "Once they start research and testing on captive werewolves, they'll discover that it wouldn't affect the werewolves at all if not for the silver compound."

Blair grinned. "And prove to themselves that silver is a weapon. Sneaky. I like it."

"I'll arrange for a larger shipment of the darts to be delivered to you, without charge as before. They'll assume I have some cunning plan to benefit from future sales and laugh themselves sick when they decide to steal it from me."

"It will take time to get teams nationwide trained and supplied with tranquilliser guns and your darts. In the meantime…" Blair said, leaving his question unspoken.

"If we were somehow to receive notice of attacks the same time as you do, we will try to respond if the threat is sufficiently dire. We can't be everywhere at once, and we are risking our lives and our freedom," John said. "But we can only risk intervening if you can guarantee that your people will look the other way when we do … what is necessary. We can't fight both sides at once, and I have no desire to hurt a police officer or soldier doing his or her duty."

Blair bit his lip. As a police officer he couldn't possibly approve of such deadly vigilantism let alone actively abet it. If he crossed this line, could he still call himself an officer of the law? Then he saw Professor Jamieson's face again, in that fraction of a second when she knew she was doomed. Then he nodded. "I'll only call upon you if the situation is totally out of control. But if I do, then I'll do everything in my power to clear the way for you." He hesitated, and then said, "But I need to know, how you did the things I saw you do. No amount of training…"

Tara said, "In addition to aircraft design, my father is experimenting on bio-engineering. Improving and enhancing human performance through technology. But his work is very much in a preliminary stage. The treatments can have very dangerous, even fatal side effects." All this was true, and she let Blair assume that this was the source of their inhuman abilities. She and John had both agreed that they still couldn't trust Blair with their secret.

"What are you going to put in your report? You have two dead girls downstairs," John asked.

"Officially, they will be reported as two more victims of the unexplained creature attacks. Off the record, my superiors, MI5 and Dstl, and the PM and Cabinet of course, will be shown the video and witness transcripts. Whatever conclusions they come to will be based on the evidence and what is politically expedient," Blair said.

"I'll have another batch of the darts delivered as soon as possible." John looked into the Commander's eyes. "If you like I can also deliver a box of twelve gauge shotgun shells loaded with silver shot, for your personal use."

Blair found it hard to meet the strange industrialist's gaze, which seemed to glow with a depth of experience and knowledge the likes of which he had never before seen. "I … I would appreciate that. Thank you."

"I hope you're aware that the number of werewolves is likely to be increasing at an exponential rate. There are going to be a lot of the bastards around soon, and that's not even counting the ones that Viktor manages to recruit. I suggest that if you ever come up against Viktor or his followers, run. Run as fast and as far as you can. You've seen what werewolves can do as nearly mindless beasts. Imagine one who also has the intelligence of a man or more."

Blair shuddered. "Thank you for that pleasant thought. I won't get any sleep at all tonight."

***

"Did you mean that, when you said we would only respond if he can guarantee our immunity from the law? It's unlikely that he can really do that without eventually drawing suspicion upon himself," Tara asked as they ran across rooftops and through back alleys towards the modified van that had brought them here.

John nodded. "Tara, we're not superheroes. In fact, many in power would probably consider us an even bigger threat than the werewolves. It won't help anyone if we end up being dissected in some super secret laboratory."

She looked disturbed at this. "Do you really think they would do that? I now I've joked about it but …."

John chuckled grimly. "Remember who you're talking to. Good, god fearing people have been trying to kill me in numerous horrible ways for centuries."

"But I'm not..."

John gripped her arm, squeezing hard enough to hurt. "Thinking like that will most definitely get you killed. Your father's implant alone has made you a target, let alone being a vampire. We can trust no one outside of our current circle without being very cautious and suspicious indeed."

"So what do we do in the meantime?"

"I won't require that you participate, but I have a score to settle with Werner's people, and I need to send a message to Werner himself," John said, his voice low and deadly.

"They would have killed my father and Emily as well as Duncan and all the innocents at your facility. I'm not going to flinch or abandon you if you're going after Werner," Tara replied, her voice equally grim.

Chapter Twelve

Viktor had given an email address to the surviving member of the Russian kidnap team, so he relaxed and waited, while his pack scoured the city for all the information regarding the mobster that they could find. This would be his first confrontation with a professional criminal boss and he didn't want to make any mistakes. Two days after the disastrous kidnapping attempt, he received a message. "Let's meet and talk. Somewhere neutral. Tomorrow, 2 p.m." The email went on to name a bar in east London and was signed off by Dmitry Vasnetsov himself. Viktor looked the bar up on Google and discovered it had private tables under railway vaults. He smiled. It all seemed innocent enough, except that his pack's research told him that it was one of Vasnetsov's properties. He owned the business. The information wasn't a deep dark secret and they had discovered the fact by simply asking around. This could either be a trap or Vasnetsov simply wanted to ensure his privacy when talking business. Most likely the mobster was hedging his bets and was prepared for either contingency.

Jenny laughed when Viktor told her. "He's going to resort to threats and then violence when he doesn't get his own way. I've lived with people like him all my life."

Viktor had acquired Jenny as a companion quite by accident, and he had kept her around first because she was a rarity, a werewolf who retained some degree of control when she changed and who could control when she changed. The second was that she was sexy and good in bed. But he was surprised to discover that she had a sharp mind and an encyclopaedic knowledge of the streets and the shadier side of London, garnered from her many regular clients in her former life as a prostitute.

Jenny was also totally ruthless and became fanatically loyal to Viktor when she realised that he would actually protect her and care for her without demanding sexual favours in return. In the event she had soon gone to his bed, but it had been her choice and for that alone she valued him. She didn't blame or hate men since she had entertained women as well, but she was fed up of being told what to do by others, be it the police or the many flavours of criminals, whatever their sex.

"How would you suggest that we play it? Should we negotiate first?" Viktor asked, curious to hear her view.

The shake of Jenny's head was unmistakably emphatic. "No. People like him only understand and respect power. If you go in and offer to negotiate, he will see this as weakness. Vasnetsov would only agree to negotiate if he was either hopelessly out-gunned, or he held the winning hand himself, in which case his negotiation would be in the form of a list of demands backed up by an 'or else'."

This was pretty much what Viktor had expected but he was pleased that Jenny saw it so clearly too. Often street people were so beaten down that they looked to appeasement as the first option under any circumstances. He tapped the table thoughtfully. "Then should we bother meeting at all, or just start hitting him and keep on doing it until he waves the white flag?"

"We could, but he's not going to be terrorised. He can't afford to show that kind of weakness, or one of his men will replace him. It means a fight to the death."

"What's the alternative?" Viktor asked, his tone approving and encouraging.

"We need a demonstration, a powerful and convincing one, but one that doesn't make him look bad to the rank and file.

Viktor had already figured this out and he smiled. "So we walk into his trap, just like we did with the street gangs?"

"But we're not trying to terrorise him. We need to make him an offer he can't refuse, but he must think that he still has a chance of keeping his power and position. We would just be another player in the game. Perhaps even an ally, once we've proven ourselves. The power behind the throne. Women are good at that," she said grinning.

Viktor nodded. "I agree. There is a lot of day to day drudgery in running a criminal enterprise, even if they don't have the paperwork the government has. Let Vasnetsov keep that and the trappings of power, so long as we have the final say."

Now Jenny smiled. "*You* have the final say, you mean." Power made her hot, and Viktor made her melt into a puddle. Oddly, the fact that she couldn't manipulate him made Viktor even more attractive. She knelt down beside his chair and rested her head upon his lap. "And when we do the same for each mob, we'll control the London underworld." Viktor's hand stroked her hair, and she rumbled deep in her throat like the sleek and deadly predator that she had become.

Viktor responded with a silent smile. "Our only real opposition is Tara and John Seward, who know what we are. But they have much bigger things on their plate than us at the moment. Let them deal with the authorities and politicians, and in doing so, draw Werner's attention away from us until we are too strong for anyone to threaten."

Jenny rubbed her face against the fabric of his trousers. "And then what?" she whispered in a conspiratorial tone, like a child listening to a favourite fairy tale that she had heard many times before.

"Then, my darling Jenny, we shall live like royalty," Viktor said indulgently, his hand sliding down her neck to her bare shoulders.

***

Like most men of his kind, Dmitry Vasnetsov had

risen to where he was by being more clever and more ruthless than his enemies, as well as his allies. But he knew that loyalty was as important as the willingness to kill. Loyalty to those who looked to him for leadership and protection, as well as loyalty to those above him. There was always someone above you, somewhere. That was just the way of the world. He had listened to all the reports about this new player in the underworld. He had summoned cocky gang leaders and he had seen the fear behind their eyes. He had personally seen the carnage in the van before it was quietly disposed of. He didn't want the police involved in this. The street punks talked of monsters and claws that killed in the dark. It was hard not to associate this with the terrifying and unexplained attacks happening in the streets. Could this Viktor somehow have one or more of these things under his control? Of course he had heard of werewolves, or Bodark in Russia, but he had always dismissed these things as myths. No one he knew had ever seen one, until now. Werewolf or not, he had great faith in the power of bullets to solve problems, and if necessary, they would solve this one.

Although he was a proper Russian, he lived in Britain now and he tried to be English too. He arrived at the bar early and ordered lunch. Dmitry liked his food. He ordered smoked salmon with soda bread as a starter, and a Porterhouse steak with buttered broccoli, mash and gravy. But when it came to drink, it had to be vodka. A bottle of Kauffman Luxury Vintage Vodka sat on the table. His bottle. Since this was a business meeting, he also had a carafe of mineral water too. He sat alone, with two bodyguards standing discreetly nearby, scowling at anyone who came too near. He could have had the place closed to the public, but he wanted Viktor to feel safe. Werewolf or no, this Viktor person obviously had some good people working for him and he was even more clearly a murderous psychopath. Dmitry would kill someone as soon as look at them, but like all modern mobsters, be was also a businessman. Money was everything, as was public image. If Viktor could be convinced to go away, or to work peacefully with his organisation, then fine and good. If not, he and his people would all quietly disappear. It wasn't hard when you could pay. There were cleaners who would discreetly remove the bodies and all trace of the crime using the same methods as the police forensics teams would use to find them. Only amateurs got caught. He checked his watch. Good, he had ample time to enjoy his meal before this Viktor arrived.

As it turned out, the timing was perfect. The table had been cleared except for the vodka and Dmitry was just taking a sip when his bodyguards announced Viktor's arrival. He frowned in disapproval when he saw the woman with him. He knew her type, the bold pose, the hard eyes, all spoke of a professional. He wondered why Viktor would bring a plaything to a serious meeting. Did he mean it as a sign of disrespect? Bravado? Or was he planning a celebratory screw afterwards? He watched the pair of them walk up to the table, leaning back casually in his chair, vodka glass in hand. "So you are the one who frightened all those children and killed my men. Tell me why I should not have you taken out and shot right now?" The tables around him were either empty or occupied by his people, and the bar had been swept for listening devices, so he was not afraid to speak his mind. His visitors had been thoroughly searched at the door, including the woman, so he knew they weren't wearing transmitters either.

Viktor smiled broadly. "It is a poor tactic to threaten your opponent before you know his strength."

Dmitry brushed Viktor's words away with a wave of his hand. "You are here alone. My people in the street saw no others following you. You have no power base in London, or I would have heard of it before now. You

233

think to terrify me with a few dead bodies. Let me tell you, Dmitry Vasnetsov is not so easily frightened. Still, I am not an unreasonable man. If you have something to propose, then tell me what it is instead of both of us waving our dicks in the air."

Without being asked, Viktor sat down, and Jenny moved to stand behind his chair. "Very well. To business. I slapped the street gangs around in hopes that you would realise that I was serious and had the ability to back up my words with action. I didn't strike at your men until they came at me first. If anyone showed disrespect, it was you."

Very slowly, as if reprimanding a particularly wayward and thick headed child, Dmitry said, "This is my territory. No one does anything here without my permission. Those gangs you attacked were my business associates. They have now turned to me for redress and although your ability and daring impress me, I cannot allow your actions to go unpunished." He sipped his vodka and made a gesture with his finger. His bodyguards stepped forward and two of them pressed the muzzles of their pistols against the back of Viktor and Jenny's heads. "Why don't we continue this conversation somewhere more private," he said, almost genially. Dmitry was always genial when someone was about to die. They had managed to ambush the gang leaders and frighten them with some magic tricks and masks. But that was not going to work here. His men were pros. He finished his vodka and then stood up. "Come, follow me. And do not make the mistake of thinking my men won't shoot in a public place. This place is mine, and no one here would dare to testify against me, of if they did they would never reach the court. But the noise and resulting mess would be bad for business, so I would prefer that it happen elsewhere. Besides, I have a few more questions for you."

Viktor caught Jenny's eye and gave her an almost

imperceptible nod. Being taken for a ride was exactly what he had expected, and Dmitry was being most obliging. He didn't resist when the two of them were hustled towards the back of the bar, through the steaming heat and cooked food smell of the kitchen, and out into the narrow alley at the back of the building. There, a dark blue Mercedes Benz awaited, engine running and a tough looking driver with Russian prison tattoos behind the wheel. The back seat was wide enough for Victor and Jenny, sandwiched between the two thugs who had threatened them with guns in the bar. He could sense the presence of his pack in the surrounding streets and roads, except for the two that were carrying out the second part of today's plan, and he knew they would follow the car even though he wasn't too concerned in the event that the Russians managed to lose them. He wasn't that familiar with London, but was surprised when they finally ended up in front of an abandoned public swimming pool. Even more interesting was the fact that the Russians had a key to a side door. They were roughly shoved inside as the car drove off, presumably to find a less noticeable parking spot. They were led right down into the drained swimming pool, where two chairs sat in the middle of the large rectangular tile lined space just before the bottom fell steeply into the deep end. He would have expected mould and dampness, but the entire building was surprisingly dry, and if anything it was covered with a film of dust and city grime, the disturbed dust floating visibly in the shafts of light from the windows that ringed the entire huge space. He was thrust rudely onto one heavy chair and his hands cuffed behind the sturdy back, and he watched as the same was done to Jenny. He felt a rush of anger when the mobster took the opportunity to grab a feel of her breasts while grinning at his companion, although Viktor's face remained calm, almost bored.

Dmitry clapped his leather gloved hands together.

"You think you are very tough, yes? That you have no fear? Many that come here start off like you, but soon, very soon, they are crying for their mothers and shitting themselves. They beg for mercy and die like pigs." He spat on the tiled floor and without warning slapped Viktor across the face hard with a vicious backhanded blow. "Did you think I would be too frightened of your reputation to touch you? That you would walk into my place and dictate to me?" His face twisted into a mask of rage as he spoke. Then just as suddenly he was all smiles and the urbane businessman again. "My men are going to make an object lesson of you and your whore. Anyone else who thinks to challenge me will see what happens to you and shit themselves in fear." He grabbed Viktor's hair and twisted his head up and around to stare into his prisoner's eyes. "I am curious. What did you think you could achieve today? Surely you did not imagine I would just hand over my territory and businesses to you? Well? Say something before I have your tongue cut out of your head."

The split lip and the cut inside his cheek had healed so fast as to be almost instant, and Viktor's face was unmarked when he smiled. "Yes. I did expect that you would hand over anything I want, your possessions and your organisation, and you will do it willingly."

Dmitry frowned. "Are you mad? Is that it? Are you a group of madmen intent on committing suicide?" He looked surprised when his cell phone vibrated in his coat pocket. Very few numbers were white listed to get through when he was working. He looked at his men who shook their heads and shrugged.

"I suggest you answer that," Viktor said, his excellent hearing detecting the faint buzz.

With the first beginnings of alarm tingling along his spine, Dmitry fished out his phone. His heart froze when he saw his wife's icon on the screen. "Hello?" He felt black, rotten ice fill his bowels when a man's voice answered. A voice he did not recognise. "We have your family. Listen..." There was a moment of silence and then the sounds of his wife and daughter screaming. Then the line cut off.

Viktor used the momentary distraction to will the change to come over his body. As strength and vitality stormed through his being like a huge gulp of brandy, he snapped the handcuffs holding his wrists, crushing the back of the chair into kindling at the same time. He sensed Jenny's change happening just a moment slower. She was getting a much better control over her transformations into werewolf form and in controlling herself after the change, and he reminded himself to tell her how pleased he was.

The Russian mobsters gaped in unbelieving horror at their erstwhile prisoners, the impossible sight stunning even these hardened killers.

Dmitry's mind finally associated what he was seeing with the news reports of monsters in the streets. "Shoot them! Kill them you fools!" he screamed as he shifted his phone to his left hand and snatched for the pistol in its holster in the small of his back.

Viktor left the bodyguards to Jenny and focused his attention upon Dmitry. Although in his mind he now saw a strange, nearly hairless creature, enough of Viktor's mind remained, like some imperfectly remembered but insistent memory, the werewolf knew what it had to do. It knew that it was not to kill this Dmitry thing, but to render it helpless. It uttered a barking growl and pounced.

Despite the double shock of his kidnapped family and Viktor's insane transformation, Dmitry managed to snatch out his compact Glock automatic pistol. He pressed it into the creature's belly and pulled the trigger, once, twice, the recoil jolting his bent arm and imperfectly positioned wrist. But before he could fire a third time, the thing's great paw closed around his wrist

237

and squeezed with a force that made his bones creak. He screamed in agony as his wrist bones fractured and the pistol fell from his nerveless fingers. He kicked and punched with his free hand, but he might as well have been a child for all the effect his blows had on his opponent. For the first time since he grew out of his early teens, he knew the feeling of utter helplessness. He screamed again, even louder this time when the thing he was fighting twisted his arm up and around like pulling a chicken wing from a roasted bird and almost casually dislocated his shoulder. With his right arm hanging uselessly at his side, he cried out in terror when the thing grabbed his other arm, its paw closing around the elbow. Once more he fought and struggled, even though the pain of jerking his dislocated shoulder around made the world swim. This time sharp, steel hard claws dug into his arm like five small daggers. He felt flesh tear and blood flow from deep wounds. He froze in terror and began to cry when the creature started to twist his arm. No! Please, I beg you, don't…" He bit his lip until blood dripped down his chin. His faced darkened and blue veins bulged in his temples and along his neck as his other arm was slowly and irresistibly twisted around and up. He fell to his knees in agony as tendons tore and he heard the loud pop of the ball joint popping free of his shoulder. Spittle mixed with blood ran down his chin and onto his chest, staining his expensive hand-made shirt and suit. There were more screams and he realized that they were coming from his men. He knew those screams. They were sounds he had heard many times as men and women were hurt beyond bearing, beyond possibility of survival, but denied the mercy of death. But in the past they had come from his enemies and victims. But this time was different. Fingers, human fingers gripped his hair and lifted his head, just as he had done to Viktor. He was forced to watch as the monster that he knew was the woman Jenny, ripped his men apart, literally tearing lumps of flesh, fingers, and then entire limbs from their bodies. Worse still was when she popped the dripping flesh into her mouth and tossed her long, fang filled jaws as she swallowed, the way a dog would gulp down a treat. He was made to watch as she disembowelled the two men, his best and most faithful killers, while they still lived and suffered. Viktor did not allow him to look away until there was nothing left but butchered meat and vast quantities of blood scattered across the old tiles of the pool. He tried to shrink away when the female monster brought her muzzle right up to his nose and slowly licked its lips, a wide canine smile on her face, but the grip on his hair was relentless and unyielding.

Viktor, who had already changed back, smiled approvingly at Jenny and nodded. He watched as she smoothly and miraculously changed back into human form, and then he twisted Dmitry's head around so that he looked into the mob boss's eyes, an exact reversal of their previous roles. "I have your family. My people know who and where all of your relatives are, your mother, your father, you two sisters, your grandfather, your nieces and nephews, yes even the ones in Russia. Oh yes, and your mistress in the apartment in Knightsbridge. Unless we can come to an … understanding, what happened to your men will happen to all of them."

Unable to get up from his knees due to the agony and his useless arms, Dmitry looked up at his tormentor. He licked his lips and forced himself to speak clearly rather than to babble in maddened panic. "Wh-what are you? No human could …" His eyes flicked towards the remains of his men and he flinched at the thought of his family.

Viktor chuckled. Jenny's chair was still intact although lying on its side and he picked it up, set it on its feet and then lifted Dmitry, heedless of the pain he was causing the crime lord and sat him down on it. "Let's just say that we're gifted. Did you ever watch any of the X-Men films?"

Confused by this sudden change in topic, Dmitry's eyes narrowed in effort. "I watched one with my … my daughter." His eyes widened. "You are mutants?"

Viktor looked at Jenny and laughed. He patted Dmitry on the cheek. "Why don't you just concentrate on what the X-men could do?" He pointed at Jenny. "We're not afraid of your bullets. We can kill anyone you send after us, as you already know. And now I'm telling you that refusal to cooperate with me will have serious consequences for your family. How long do you think your men will remain loyal to you if their families begin to be slaughtered because they are associated with you or because you are uncooperative?" He stopped and rapped Dmitry on the top of his head. "I know what you're thinking. You'll agree to anything I want now, but the moment you and your family are safe you'll try to hit back. You fear you'll be seen as weak otherwise. First, let me assure you that I have no intention of taking your place. I have other, more important things to do. I shall just become your silent partner. You can carry on living and doing business the way you always have, except that a certain share, say thirty percent, of your net proceeds come to me. In exchange, no one will know this ever happened. Your men will have mysteriously disappeared. You can go to a discreet hospital to recover and then come back, good as ever. You will even have my protection from your rivals. But cross me in any way at all, try to hide income, or be late with your payments, and all the demons of hell will fall upon you and yours."

Dmitry nodded slowly, his mind already working on how he could turn the tables on Viktor by gaining his trust, by appearing broken. "It seems I have no choice," he said bitterly.

"Tsk, tsk, Dmitry. I can call you Dmitry, can't I? We're going to be partners after all. I can see the wheels

240

turning in that brain of yours. You're a tough man. You've seen death before, been tortured before. You won't give up so easily. So I think one more object lesson is needed."

"No! Wait! I've said I agree to all your demands..."

Viktor stopped the man's protests by squeezing one of his dislocated shoulders. "Listen carefully. This is important. I want you to tell me which you prefer. That your wife and daughter each lose a toe or a thumb."

Dmitry shook his head. "No, no, you can't make me .... "

"Choose or I shall have either your daughter or your wife torn apart and fed to the survivor."

Tears began to run down the mobster's face. "You're a monster. You..."

Putting his finger to his lips, Viktor said, "I am indeed a monster. A real and very dangerous one. Last chance. Choose. Now."

Dmitry Vasnetsov, head of the Russian Mafia in London began to cry, sobbing like a heartbroken child.

Chapter Thirteen

John entered the meeting room and nodded at the others who had also been summoned to the meeting by Rowland. When everyone was seated, he said, "Well Roland? Do you have something to tell us?"

Rowland looked grim as he tapped the notebook computer on the table in front of him. He glanced at Emily, who nodded encouragingly. He took a deep breath and touched a button built into the table. The glass of the windows darkened in response to an electronic signal and the lights dimmed. A projector built into the ceiling came on, throwing an image on the large whiteboard. A map of Great Britain appeared.

"These are all the reported werewolf attacks and sightings to date." Red dots appeared on the map, with the largest concentrations clustered about the cities.

Tara gasped. "That's a lot more than I realised."

Rowland said, "We have to assume that these figures are under reported by at least fifteen to twenty percent due to lack of witnesses, disbelief, the refusal of people to submit or pass on reports referring to monsters or werewolves. The efforts of the Government to keep the people calm actually contributed to this effect." He touched a button on the keyboard and the dots grew in number, covering the country like a rash. "I have discussed this matter with John and based upon his experience and the cases where there were actual and uncensored reports, it appears that the average rate that victims themselves become werewolves is about one in four, twenty-five percent."

Emily shook her head. "Wait a minute. If there have been werewolves going back centuries, why haven't we seen such wide spread occurrences before. Surely werewolves would have been accepted as being real by now if they had."

"I can answer that," John said. "I've been living

with this concern for a long time. First of all, until we all became modern and civilised, the common folk truly believed in the forces of darkness. Demons, ghosts, vampires, and werewolves alike. Country folk, what were called peasants, had a simple and straightforward approach to supernatural matters."

"Let me guess, pitch-forks and torches," Tara said with a grin.

John winced at some painful memories and nodded. "Precisely. There was no thought of human rights or fair trials. If someone was suspected of being a werewolf they would wait until the person was in human form and preferably asleep, and then they would kill him or her. It didn't always work, and when that happened they put up a collection to hire a hunter. Anyway, most newly made vampires and werewolves died. The canny ones hid and blended in, carefully spacing out their kills and choosing their victims. And the other reason nothing like this ever happened was the lack of modern transportation and communication. Viktor has done something that no werewolf has done before, which was to carry out a deliberate campaign of infection on a nationwide scale."

"Precisely," Rowland said. "Like all diseases there is always a turning point where it becomes so wide spread that it becomes a pandemic."

Tara's eyes widened. "Are you saying .... "

Her father nodded. "I'm afraid so. Given that the authorities do not seemed inclined to carry out a campaign of extermination, and in fact are reluctant to even admit that a problem exists, I fear that we have already passed the point where the infestation can be controlled without drastic, even draconian measures. And given that the werewolves don't remain in their monstrous form, but turn back into ordinary men, women, and perhaps even children, I cannot foresee the authorities ever approving such measures until it is totally hopeless.

"Isn't there anything to be done?" Tara asked.

"As I see it, the problem is to prevent mass panic and having the public taking things into their own hands. In small villages, the damage was normally minimal, but imagine the hysteria of the Salem witch trials, but with real, tangible, and very deadly monsters who were undetectable until they actually attacked and in huge modern cities like London. Civil order would collapse. Neighbours would start killing each other on the merest suspicion," John said heavily. "It will soon be impossible to hide the existence of werewolves. But it might be possible to hide the fact that they change back into humans and vice versa, often at random. In other words, the public must be convinced that it is a one way process. The infected turn and stay that way. The authorities will have to set up special squads to capture or kill the werewolves. Simply trying to shoot or blow them up would turn the cities into war zones. But with the tranquilliser formula I am providing them, this should be possible without mass destruction."

Tara looked horrified. "But that would mean setting up huge prisons holding what are in effect prisoners for life, locked up without trial or hope of release. And the numbers would grow and grow."

"That's right. And in the long run it won't work," Rowland said, looking at John. "Eventually they are going to capture werewolves like Viktor. Imagine them making a jail break and releasing thousands of angry werewolves all at once. But you already knew this," he said staring at John accusingly.

John shrugged and nodded. "Which is why we can't be involved in any of this beyond providing technical advice. We have an even more serious problem. Viktor has a longer range plan in mind. I'm sure of it. An army of intelligent and disciplined werewolves will be very hard to stop."

Emily cleared her throat. "I don't want to sound like an anti-government crackpot, but what about the military. There is no way they are going to be able to resist trying to turn the werewolves into weapons or soldiers. I shudder to think of werewolves like Viktor given weapons and military training."

Duncan, who had remained silent until now, nodded in agreement. "I know the military mind. The thought of werewolf special forces will be irresistible."

"I've been reviewing the fragments of the alien memories that I have managed to access and make sense of. I think that in the alien military, that is exactly the role the werewolves played. They made up the Special Forces units for ground combat. The vampire race were the administrators, pilots, and technical personnel," Tara said, her eyes focused on her inner visions and the implanted memories that were still more like mad nightmares that came to her mostly in her sleep.

John sighed and placed his hands flat upon the table as if he would hold something down. "Those are just more reasons why we need to prepare, perhaps for all-out war. The vampire race were strong enough and advanced enough to ally with the werewolves on an equal footing. I fear that the human race isn't at all ready for this challenge. We know that Werner has some of the werewolf vaccine. There's no chance that they'll be able to resist experimenting with it. And we don't know if and how many of Viktor's followers have gone overseas. Europe first for sure, Eastern Europe including Russia, and possibly Asia are bound to follow."

Rowland looked around the table and gestured helplessly. "But there's just the few of us..."

Tara's eyes narrowed. She pointed at John accusingly. "There's something you haven't told us."

John looked slowly from person to person, as if judging their souls. "You're right. Largely because it wasn't my secret to reveal. I think I already told you

Tara, but you simply haven't considered the ramifications of my words in detail."

Tara reviewed her now encyclopaedic and searchable memory. Then she gasped. "There are more vampires! I had assumed you meant that there were a few isolated vampires hiding here and there and going out for a sneaky suck of blood when they got hungry but I'm wrong, aren't I?"

John chuckled at her depiction. "I'm afraid so. Unlike werewolves, many more people who turn because of vampire bites retain their original personality and memories. Unfortunately most are overwhelmed by the thirst for blood or go mad thinking they are monsters and end up behaving like one. But a small but significant number manage to control themselves and conceal themselves in the middle of normal human society. Over the centuries a loose community of vampires has formed around the world. Nothing as formal as the vampire families envisaged by modern fiction, but more like mutual aid societies. Vampires get lonely too, and the original alien vampire species was apparently very gregarious, so vampire ties can be very strong. Very few have ambitions to become a hunted monster, but there are always some who think that their powers make them superior. The trouble is, they tend to draw unwanted attention to the rest, and that is where the vampire societies are most active."

"They police their own kind," Duncan said.

"In a way. There are no ancient laws and rituals and there are more than one society or group. If a vampire deals drugs or robs banks in the usual style, no one cares even if these criminals tend to be a bit harder to apprehend than usual. But if they start giving public demonstrations of their powers, then the societies in the area will step in and try to persuade him or her to be more um, discreet." He nodded at the werewolf that Rowland had put up on the screen. On occasion they have taken down werewolves too. If normal humans start believing in werewolves again, they might also start believing in vampires as well."

"So you think these fraternal vampires will be willing to help?" Tara asked.

"Not all, and not easily. But as things get worse, I'm confident that we can recruit a number of them to our cause. There is a chance that we can make at least some people, like Commander Blair believe that vampires can be allies instead of a threat."

Emily looked questioningly at John. "Are you a member of one of these societies?"

"Not exactly. Let us say that being one of the oldest of our kind around, I am occasionally consulted for advice and asked to arbitrate disputes. But I've seen more than enough politics and backstabbing during my human lifetime and took pains to remain outside of their social organisations."

"That couldn't have pleased them," Rowland said, having experienced his own share of problems with bureaucracy and vested interest groups who had wanted control of his inventions and the things he worked on.

John's smile revealed a trace of the ruthless warlord whose name had been once feared far and wide. "I made it clear that I desired to be left alone and that they interfered in my affairs at their peril."

"What about the synthetic blood? Couldn't you supply it to them so they can avoid hurting people?"

John nodded at Tara. "Why don't you ask her for an answer?"

Tara bit her lip and slowly said, "It's difficult. Imagine telling large groups of people to stop eating food and living off of a synthetic biscuit."

"Even if I produced a range of flavours, it would involve a huge and very visible distribution and supply network. I couldn't simply open up shops on the high street, or even sell it through the Internet. Someone is bound to notice sooner or later. And that very network would expose all the vampires who took part," John said.

Tara frowned. "Then will they be willing to work with us now?"

"They will when they realise what is at stake. It will take time, but fortunately things are not at a critical stage just yet, so time is still a luxury we can afford for now." He turned to Rowland. "I have a database of names that I have accumulated over the years. I shall give you a copy. Perhaps you and Emily can begin updating that list, after which we can make plans to contact them. I shall assign some IT staff that I trust to help you with the work. I do have some friends amongst them. We can start with them."

"I'm not sure how the authorities and military are going to react to the news that there are vampires living amongst us and worse still, that they have their own society and organisations," Duncan said doubtfully.

Tara studied John thoughtfully. "Which is why we're going to wait until they're desperate and come to us, or at least to John for advice and help. But it's going to be bad in the meantime."

"We'll do what we can to work with Commander Blair, but I fear that you're right Tara. We have no choice but to wait until they come to us. But in the meantime we can get ready. For one thing, Duncan can start building up a group trained and equipped to fight werewolves. Unlike the police, we can use silver bullets and other silver weapons and armour. We can use simulators and trainers in experimental exoskeleton suits to get the men used to fighting opponents who are faster and stronger than they are. We'll make Unit Vampire a reality." His fingers tapped the table thoughtfully. "But first, I need to send Werner a strongly worded message. He needs a slap on the wrist, and after what he did to my home and all of you here, I'm inclined to make it a very pointed one indeed."

Tara was surprised to see the approving and excited expression on Emily's face. "You approve?"

Emily put her arms around Rowland's and leaned her head against his shoulder. "They tried to hurt Rowland, and all of us of course. I firmly believe in 'Do unto others before they can do it to you'."

Tara was both amused and a little horrified at the young bio-engineer's bloodthirsty attitude. She couldn't bring herself to think of the young woman as her stepmother, but it was obvious that her father was smitten with her, and she worried about what would happen when they had their first fight. "It's in all our interests to persuade Werner to leave us alone. But how do you propose to do it?"

John smiled. "Werner feels untouchable in Washington with the protection of his own security as well as the government bodies like the FBI. We need to disabuse him of that fact. First we need to find his primary agent in Britain, and convince him or her to go home … or to go away – permanently. Then I'll take a little trip to the US."

"I should come with you. It's my fight as well as yours," Tara said.

"Not this time. I don't question your commitment or your ability, but I have made long standing arrangements to get me in and out of most countries in the world without being spotted by immigration, customs or the intelligence services. These have taken generations to put in place and I won't be able to do the same for you at short notice. You won't do anyone any good if you're in a US federal prison or are forced to massacre a load of American police officers in order to escape." But you can definitely help me with whoever he has in Britain, he offered, smiling at her glum expression. He checked his smartphone for messages. "I've been waiting for information from my contacts and friends in the government. Ah! Here we have it. The survivors of the attack on this facility were spotted by security cameras leaving the area. It took a while to trace their movements, but they've finally found them. Since I didn't report the raid, and they police haven't turned up here to investigate a reported disturbance, I think we can safely assume that we have a clear field to act. I wouldn't be surprised if Werner's people actually used their influence to suppress any investigation."

Tara grinned bleakly. "Well they're going to regret that. We have some debts to pay."

***

Tara casually leaned against the wall near the junction of Liverpool Street and Bishopsgate, a compact camera around her neck and a bluetooth earpiece attached to the side of her face. "This isn't a very good place to get sneaky. We're bound to be spotted if we go up the outside wall."

John, who was strolling down Liverpool Street replied, "There are some buildings further down the road which we can enter and get up onto the roof. From there we can get to the hotel roof and inside. Fortunately the Victorian architecture provides for all manner of windows and architectural embellishments that will aid our entrance and exit. Actually, I find the situation rather humorous."

"In what way?"

"The hotel used to be the Great Eastern Hotel, built in 1884."

"So it's an old hotel. Why is that funny?"

"It so happens that it is the very hotel that Abraham Van Helsing was supposed to have stayed in during his sojourn in London while pursuing my literary namesake. Now we have a modern day vampire hunter staying there."

Tara chuckled. "Van Helsing stayed here? That's

an incredible coincidence fit for a modern day horror film."

"Only this time, the vampire has the opportunity to visit the hunter in his bed instead of the other way around." John had located the rooms occupied by the Americans through the simple expedient of hiring a reputable firm of private investigators cum security consultants. The surveillance cameras had provided a clear image of the faces of two of the attackers, and with that it had been a simple matter for the investigators to discover their rooms and the rooms of the rest of their party. For a generous fee the consultants had agreed to place listening devices in the men's rooms and it was not long afterwards that they identified the leader of the group, a Mr Dan Jackson, whom the investigators confirmed was an employee of the Werner Corporation in the USA. Both of them immediately recognised the name from the dying sniper team member's final words. With that, John had decided to pay the modern day Van Helsing a nocturnal visit. They had come here in the daytime to scout out the area before mounting an actual assault.

Joining Tara at the corner of the street across from the hotel, John smiled. "I think we're getting too dramatic. This is London, not Romania. How would you like to spend a night in the hotel? I hear that they have excellent restaurants and bars."

Tara grinned. "At last, some luxury. I was getting a bit fed up of all this crawling around in the muck. Hmm, I'll have to do some quick shopping."

"I see I've unleashed a monster of a different kind," John said with a chuckle.

***

The reservation and billing was done through one of John's myriad of companies, and they would be checking-in under aliases. As British citizens neither of them would be required to present their passports, so all that was required was for John to obtain two new credit cards under their aliases, again issued through a corporate account.

It was late afternoon when they drove up to the red brick building of the hotel in a rented limousine. The same process that allowed them to transform into their vampire form allowed them to make subtle changes to their features, including the shade of their hair, so even someone looking out for John Seward and Tara Harker wouldn't give them a second look. They were just another well-to-do couple coming up to London for a show and dinner.

Even though her family were not poor, Tara had seldom had the opportunity or inclination to stay in a luxury London hotel and she looked around in curiosity after they had checked in and been shown to their room. The day was clear, so the natural light coming in through the atrium made the interior look bright and cheerful, and she eagerly explored the hotel, followed by an amused John. They had a drink in the hotel pub, and then an early dinner in one of the restaurants, sitting and chatting like an ordinary couple as they ate.

Looking over the small table at John, Tara said, "I'm quite enjoying myself. I find that a bit disturbing. Shouldn't I be more nervous and anxious? That would only be human. I was always terribly nervous before a test flight. It was only when I got into the cockpit that I became cool and emotionless. Do you think the you-know-what is suppressing my emotions?"

John considered this carefully. "It is possible. My own case is not a good exemplar since I had so much practise in dealing with unpleasant and frightening circumstances, starting from my slavery under the Turks as a child. But I think you're giving yourself too little credit. You've become a formidable warrior in your own

252

right and you're entitled to feel confident. Just don't let it go to your head," he added cheerfully.

"I suppose you're right. Besides, it's better than throwing up like I did before my first test flight. Mmm, this steak is good." She was silent for a while as she enjoyed her food, and then another question came to her. "Is there any truth to the hypnotic powers thing? I haven't noticed any sign of it."

"You mean like in the films when the vampire makes the pretty female victim swoon or go into a trance? Well, actually we can do something of the sort, but it's rarely as neat or convenient as in fiction."

Tara was immediately intrigued and leaned over her plate. She pointed the tines of her fork at him. "Go on then. Tell all."

This made John smile. "I was going to tell you, but you have enough to learn and perfect already. Science has shown that both in intensity infra-sound as well as ultrasonic sounds can affect the human nervous system. Normally they produce anything from feelings of unease or even panic, to pain in the head, loss of balance, and several crowd control systems are already being developed using them such as the EPIC system from America. Most have not been very effective because as a military weapon they need it to work over a reasonable distance. Policemen and soldiers can't lug whacking great speakers and amplifiers around with them on the off chance they might be needed. However, if you're within arm's reach of a person, it is a different matter entirely. It's really an extension of the vampire's sonar system. The vampire race must have developed it as a natural defence. When attacked, it could stun its enemy or inflict such pain and nausea that the attacker would let go and pull back. As a last ditch or surprise weapon it can be very useful."

"So not hypnosis but puking? That's not very romantic," Tara said, disappointed.

253

"Real life is rarely romantic," John said, smiling sympathetically. "But making your opponent piss in their pants can be rather amusing."

According to the investigator's reports, Dan Jackson habitually came down to the same restaurant every night at seven p.m. for dinner. Tara and John were sitting sideways to the entrance, and both of them spotted the man come in, recognising him from the covert photographs the detectives had taken. They took their time with their meal and the after dinner coffee, and watched as Jackson finished his meal and went back to his room. The other men seemed under orders to have their meals in their rooms. This was actually convenient for what they planned.

Even though the hotel doors would have proven to be no real obstacle to their vampire strength, that would have been suspicious. In addition, they might be spotted by security cameras or staff. Instead, they would go out the window of their own rooms and re-enter through the windows as well. Their camouflage suits would render them practically invisible on the red brick wall, and they each carried suction cups and glass cutters. "That was a marvellous dinner, darling. I'm feeling a bit sleepy after all that food. What say we take a nap before going out?" John said.

Tara grinned, noting the way the people at the neighbouring tables were listening. "Why a nap sounds like a wonderful idea, honey." She took his arm and strolled out giggling. Once they were in the privacy of their room they quickly changed into their combat suits which were part of their luggage. Since they weren't facing werewolves, they were each armed with a high powered air pistol firing pellets containing a special mixture of etorphine and nerve toxins. There was no risk of the pellets penetrating walls and harming innocent holiday makers, and the guns were relatively quiet, the brisk snap when it fired barely audible outside the room and easily mistaken for the popping of a champaign cork or something similar. They really didn't need the guns, but a bloody massacre in a five star hotel wouldn't endear them to the authorities or help to differentiate them from the werewolves, and would only make Commander Blair's life more difficult.

The remaining mercenaries were accommodated two to a suite on either side of Dan Jackson's own suite. The plan was for them to take out the soldiers first and then deal with their leader together. Tara had been angry enough to be tempted to kill the mercenaries who had attacked them by draining their blood, but again providing the public with indications that there were vampires as well as werewolves loose wouldn't be in anybody's best interests. She smiled when John bowed and said "Ladies first". As she climbed lithely out the open window she wondered if being a vampire disqualified her from being a lady. Murdering people in their sleep most likely did. She glanced down to ensure that there were no tourists or urban bird watchers staring in her direction, and then crawled along the wall, going up one floor and then counting the windows to locate the right suite room. It would be embarrassing to say the least to break into the wrong room. A glance to the side showed her John gliding smoothly up the red brick wall. It had chilled her the first time she had seen him do it, reminding her of how far from human he was, and then that she was just like him now. He reached his window first, and she saw him waiting for her so that they would enter at the same time. She extracted the suction cup from a utility pocket of her suit and attached it to the window next to the catch. It had been both a thrill and a shock to discover that her claws were hard enough to cut glass, and she made a note to ask her father to analyse the composition of her claws. She winced at the tiny squeak as she crew a rough circle around the suction cup. The catch and window were well maintained and opened with barely any sound, and the heavy curtains hid both her entry and the breeze that blew in through the opening. The air pistol slid from her holster as her feet touched the floor.

***

John skilfully cut the glass, but just as he was about to open the window, the occupant of the room parted the curtains, either desiring to take in the view or to take a smoke. At any rate, his eyes widened comically and the blood drained from his face at the sight of the man clinging to the outside of the window. His mouth opened to shout a warning, but before he could utter a sound John's hand darted through the hole he had cut in the glass and grabbed the unfortunate mercenary by the throat. With no time for subtleties, John sank his claws into the man's flesh and ripped his throat out with a single convulsive movement of his arm. He winced as a torrent of blood splashed the unbroken glass of the window as well as his forearm. So much for a clean kill. Still, a ripped throat could be blamed on a werewolf, unlike the two neat puncture marks on the throat made famous by countless appearances on TV and the cinema. He released the man when he was sure that the mercenary was dead and then opened the window and slipped in. His sensitive hearing caught the snap of Tara's air pistol. Apparently she was having better luck than he had. Drawing his pistol he stepped over the corpse and glided silently across the bedroom. The door was closed so he turned off the room lights and paused with his hand on the handle to listen. But it was his sense of smell that gave him the first warning. Just as he was about to open the door, he caught the scent of gun oil wafting in from outside of the room. He froze, his shoulder against the wall, clear of the door in case the mercenary fired through the panel or kicked it open, and waited to see

256

what the man would do.

There was a soft tap, and then a whisper. "Hank. Hank, are you awake? I couldn't sleep. That fucking vampire is giving me nightmares. Jackson refuses to believe us so he might send us out there again once the new guys get here. Hank, is there something wrong? I heard you make a funny noise. Hank? I'm coming in."

John rolled his eyes. Apparently he had been too successful in frightening his enemies, but on the other hand if Jackson hadn't believed his men, it was likely he hadn't reported the existence of vampires to his superiors in America either. That meant if he could silence all of this group, their secret could remain a secret for a while longer. He felt the handle turn under his hand and he pulled further back so that the light from the living room wouldn't expose him. The door slowly opened.

"Hank?" The man pushed the door open wide enough to push his head and shoulders into the room. He held his gun at his side, pointing at the floor, obviously unwilling to risk shooting his companion by accident in the dark. That was the last sound he made before a long boned hand tipped with razor claws closed about his throat and something ripped the pistol from his hand.

***

Dan had not gained and retained his position without a healthy dose of paranoia. The story of the men who had returned from the raid had been totally unbelievable. Monsters, yes. He could accept just about anything at this point, but Dracula? How stupid did they think he was. He had written up his report to Werner, but at the last moment his finger had not been able to click on the send button and it still sat accusingly on his notebook's screen. He just didn't know enough. For all he knew, this Seward person could have somehow bought all of his men off and sent them back with this ridiculous story, or they may have been humiliatingly beaten by the guards and just didn't want to admit it. He was even ready to consider the possibility that Seward's people had somehow found some werewolves and a way to control them. But he knew too little at that point and Werner would be furious if he submitted a load of shit without confirming it first. The fact that the heavily armed raid had clearly failed was bad enough. He might even lose his job. But a brainless report could lose him his life. Instead, he had dropped electronic bugs in the men's rooms the moment he had the opportunity, and he had left the sound on twenty-four hours a day since then, muting it only when someone came into his room, hoping to catch an unguarded comment that would tell him more. Frustratingly, he had heard nothing of use at all, the men being either too clever or to truly frightened to say anything that didn't tally with their reports. He decided to give it one more night and then he would submit the report anyway and face the consequences of his incompetence.

Dan had been unable to sleep, lying in his bed and staring at the ceiling when he had heard the sounds. The first was a sharp crack that had made him jump. He wouldn't have heard it through the walls but it came through loud and clear from the bug. Then there was a faint tinkle of broken glass and the thud of something soft and heavy like a body colliding with something, and more sounds of movement, two more of the sharp snapping noises, and what sounded like gurgling. His body tingled and he jumped upright. His mind recalled what his men had been saying and the sight of the dark living room of the suite suddenly chilled him. Another snapping sound made him jump, followed by a horrible choking groan and there was the unmistakable sound of a falling body. He didn't wait for more. He snatched the pistol from under his pillow and slipped it into the flat pancake holster on his belt. He was fully dressed except

258

for his shoes so he slipped them on and grabbed the small backpack that held his passport, more ammunition, a wad of money in various currencies, a spare cellphone and the various other useful items that made up his bug-out pack. He threw it on and headed over to the entrance to the suite. He listened with his ear pressed against the door, and then risked a glance through the peep-hole when the light in the hallway showed that no one was standing right in front of the door. The wide angle lens revealed that the hallway was empty. He pocketed the hotel room key-card, turned off all the lights, and silently opened the door, the pistol held low and ready at his side. When no one attacked him he slipped out of the room, carefully closed the door and silently ran down the hall towards the elevators. If he had been mistaken he could always say he went for a walk and return to his room, but if he was right and they were under attack, then his only ally was speed. He had to be gone before they got around to him. He was a professional and already had a contingency plan. He sighed in relief when the elevator doors closed smoothly in front of him and the cage headed for the ground floor. He stepped out of the elevator and strolled calmly across the lobby. Once out on the street, he walked briskly towards Bishopsgate, all his senses and skill tuned to detecting followers or watchers, but he didn't see anything. He paused at the corner of Liverpool Street and Bishopsgate, straining his every sense and using all of his considerable experience to detect any possible threat. For a moment he hesitated, remembering the unsent report. He considered going back to send it, but he decided that if he survived and escaped he could always write another one or at least call Werner and give him a verbal report. However it was much harder to encrypt a cellphone call or email without special equipment than it was to encrypt a document file on a computer, and what he was dealing with required the maximum of security so a call would necessarily leave a lot of important detail out. Werner was under no illusions about the degree of scrutiny the NSA and other intelligence agencies ware sure to have focused upon him due to his involvement in so many highly secret and sensitive projects. When the pause became dangerously long, Dan shrugged and turned the corner and headed for the glass covered entrance to the main concourse of the Liverpool Street Train Station. There he could lose himself in the evening crowd and buy a ticket to a random destination during which he could ensure that he was not being followed before setting up an alternate base from which to communicate with the US and to carry on his operations, provided he still had a job after today.

***

John and Tara entered Dan Jackson's room from separate windows, reducing the chance that they would both be hit by an ambush or booby trap. But the moment they stepped into the suite, their keen vampire senses told them that no living creature above the level of insects was present. John still went to check the bedrooms and bathrooms just in case Jackson had somehow managed to conceal himself from them.

In the meantime, Tara searched the sitting room for items of interest or indications of where Jackson might be. The notebook was the most obvious item in the room, and she went over to look at it. Jackson didn't use a passworded screen saver, since those were pathetically easy to break, so a touch of the touch-pad brought the screen to life with the unsent report detailing the attack and John's dramatic appearance. "John, come and look at this," she called out. "It looks like Werner's people in the US don't know about us yet."

John appeared, holding up wireless relay and recording equipment. "And here's why our friend isn't here. He heard us taking out his guards and very wisely departed at speed. So you think our secret is still a secret for the moment?"

"From Werner at least. It seems that Jackson wasn't very sure what to make of his men's account of what happened at our facility and hasn't sent anything yet. We've just killed the last of the actual attackers, although there might have been some drivers or pilots who were there as well. It's likely they were locals hired for the job, and they wouldn't have been part of the actual attack."

John nodded at the notebook computer. "Take that. We can leave it somewhere outside until we can recover it. But first we need to find Mr Jackson. If we can silence him, Werner will never know what happened, other than their people all died or disappeared. For all they know, the men may have mostly deserted or turned on their employer due to some dispute, killing the ones that remained loyal."

"Providing Jackson isn't around to tell his side of the story," Tara said as she unplugged the notebook and pulled out the power supply and charger from the wall socket. There would be no trace to suggest a missing computer when the police finally came upon the scene. Tucking the notebook and cables into her back pack, she climbed smoothly out of the window. At first the idea of clinging to the side of a building had been frightening, even when she was sure she wouldn't fall. But with much practise she had become quite used to it and she joined John outside, scanning the streets, vehicles, and buildings below for any sign of Jackson. Her eyes were as sharp as those of a falcon, and the faces of the people in the street were clearly visible to her even in the semi gloom of the street lighting. "He might be still in the hotel, or even in another room."

John shook his head. "Unlikely. Jackson is a professional, and an experienced one to be trusted with heading up an illegal military operation in a foreign country and a member of NATO at that. A screw up could be highly embarrassing to Werner and through them the US government. He wouldn't hang around a compromised location. He would run, as far and as fast as he could. He would look to lose himself in crowds …" His voice trailed off as he focused upon his search.

"There! At the street corner. It's him, I'm sure of it," Tara said. Her HUD showed a "Target Lock" icon, so her alien senses must have agreed with her conclusion.

John looked in the indicated direction and immediately spotted Jackson's tall fit figure, just before he turned the corner and went out of sight. "You're right! Let's get after him." He led the way across the length of the Victorian building, nearly invisible from the ground in their suits. However in order to get down to ground level, they needed to descend, increasing the risk of being spotted. But with some patience and quick reflexes, both he and Tara managed to get to the pavement, picking the moment when no one close by was looking their way. Turning his camouflage off, he set off in pursuit of the Werner executive, his surroundings both familiar and strange, the memories of centuries of gradual change dancing past his mind like long banners rippling in the wind. He had walked this way, headed for the Liverpool Street station countless times, bent on errands both fair and foul, and even on rare occasions with thoughts of love and romance lightening his steps. But more often his long life had been filled with death. The death of family, of friends, of faceless prey, and most important of all, of his enemies. But the familiar thrill of the hunt made his apparently immortal heart beat faster and he had to resist the urge to run down the crowded street, weaving through the slow moving humans like a dark shadow. There had been times over the long years that he had stalked the streets of London like the avatar of death itself, filling the night

262

with fear and dread, but this was not one of those times. He was a respected and well liked member of society and he intended to retain that status for as long as he could, and in order to do so, Dan Jackson had to die. He walked on, leaning forward eagerly like a leopard that had caught the scent of prey, while his vampire senses told him that Tara Harker followed close behind. "He's heading for the trains," he said over his shoulder.

"That makes sense," Tara replied. "Large crowds of strangers and many different and very anonymous paths out of the city. Once he gets on a train we'll lose him, at least for long enough for him to communicate what he knows to someone." She was forced to walk fast by John's long legged stride and she knew she was attracting attention. Knowing that obscurity was impossible, she unfastened the neck and front of her suit peeling the soft flexible fabric apart until the upper curves of her breasts were revealed. Her stride changed to emphasise the smooth scissoring of her long legs and the rocking of her hips, and suddenly she changed from an oddity, and annoyance on the street, to a beacon of sexuality, like a lingerie model on a catwalk, shifting the focus of the observers around her to admiration, lust, envy, even jealous hate. But now at least no one saw the hunter, the predator. Beautiful women were often in a hurry, headed towards some assignation or coming from one. She smiled when she saw the looks around her change, and the smile only served to increase the sexual aura that shielded the reality of her from everyone. This was no vampire power, but the natural powers given to every attractive woman. But like every piece of equipment that came into Tara's possession, she had learned to drive her body to its limits and to make full use of it the way she would any new experimental aircraft. It was what made her a superlative test pilot. As she watched John stride through the crowd like the prow of a battleship cutting through the waves, she realised

263

that he had long ago learned that same lesson. He could be warm and cheerful, or terrifying and commanding at will. She had no doubt that they would catch up with Jackson. The man, as well trained and professional as he might be, didn't stand a chance.

***

It might have seemed an incredible, unbelievable coincidence, but in truth it was not so great of a coincidence when the nature of the station was taken into account. Werewolf attacks were happening with increasing frequency in London and an almost wartime atmosphere filled the city. Surprisingly, rather than the mass panic that the experts always anticipated with such relish, most of the populace actually pulled together to help each other and to sound the alert whenever a werewolf sighting was made, once it was accepted that the creatures were not the result of drug inspired hallucinations or some kind of deadly hoax. SMS messages, all manner of social media, as well as simple phone calls kept the majority constantly alert to the latest sighting, even when the sightings were often false. More than one person had already been seriously beaten up by angry crowds when they posted fake alerts. The very inexplicable nature of the threat made it easier for the people to band together, undivided by political or economic forces. Everyone was potential prey, the rich, the poor, the powerful and the homeless. But the very size of the city and its huge population made it possible for everyday life to continue. The werewolves couldn't strike everywhere at once, and unlike a terrorist's bombs, the monsters could only kill one person at a time. When entirely determined by the werewolves' instincts and hungers, the attacks were almost completely random, depending on the timing when the change came upon the infected, and what their normal routine happened to be.

But in some cases the attacks were directed by intelligent purpose, by Viktor's followers who were tasked with creating the maximum of havoc and to distract the police from the affairs of the criminal underworld so that Viktor could wage his campaign of terror against the mobs and the firms unmolested by the forces of the law. In such cases, places which presented the largest concentration of victims and easiest access by strangers were obviously the most attractive to Viktor's men and women. Places such as Liverpool Street station.

The strike had been carefully planned. Two of Viktor's pack had boarded a train outside of London and ridden it into the city. Once the train started moving, they went off in search of prey. By carefully picking their targets they were able to attack out of sight of the other passengers, each of them infecting a victim, leaving them near death but with the minimum of blood and mess. They had become very good at this from repeated practise all over London and in other cities. When the train pulled into the next station, the werewolves, now cleaned up and in human form, left the train with the other passengers. The two victims, one male and one female, had just begun to stir, their bodies twisting and rippling as the alien medical nanites struggled to save their lives by repairing their hosts in the only template they had, which was that of the werewolf-like species that they had been created for, when Dan Jackson descended the stairs into the main concourse pursued closely by John and Tara. The train was about ten minutes away from the station when the newly created werewolves completed their transformation and as a necessary consequence of their change, they were ravenous. For some inexplicable reason, both of them chose to head forwards into the first class carriage. They burst through the doors roaring in fury and blood-lust. Unfortunately for the passengers and crew the creatures retained sufficient human knowledge to recognise the noisy screaming creatures as helpless prey and so they threw themselves forward without the primitive hesitation and threat displays natural when faced with unfamiliar creatures of significant size.

The male werewolf pounced upon the most obvious target, a steward pushing a snack trolley down the aisle. Its jaws closed on the uniformed man's shoulder, fangs tearing effortlessly through the fabric and into soft sweet flesh. The taste of blood drove the creature into an absolute frenzy, all thought submerged beneath the need to feed. It's claws ripped at the man's chest and abdomen, shattering his ribcage with the sickening sounds of snapping bones and tearing flesh. A flick of the werewolf's paw sent coils of intestines flying outwards to drape themselves over an already hysterical matron, who took one look at what was clinging to her body and collapsed in a dead faint, falling on top of the young woman beside her and pinning her to her seat.

The female werewolf was a second behind, scrambling over the backs of the luxury seats. Drawn by the blood and scent of raw bloody flesh she sprang from seat to seat until she was above the pinned girl. The werewolf's paw shot out and gripped the girl by her long hair and pulled her bodily from her seat. Despite the girl's desperate struggles, the werewolf bent her victim backwards over the headrest of the seat and sank its fangs into the girl's breast.

Two men, braver or simply more driven by instinct, snatched up steel trays from the trolley and attacked the werewolves who were too busy gorging themselves to react to their puny threat, at least until the men began beating on their heads with the trays.

Both werewolves looked up simultaneously. Having no language, much like young human children, they still managed to communicate via body language, growls and whines. Although their minds were almost like those of new-born children, they were able to draw upon the deeply ingrained knowledge of their former human brains. Despite their appearance, they were based on the form of a highly developed alien race, and they learned very quickly and were by nature a cooperative species. They both realised that it would be better to subdue all of the creatures first before settling down to eat in peace, and with a meeting of their eyes, they set about doing just that.

**

The driver of the train faintly heard the screams, but only shook his head, assuming that a bunch of passengers had gotten rowdy. It was unusual for the first class section, but not impossible. The young and wealthy were often worse than their less fortunate peers. The train was approaching the station, and all of his attention was focused upon the track and signals in front of him, his hand on the speed regulator in preparation for the gradual slowing down that would cause the minimum of discomfort and inconvenience for the passengers. A thump on the door behind him made him frown, but before he could turn, the metal door smashed inwards as if propelled by an explosion. He barely had time to scream before hook-like claws ripped out his throat, his clinging fingers moving the throttle to maximum speed and his spasming foot holding down the DSD, or what was traditionally known as the "dead man's switch" for long enough to make it too late for the built in safety devices to slow and stop the train. The female werewolf grunted and turned around, eager to get back to her companion and the feast that lay all around in the main carriage.

**

Dan Jackson looked around the station, which he

had only visited once in order to familiarise himself with its general location and layout in case of an emergency such as the one he now faced. With his back to a huge painted iron pillar, he searched with his eyes until he found the bright new electronic arrival and departure board. Once he had located it, he headed in that direction in order to pick a train that was scheduled to depart soon and for a decently distant destination. He had just reached the bottom of the display when a commotion broke out. A nearly unintelligible announcement was broadcast over the station PA system, echoing around the huge, high roofed structure. The urgency in the announcer's tone drew the attention of most of the people in the station, who looked around in puzzlement, trying to spot the reason for the shouting. A buzz of conversation filled the station, and the people on the platforms, sandwiched between the long caterpillar-like forms of the empty or emptying trains looked up and down the long concrete piers uneasily. Some began to hurry towards the main concourse while others tried to decide between boarding their trains or waiting to see what was wrong. Most people were highly aware of the possibility of terrorist bomb threats, and more recently, of the nearly impossible to believe werewolf threat, and panic rapidly began to spread through the huge station. This was made worse by a strange screeching and rumbling coming from the open end of the station, and then some people realised what it meant.

***

Standing at the top of the stairs that led down into the concourse, John and Tara had just spotted Jackson when the unexpected announcements began to blare from the loudspeakers. John, who had lived through the age of steam and had personally witnessed several train crashes, immediately realised what was happening. It seemed impossible with a modern train, but now was not the time to debate the point. "Runaway train coming into the station!" he snapped.

Tara pointed at the Werner operative. "We have to get to him before all hell breaks loose," and jumped over the railings onto the floor below, much to the amazement of the already confused people standing around the area.

John followed without hesitation and added to the confusion. He started to run after Tara, and then paused. "Run! An out of control train in coming into the station. Run for your life!" he shouted. Without waiting to see if his warning did any good, he raced towards the beacon of the arrivals and departures board.

Tara cursed as she forced her way through the confused crowd. She was almost within reach of Jackson when there was a horrific mechanical roaring from the direction of the platforms, followed a second later by a train moving at full speed which drove full tilt into the crash barriers. She turned to look, just in time to see the amazing sight of several carriages jack-knife into the air before toppling over sideways and on top of the platform and the train next to it, spewing wreckage and human bodies all around. The impact shook the entire station, sending clouds of dust flying into the air, followed by panels of glass shaken loose from the roof, falling like gigantic and deadly snowflakes towards the crowded concourse. People were crushed and smeared against the concrete of the platforms to either side of the smashed train and bodies flew from the shattered carriages to land upon bystanders like boulders flung from a medieval catapult. Then the silently falling glass panes reached the ground. One fell vertically like a guillotine blade, cutting an unfortunate traveller neatly in half, head to crotch, while others struck at various angles hammering people onto the ground. Many more hit the ground and shattered with terrific force, sending razor sharp shards of glass flying in all directions and slicing into legs and bodies.

269

Screams of pain and terror filled the station, most of the uninjured too stunned by the tremendous impact to run.

Then there was a long moment of stunned silence, when everyone realised that the immediate danger was over. The loud cringe making sound of ripping squealing metal made all eyes turn towards the wrecked train. The roof of the bent and twisted first carriage suddenly bulged, and then the metal tore, ripping like paper as a muscular, hair covered arm pushed it aside. The hole grew bigger and bigger, and then the head and shoulders of a werewolf appeared. With a powerful shove of its arms it sprang out of the improvised exit to land crouching on the slanted roof of the carriage. There was blood on its muzzle and all over its body, but there were no apparent injuries. Then a second werewolf appeared, and they stood side by side, red eyes blazing, jaws open and snarling, clearly infuriated by their unexpected ordeal. Then both extended their claw tipped paws out to their sides as if preparing for a huge hug, and they roared their defiance at the gathered crowd of stunned humans. One of them, the larger one, sniffed, catching the scent of fresh blood, as did the other. Then as if driven by giant springs, both of them leapt into the air, bounding across the tops of the trains and empty platforms, heading directly for the huddled crowds.

The combined shock and threat of the colliding train and the unexpected appearance of the werewolves was too much, and the crowd reacted with blind panic. A mad scramble commenced, starting with the people closest to the crashed train and the werewolves that were rushing towards them. The people further away were slower to react, and as always in such situations the two groups collided in the middle of the concourse when one group failed to run or move aside quickly enough. People were trampled, and others retaliated, striking back at what they thought were attackers. Soon there was a full-fledged riot going on, as well as deadly pile ups at the exits with the slower being knocked down and trampled to death.

The werewolves had already eaten, and would not ordinarily have been in a rush to kill again, but repairing the severe injuries incurred during the crash made them ravenously hungry again. Even so, they paused at the edge of the concourse, eyeing the helpless prey like diners studying a buffet spread.

But suddenly the situation changed when a pair of British Transport Police Armed Officers opened fire on the stationary werewolves with their LMT Defender assault rifles. Each of their rifles barked and the officers grunted in satisfaction when their targets staggered under the impact. Unfortunately for them, the light high velocity 5.56 mm rounds lacked the power to do the kind of damage that could have even slowed the werewolves down. Their satisfaction changed to apprehension when both creatures straightened up and swivelled their heads so that their muzzles pointed directly at the police officers who had attacked them. "Shit! Fire! Fire!" one of them shouted, shouldering his weapon again and shooting rapidly at the apparently unharmed monsters.

But the pair of werewolves burst into violent action, bounding from place to place in a blinding zig-zag motion which demonstrated that they understood the threat of the weapons being used against them.

The officers began to back up as the werewolves bounded rapidly towards them, moving so fast that neither officer was able to hit them again, their bullets hitting trains or going on up to shatter the glass of the roof canopy. Then their backs came up against the madly struggling crowd, halting their retreat. A moment later the werewolves were upon them, and they realised that their weapons were of no use at all.

***

John had almost reached Tara's position when the crash happened, followed a moment later by the appearance of the werewolves. "Damn! Tara, you take care of Jackson, then come back to help me if I need it." He didn't need to say that he was going after the werewolves. He eyed the rapidly forming stampede, then broke free of the crowd and headed for the nearly vacant platforms and trains. Like some kind of impossible vaulter, he sprang up onto the roof of a train and then leapt across the width of the platform and onto the next one. When the track was empty he jumped across the track onto the next platform with an ease and grace that would have made any Olympic athlete retire on the spot. As he ran he considered his option. He couldn't use his pistol because of the crowd and because it wasn't loaded with silver, and the same went for his sword since the follow through of his strokes would kill those standing around and behind him. That left him with his dagger, claws, and fangs. His next leap carried him onto the side of one of the jack-knifed carriages which had toppled over onto its side. Running lightly along the smashed train, he accelerated until he was a silver grey blur. His camouflage was not active as he needed the crowd to be able to see him, although he could activate it almost instantly in the event he needed it. He could see that the two brave but unfortunate police officers were down, torn to pieces by the enraged werewolves.

The nearby crowd were attempting to flee but the panicked jam formed a solid wall of bodies and they could only move sideways across the width of the concourse. Instinctively drawn by the movement and sight of fleeing prey, the werewolves split up, one going left and the other right across the ends of the platforms and pouncing upon the slowest to flee, bringing them down with a single savage slash of their claws or a snap of slavering jaws that severed hamstrings and even bones. They plunged into the fleeing mass like furry threshing machines, sending blood and body parts flying in all directions.

John dove off of the train, somersaulted, and landed running. He turned left, picking the larger of the werewolves as his first target. Holding his knife out in front of him like the point of a spear he charged towards the creature's back. Even as he neared he saw the monster's ear flick and threw himself into a forward dive, the werewolf's raking claws just passing over his head. The silvered dagger slammed into the creature's side just below the ribs. He twisted the blade when he felt it go in, and then pulled it out as he crumpled into a tight ball and rolled away out of range of the werewolf's furious retaliation. He narrowly missed falling into the deep pit of a set of tracks as he rose smoothly to his feet, just in time to meet the wounded werewolf's enraged four legged charge. Spinning aside at the last moment like a bull fighter, he flipped the blade downwards and drove the dagger into the creature's back as it passed, pulling it free just before it would have been torn from his hand.

The shock of the silver blade threw the werewolf off balance and it skidded on the hard smooth tiling of the floor and tumbled with a roar down onto the tracks, but not before a rearward kick of its leg caught John's thigh, the tremendous impact knocking him off his feet and sending him tumbling into the crowd. People of all ages and sexes screamed and shouted in alarm when his body crashed into their backs, crushing them against the rest of the crowd, breaking bones and spraining muscles. Despite the fact that his leg felt like it had nearly been ripped from his hip, John got to his feet and drew his sabre. The creature had made the mistake of separating itself from the bystanders, giving John room to manoeuvre and to wield his blade. Dashing forward, he reached the edge of the platform just as the werewolf climbed up and out of the pit. He immediately attacked, cutting and thrusting at the creature while it still had the pit at its back, hampering its ability to dodge. But before he could finish the creature off, a set of powerful jaws closed about the biceps of his left arm, dragging him back and away from the first werewolf. He had to clench his teeth to prevent himself from crying out in pain as the werewolf shook and twisted its head in an attempt to tear his arm off. The fabric of his suit held against the fangs, but provided little protection from the crushing pressure of the creature's jaws. Even though the agony made his vision turn red, he braced himself against the pull of the werewolf using all of the vampire strength in his muscles to prevent his arm from breaking. He twisted around to face it and his foot shot up in a forward snap kick that drove his own claws into the creature's belly, raking across the hard muscles of the monster's abdomen. Although he knew the wound would heal almost instantly, the injury still winded and hurt his attacker just enough to delay the raking blow of the werewolf's claws across his face, and to allow him to slash his sabre across the front of his body from right to left, severing two of the creatures fingers before sinking deep into the spot where its thick neck joined its body.

The cut wasn't strong or deep enough to sever its head, but the werewolf's jaws snapped open and its upper body recoiled as it roared in agony from the poison of the silver in its blood. The savage wound remained open and bloody and it clamped its paw over the gaping cut in its neck.

John reversed the motion of his sabre and hammered its heavy silver pommel up against the bottom of the monster's blood drenched muzzle with a blow powered by all the strength of his legs and back.

The werewolf's jaws were slammed shut by the blow and the silver split the flesh of its chin and lower lip and it was hurled backwards lifting the creature up off its feet and onto its back where it lay momentarily stunned.

Warned by his sonar and the movement of the air, instead of finishing off the downed werewolf he swirled around to his right, the sabre painting a diagonal silver spiral in the air and its razor sharp edge caught the male werewolf in mid-air, cleaving into the side of its skull with the sound of an axe striking the trunk of a huge tree and slamming it to the side so that it landed flat upon its belly, arms and legs splayed. John spun the sabre in a tight loop around his wrist and then vertically down. With a meaty thwump the sabre sliced into the male werewolf's neck with meteoric force and the monster's head flew free of its body. Bringing his feet together he twirled with the sabre extended at the length of his arm to face the female werewolf who was just climbing to its feet, shaking its head sending droplets of blood flying through the air. He took a step to the side, his foot gliding over the floor, never quite losing contact, as the werewolf started to circle him, its fangs and claws threatening his left side. He matched the creature's circling pace and for more than thirty seconds they moved around each other like a pair of oddly matched dancers.

Demonstrating once again that it was much more than a dangerous animal, the werewolf suddenly feinted a bite at John's left knee, but then twisted in an almost snake-like movement and lashed out with its claws, raking them down the inside of John's wrist and the fingers that held his sword, sending the sabre flying away to narrowly miss impaling one of the fleeing passengers.

But vampires had fighting moves of their own, and even as the creature lunged for his throat John seemed to take wing, bounding vertically into the air with his arms outstretched like wings and narrowly escaping the werewolf's jaws. He performed an acrobatic flip in mid-air completely inverting his body even as he was still rising. Then he plunged down his arms snapping to his sides and adding a tiny bit of momentum to his downward dive. His body twisted again just before his own fangs sank deep into the back of the werewolf's neck while his legs clamped around the creature's waist and squeezed with the force of a metal vice, driving the breath from the creature's lungs. He whipped his dagger from its sheath and slammed the blade between its ribs and into its heart. The werewolf collapsed beneath him. Arching his back, he pulled the werewolf's head back with his teeth and clamped his free hand under its muzzle, levering its head back and allowing the silver coated blade to sink into its throat. With an inhumanly powerful pull of his arm John cut the werewolf's throat, the tip of the dagger grinding against the creature's spine. He bent his legs and braced his knees against the shuddering werewolf's back, dropped the knife, and with both hands he pulled, every muscle in his body straining to the utmost, quivering like a bow. Suddenly there was a wet snap and the sound of tearing flesh as he ripped the werewolf's head off of its body. Holding the severed head in his hand he looked around, remembering that he was in a public place.

But the only people looking in his direction and not fully occupied with trying to flee, was a teen-aged couple who stood holding hands and staring, open mouthed.

"Awesome!" breathed the girl, her eyes going from John's blood streaked and fanged face down to his buttocks which were tightly outlined by his silver-grey suit.

Unaware of the focus of his girlfriend's attention, the boy nodded enthusiastically. "Yeah, what she said."

John put the head down and smiled at the pair. "Um, I'd appreciate it if you didn't tell anyone what you just saw."

Still nodding the boy said, "No problem. You

saved our lives. We didn't see anything, did we Lucy?"

Lucy licked her lips and shook her head. "Nope, didn't see a thing," she said and giggled, blushing.

John looked around. "I have to go now. You'd better leave too when you can. The police and everybody else will be here soon." He watched the young pair run off and shook his head in amused despair when the girl looked over her shoulder and blew him a kiss. He could sense where Tara was and set off running in that direction. Jackson shouldn't be any threat to her, but the man was a professional killer, and despite her powers, Tara was not invulnerable. He realised that his image had to be captured on at least one security camera, but now that Tara was able to change her appearance he wasn't too worried. It was unlikely that the camera had caught sight of his fangs or his claws. The rest could be explained away by extreme agility and martial arts skills. People were used to seeing impossible fights in the cinema, especially with the popularity of superhero films.

***

Her ears still ringing from the tremendous crash of the train slamming into the station, Tara turned around and then cursed when she saw that Jackson was gone. She looked around, her enhanced vision bringing every visible face sharply into view, but she didn't see the man's face anywhere. Her eyes narrowed and then she ran towards one of the huge metal pillars of the station. She had spotted the security cameras and moved around the pillar until she was blocked from view by it. Seeing that there was no one looking in her direction, she started to rapidly climb up the pillar until she was high enough that she had an overhead view of most of the station. At first she felt a rush of dizziness as her vision zoomed in and out like a telephoto lens, but then her mind adapted to it and she marvelled at how clearly she saw each face. Suddenly a circular cursor appeared in her HUD and it began to rapidly jump from face to face, and she realised that the military component of the alien nanite system had cut in and was aiding in her search. The cursor locked on a head and began to flash. Tara concentrated on the person and her vision zoomed in. Even though she was looking at the person's back, she immediately recognised Jackson. He was headed out for the open rear of the station that was a wide open wall-less space filled with railway tracks. Several trains had halted just outside of the station building and one was half way in. Jackson was making his way along the side of the huge station building and would soon disappear outside. Tara realised that she was above the range of the security cameras which were not designed to watch pigeons and bats. The wall of the building was too far away for her to jump to it, so she headed up to the huge wrought iron arches and painted cast iron decorative panels that supported the great span of the roof and then began to rapidly crawl upside down along the roof like a gigantic spider. She found herself humming the theme from the old Spider Man cartoon and grinned, despite her grim purpose. Even though she had to follow the metal supports and mouldings, she was able to move faster than Jackson who was jogging steadily along. She dropped to the ground at the end of the station building with Jackson about ten metres in front of her, moving parallel to the tracks and obviously looking for a spot on the embankment where he could climb up and out. All train traffic in the area had come to a halt by that time so she was able to run along the track without fear of being run over.

Alerted by the crunch of gravel under Tara's boots, Dan Jackson glanced over his shoulder. Seeing his pursuer, he swore and ran faster. But when he looked again the woman was still gaining on him. She didn't look any different from a normal person, nor was she even particularly tall or powerfully built, so he decided to take her out before anyone else showed up to help her. He reached under his coat and drew his SP2022 SIG Sauer pistol. Through Werner's influence he even had a concealed carry license for it, which in Britain was nearly impossible to obtain legally outside of government service. He already had a round in the chamber and the pistol was capable of double action fire, so he didn't have to do anything except to stop and turn around. He took a half-step back, raised the gun into a firing position and gave himself a second for his breathing to steady as he took aim at the approaching woman. To his surprise she didn't weave or dive to the side, and he wondered if she was just another passenger trying to escape the same way he was, but when she kept coming even though she must have seen his gun, he knew for certain she had to be one of the people who had attacked his men in the hotel. All of this went through his mind in a fraction of a second even as his finger tightened on the trigger. He lined up the three white dots of the sights on the middle of the woman's chest and fired twice in rapid succession. The woman darted to the side just as he fired and he felt a flash of surprise and annoyance. He rarely missed with a target that was out in the open and was not shooting back at him. His irritation changed to shock when he fired again and missed. She barely seemed to dodge, but his bullets went past her body anyway.

The alien nanite system was growing increasingly integrated with her nervous system. Without even trying, she detected the subtle movement of Jackson's hand and the gun itself just before he fired, and even without referring to the warning icon on her HUD, she felt the urge to dodge to the side at exactly the right moment. She might have dismissed the first as a fluke or just her improved reflexes, but with the second she realised that the alien artificial intelligence in her body was actually computing the movements needed and sending a signal to her brain and nerves. It didn't take over her body, but simply implanted the desire to move in the right direction and the degree of effort required so that she just did it the same way she would catch a ball or dodge a collision with an oncoming pedestrian in the street. She could have drawn her pistol and shot Jackson down right then, but her anger wouldn't allow it. She wanted to feel him die under her hands.

Dan tried to fire a third time, but she was too close and it was too late. A sharp blow simultaneously struck both of his wrists, the force of it driving both arms sharply to his right and numbing his hands. The pistol fired, hitting the embankment and pulling the gun from the nerveless grip of his fingers. He was a master of several martial arts and his shoulders automatically twisted as he attempted a shoulder check against Tara's chest which would have shattered her sternum if it had landed. But instead a hard push to the rear of his shoulder diverted the power of his blow harmlessly to the side and he grunted in pain when a palm strike to his side cracked ribs. Then he screamed in agony when he was stabbed in the back by what felt like multiple knife points and a kick to the back of his leg made him drop to his knee. He tried to roll away, but clawed fingers clamped down on the top of his head piercing the flesh and grating against the bone of his skull. The agony was blinding and he froze when he found that he was unable to turn his head. If he tried to twist or roll now he would break his own neck. Instead he reached up with both hands despite the his cracked ribs, searching for a punishing nerve grip that would allow him to break the grip on his head but when he did he discovered that the slim, normal looking woman's grip was as solid as steel and he was unable to bend even her little finger with both hands. Up to now he had been fighting using his skill and training, but finally he began to panic. He clawed at her hand and lashed wildly behind him in hopes of hitting her. His hand struck her thigh and rebounded, then he struck upwards with the edge of his hand, aiming for her crotch, but changed his mind when she tutted and twisted his head, making his spine creak and a jolt of pain run down his spine. Real, belly deep fear swept over him and he almost lost control of his bladder. This was impossible. The woman couldn't be that strong, not even a man twice her size could be so powerful. Panting and wheezing, with a stabbing pain in his chest making it hard to breathe he gasped, "Who are you, what are you?"

Tara saw the image of the dead guards and Duncan's wounds. She remembered the agony of her own broken thigh, and she felt her fangs extend as rage shook her. "Didn't your men tell you?"

The grip on his skull tightened further and his skull bones creaked. "Aaahh! Don't! They, they said some nonsense about Dracula."

"Dracula?" She chuckled. "But Dracula doesn't exist, does he," she said mockingly. "Vampires only exist in TV shows and films, right? It's all CGI and make-up." She could sense John approaching, but she wanted this man for herself. "But you're the scary one, aren't you? The powerful man, the one people fear. Does that make you proud, make you happy?"

Jackson tried to reply, but the agony that was like a crown of nails driven into his skull reduced his reply to a shuddering groan.

"You sent people out to kill me, to kill my friends, kill my father. But where is your power now, Mr Jackson?" Her fingers began to tighten their grip. "And just so there is no mistake, you're going to die today, Mr Jackson. In fact, I'm going to crush your skull with my hand as you kneel there."

At this point Jackson began to struggle and flail

his arms violently, ignoring the pain it caused him. But all to no avail. His struggles came to an abrupt halt when Tara's claws began to penetrate his skull. He replaced his struggles with pleas and begged her to let him go, or at least not to kill him.

Tara's voice was as merciless and inexorable as the grinding of a glacier. "Oh it's far too late for that Mr Jackson. But if it is any consolation, your men didn't lie to you. There are such things as vampires, and Dracula does indeed live. In fact, he's approaching at this very minute. I suspect that what I am going to do to you is a mercy compared to what he has in mind. I recall reading that when done right, an impaled man, or woman – not to be sexist, may take several days to die." With that, she began to squeeze, harder and harder.

**

From a distance, John had no trouble hearing Tara's words, and he slowed his approach to a sedate stroll. It was clear that she needed no help. Nor did he feel compelled to rescue her from an action that might plague her sense of morality in the future. He did not own her, nor was he her parent. She was a friend, and he owed her his support. She was not acting out of blind rage, nor was she inebriated, so he did her the courtesy of allowing her to make up her own mind. When he arrived at her location, Dan Jackson was very obviously and unmistakably dead, his skull crushed to splinters and his brain smashed to an oozing pulp. Tara was looking at her hand, but she was not crying nor did she appear distraught. He pulled a packet of wet wipes from his tight fitting and elastic backpack. "That looks messy. Here, clean yourself up a bit." Then he bent down to the body and pulled a large zip lock plastic bag from his backpack.

Tara looked up. "I … I had to kill him. He wasn't a

282

werewolf but I don't feel anything. Is there something wrong with me?"

"He's responsible for an attack that killed many of our people and would have killed all of us if it had succeeded. It is likely he was going to try again. He knew a secret that would have threatened our safety if he had managed to tell it to anyone. If anything, it was self-defence, although the courts might not see it that way. But that's not what you're asking, is it." He shrugged. "The sickness and self-loathing that people are supposed to feel when they kill another person is greatly exaggerated by films and TV. As long as they had a good reason to do it, a great many perfectly good and ordinary people are able to kill without being unduly upset. If you're asking whether you're an inhuman monster, I wouldn't say so, but then I'm hardly the person to give you advice on that subject, am I?"

Tara's giggle had an edge of hysteria to it, but then she sighed. "I think what worries me is that the nanites may be changing who I am, as well as what I am. The fact that you're so human is actually a great comfort. Even if you turned out to be a maniacal serial killer, at least you're motivations are perfectly normal and understandable." Then she raised an eyebrow. "Unless you're just really good at pretending to be human."

It was John's turn to laugh. "I was good at pretending to be human even before I received the alien nanites." He nodded towards the station. "If you're finished cleaning up, there might be people we could help who are trapped in the train."

"See! I can't imagine the Dracula of the cinema saying something like that," Tara said, and then immediately regretted it, concerned that she had offended him.

"The public want characters to be black or white. The good guy and the monster. Even if the monster is a romantic figure, he is still a monster and can never live

283

happily ever after. I've taken efforts to encourage that image of Dracula. But London is now my home, and its people are my people. I can't protect them from their own stupidity, but I can try to defend them from real monsters," John said over his shoulder as he started walking down the track. A touch of a control on his belt made his suit turn a dark blue making it look like he was wearing some kind of worker's overalls.

Tara imitated him and stared at his back thoughtfully as hurried to catch up with him.

***

The next day, Commander Blair studied a compilation of security videos in the privacy of his office. As head of the agency with primary responsibility for all UP incidents in Britain, he was able to confiscate all the video before any of it was leaked or circulated to other agencies. He knew this would anger MI5, who still believed the attacks were terrorist related, but at this point he didn't care. He was staring at the frozen image of the two youngsters who had been the best witnesses of the incident, given that the two armed constables had not survived. They had been identified after much investigative work, and he had ordered them brought in for questioning. Then he had the video carefully edited to remove their images and released to MI5 and all the other bodies investigating the crash and attack.

The pair of teenagers looked understandably apprehensive when Blair stepped into the room. The security camera had been deactivated by his orders and the voice recorder was off. He wanted to hear what they had to say first. "Hello, I'm Commander Blair. First I want you to understand that you're not in trouble. I just want to talk to you about what happened at Liverpool Street."

"We didn't see anything," the boy said.

"Nothing," the girl said, nodding in agreement.

Blair sat down and smiled in what he hoped was a reassuring manner. "Well you must have seen the crash, or what happened immediately after," he said.

"Umm, yeah, we saw the crash," the girl said.

"But that's all," the boy added hastily.

"I understand you're trying to protect someone. Did that person or persons save your life? I promise I'm not trying to get them in trouble either. After all, they're heroes, right?"

The girl started to nod but closed her mouth when the boy kicked her ankle. "Ow!"

Blair leaned on the table. "Look, I'm sure you two know that some weird things are happening out there. Well I've been put in charge of trying to stop it. I think that the people who saved you can help me, but to get permission to work with them I need proof that they are the good guys. That's where you come in. If they helped you, then your story could help me convince my superiors. They don't believe in super heroes."

The boy snorted. "They never do. Idiots."

"Well then, help me make them believe. Tell me what happened," Blair urged.

The boy shook his head, looking stubborn.

"Look, if they are who I think they are, they saved my life too. But nobody will take my word on it. I need more people, trustworthy people like you to help me. Nothing you say will be officially reported to anyone, not my bosses or your parents. I just need to know the truth so that I can make certain decisions. Please help me."

The couple looked at each other and whispered in each other's ears. Finally the girl nodded to her boyfriend. He turned back to Blair. "All right. I guess it's all right to tell you." He took a deep breath and then said, "He was a hero, like right out of the comic books. It was like a computer game, but real, you know? Those

285

things, the werewolves – I don't care what anyone says, I saw them, we saw them right up close, and they were for-real werewolves – they were tearing into us, the people in the station I mean. There was blood everywhere, and we thought we were dead for sure."

"But then he came," the girl said breathlessly.

Blair could see that she had a serious case of hero worship.

The boy nodded vigorously, ignoring his girlfriend's enthusiasm for another man. "That's right. He must have somehow gone around all the trains and empty tracks, and then he jumped on them. It was like, right out of a kung-fu film. He was flying through the air. He had this fucking big sword on his back and a gun on his side, but he used a dagger! It was unreal!"

"He fought both of them at the same time. Then one of them bit him on the arm and wouldn't let go. I thought he was a gonner, but somehow he got free and it was the werewolf that went down instead."

"Then when both of them were far enough away from us and the others, his sword came out, this big silver thing, curved, you now, like those um … yeah sabre things, not like the ones the Horse guards use, but with a big fat blade like in the films, and he just cut them up! It was like he had super strength or something," the boy said, bouncing up and down in his seat in excitement.

"And he wasn't just this mean killer neither. When it was over he came to us and told us to get out and to be safe," the girl added. "If it wasn't for him there would have been dozens more dead people. He asked us not to tell anyone what we had seen, and then ran off towards the other end of the station." Reminded of her promise she looked uneasy. "I hope he won't be angry that we told you."

Blair reassured the both of them that they had done the right thing and then asked a few more questions regarding the man's appearance and clothing. Although their description of his face didn't match that of John Seward, he felt certain it was him, or perhaps one of his men. But it was what the girl whispered to him right towards the end of the interview that gave him the most to think about. "I think the man, the one who rescued us, was a vampire!" she whispered, eyes very wide. "I saw his fangs, I swear!"

But when he tried to press her for more details she just shook her head and insisted that she had to go.

When he was alone in his office again he leaned back in his chair and closed his eyes with a groan. He had seen what the werewolves were capable of. He didn't believe that any one man, no matter how well trained or armed, could have taken on two of the creatures in hand to hand combat and survived, let alone triumphed. But a vampire? He knew he couldn't give this piece of information to anyone. First of all no one would believe him. They would think he was cracking up under the pressure. But more importantly, he had the uneasy feeling that he, everybody, would need John Seward and his companions in the near future. If Seward was a vampire, he seemed to be on the side of the humans. It was possible that he was some other variant of the werewolves, who had fangs too. If he really was a vampire, and that was still very doubtful, he could be a powerful weapon or at least ally. He realised that he would have to approach this whole thing with great care. For now he would keep what he had just learned a secret. The Deputy Commissioner had already approved equipping all of his teams with the supposedly experimental tranquilliser formula and plans for a super high security medical facility were being worked out. Blair had the uncomfortable feeling that Seward expected the holding facility to be a disaster, but he couldn't think of anything better that wouldn't reek of gas chambers and concentration camps. But he made up his mind to talk to Seward again soon about the subject of vampires, even though such conversations never seemed to work out well for the human in the cinema and in books. On the other hand, Seward had saved his life twice, and he felt strongly that he at least owed the man a fair hearing before doing anything else or telling anyone.

Chapter Fourteen

Viktor brushed imaginary lint off of his new Saville Row suit and looked around his huge new office. He had offered Jenny an office of her own, but she preferred a desk inside his office, so he gave her the title of Executive Personal Assistant and a new wardrobe to match. Some of her personal services were very personal indeed, but he really did find her organisational skills and advice very useful. She was also most delightfully ruthless, a trait which he greatly appreciated. He had registered a new company, Lupus Management Consultancy Services, and all of his pack who were so inclined had offices. Some of the others preferred to be closer to the street, so he used them as his field representatives for day to day affairs, such as collecting briefcases of cash from the various operations that were now effectively his. "Tell them to send Mr Li in," he said to Jenny and then waited, hands folded on his desk.

The door opened and the receptionist ushered James Li into the office. Slim and dapper the man wore a well-tailored suit made in Shanghai and wore a gold Rolex. He walked up to Viktor's desk and ignoring the fact that Viktor did not stand up to greet him, gave a slight bow. "Thank you for agreeing to this meeting, Mr Tiranul."

Viktor waved at the chair beside the Chinese Triad negotiator. When the man was seated, he went directly to the point. "Why are you here, Mr Li?"

"We have been following your um, dealings with the Russians and have noted with interest the outcome as well as the way you have established yourself in London." His gesture indicated the office and building they were in. "Unlike the Russians and some of the other of our competitors, we see no benefit in fighting with you over control. Therefore I'm here to make a proposal to you."

Amused, Viktor opened his arms expansively. "By all means. Propose away." Since he could always resort to raw violence and intimidation he saw no harm in listening.

"No matter how much you terrorise the mobs and firms in the city, you will always have upstarts and subordinates who will try to challenge you, even if it is only by anonymously attacking your interests. The larger you grow, the more ground you will have to cover. It will be like that arcade game that children like to play..." He made a hammering motion.

"Whack-a-mole," Viktor supplied.

The Triad negotiator nodded. "That is the one. Much of your time will be spent making examples of those that challenge you. If you fail, you will look weak, if you kill the wrong people, you increase the resentment against you. Push them too far and they might even ... what is it the English say ... ah yes, they might even grass on you to the authorities. Even if you fear no one Mr Tiranul, where is the profit in constant warfare?"

"I assume you have a solution?" Viktor already had a good idea what the man was going to propose, but he wanted to hear him say it. They might even have a better idea that he hadn't thought of.

"Like all overlords, you need people and an organisation, a bureaucracy, to keep your empire running. Unlike the Russians and the Armenians and the others, we will never be accepted as part of the natural order of things. Tolerated perhaps, feared if we so desired, but never accepted. That is why the Yakuza has never grown to match the Mafia or even the Colombians in America. So we have nothing to lose in allying ourselves with you. Rather than fighting for turf, we can be your people on the ground, making collections, enforcing order, and passing on your instructions. That way, you will only need to deal with major threats to your power rather than wasting your time stamping on ants. Think of it as sub-contracting. We provide a service, for an agreed range of fees. Without a power base of our own, we will never be a threat to you. In fact it will be in our interests to keep you strong."

"And in return I help you dominate the underworld," Viktor said.

"In your name. A mutually beneficial relationship, a symbiosis as the scientists say."

"If I agree to your proposal I will need to meet with your leader in person. I don't deal through intermediaries."

The Triad negotiator bowed slightly in his chair. "Of course. My purpose was to allow our proposal to be presented without loss of face on either side if you declined. The final negotiations will of course be with my superior."

Viktor smiled. "Your boss is a wise man."

"The greatest victory is one that is achieved without battle," Mr Li said.

Placing his hands flat upon the table, Viktor nodded. "Give me some time to consider and to work out the details of a possible agreement, and I shall get back to you with my decision."

"I expected no less," Mr Li said, and drew a business card from the breast pocket of his coat, offering it to Viktor with both hands. "Here is my card. Have your people call my number when you have decided." With that he stood up, bowed respectfully from the shoulders, and turned to leave.

"Mr Li, tell me something. You must have heard about the unusual abilities of me and my people, yet you don't seem very bothered about it."

Mr Li smiled. "The world is a large place, Mr Tiranul, and we have been around for a very long time. Let us just say that this is not our first encounter with … exceptional people. Unlike some, we have not forgotten or turned the truth into tales for children and TV shows."

With that cryptic statement he bowed again and walked away.

"Do you think he meant that they have …. " Jenny said thoughtfully.

Viktor grinned. "This is getting more and more interesting by the day."

***

Werner tended to work late. His office was as luxurious and comfortable as his home. He even had a private bedroom and bathroom attached to it, and he often used it when he felt the need for sexual release. His wife had her own life, and they had an understanding. She could do anything she liked as long as she was discreet. And she knew that if it came to it, there would be no divorce. She would just suffer an unfortunate accident. However, Werner was actually quite good to her and they got along well enough in public. She was still very fit and attractive, so they even had sex on occasion. He needed a socially adept wife and she like the lifestyle he provided, so they were a good partnership. She also never questioned his other women, since she knew they were just playthings and would never threaten her position, plus he was reasonably discreet and never went out in public with eye candy on his arm or flirted openly with either women or men when others could see.

He lay on his back and watched as his latest playmate got out of bed, making no effort to cover her nudity. As rich as he was, he could afford the best, which meant the best service as well as looks and figure. He only ever had sex with professionals. They knew better than to gossip, write a biography, or sell their stories to the press.

"I left my hand bag in the office. I'll be right back," she said looking over her shoulder, her eyes full of promise.

When she hadn't returned after five minutes, Werner frowned. He didn't tolerate being kept waiting, especially not by an employee. "Is there a problem?" he said, raising his voice so that she could hear him outside. When there was no reply he sighed and put on a dressing gown. If that stupid girl had stuffed her nose full of cocaine and gone to sleep he would have his assistant's ass. When he stepped into his office he found her staring at the polished wooden chest sitting in the middle of his desk. It had polished gold fittings and was decorated with a large crimson bow.

The escort looked at him with a puzzled expression. "I don't remember this being here when I came in, and the door to your office is locked, isn't it?"

Werner froze, staring at the box as if it was a large poisonous snake. He knew much better than she did just how secure his office was. Not even a SWAT team with the latest breaching equipment could get in without considerable noise, effort, and without setting off alarms all over the building and at the external security agency. And yet, there it was. He had a pistol in his drawer and he pulled it out and racked the slide back to load it. Then he pressed the panic button on the armrest of his chair. His next thought was that someone could have paid or coerced the girl to somehow bring the box in, but that didn't seem likely since he had watched her enter the office and there was nowhere for her to have hidden something the size of the box. Standing with his back to the wall, he slowly ran his eyes over the room, especially the ceiling and the ventilation ducts. But the grills over the ducts were made of steel and designed for security. They could only be removed after being unlocked from inside the room and they were still locked and firmly in place. When he was sure that he wasn't going to be shot in the back, he activated a concealed electronic lock on the wall behind his desk and the armoured door to his panic room swung open. He darted inside and pressed the button to swing the vault thick door shut.

"Hey! What about me?" the escort shouted.

"Sorry, room for one only," Werner replied, pointing his gun at her so that she wouldn't be tempted to push her way in. He sighed in relief when the door locked shut and he was securely sealed inside the steel lined room. Then he saw the writing painted on the back of the door. "It's not a bomb". Sweat broke out on his brow as he frantically tapped the pass code that would open the door again, his head swivelling from side to side as he waited for the heavy locks to disengage.

The escort looked up from her cell phone in surprise when her bastard of a client unexpectedly emerged from his bolt hole. She had no luck in placing a call, because when Werner had pressed the panic button it had also activated a signal jammer designed to make it difficult for intruders to communicate with each other. Nor had she been able to retrieve her clothes since the door to the bedroom had also locked when Werner entered the panic room. The naked woman raised an eyebrow. "I charge extra for sitting naked in a room with a bomb," she said archly.

Fighting down his growing unease, Werner went to sit behind his desk and studied the mysterious box. "Apparently it's not a bomb."

"That's nice. My fee is the same anyway. Can I leave now?" she asked. Given the way things were going, she was even willing to walk out of the office building stark naked save for her handbag.

"Shut the fuck up and don't move," Werner snapped, slapping his pistol down on the table top. He believe the graffiti when it said there wasn't a bomb inside the box. He could have waited until the security team arrived with the bomb expert, but he suspected that what was inside was for his eyes only. He untied the ribbon and flicked the clasp open with his thumbnail. He could smell the woman's perfume and the scent of her body and he idly wondered if it was the last thing he would ever smell. The box could still contain a nerve gas or Anthrax. He held his breath and gently lifted the lid with both hands. He peered inside and exhaled, both in a sigh and a soft grunt at what he saw. There was a sheet of what appeared to be parchment attached to the inside of the lid, on which was written a message in a dark red ink that looked like dried blood –

This is your only warning.

I and my friends have no interest in exploiting for money the knowledge and items you have just acquired.

If you threaten those under my protection again, you will die.

In earnest of this, I have taken the liberty of returning your man Dan Jackson to you.

D

The box was lined with red velvet and sitting in the middle was a large glass-like cube of plastic resin. Embedded within the resin was what was obviously a human heart, still looking wet and fresh. Werner sat staring at the gory keepsake for a long moment.

The escort leaned around the lid to peek into the box, but when she saw the contents she hurriedly straightened and pretended that she hadn't seen anything. This was obviously nothing that she wanted to be involved in.

The security team finally arrived, guns drawn and laser pointers painting quivering red dots all over the walls. Werner sat silent as the team ensured that the room was safe and that no traps or electronic devices had been planted. The box was whisked away for forensic examination, although he was certain that they would find nothing, just as he was certain that DNA examination of the heart would prove that it indeed belonged to the unfortunate Jackson. He made a note in his diary to have HR select some candidates to replace him. When the team finally left he noticed that the naked escort was still sitting in her chair, legs elegantly crossed and silently waiting. He admired professionalism. "You saw and heard nothing. You will be paid a bonus for the … inconvenience. Naturally I expect complete discretion from you, and I will be most unhappy if I learn that you have discussed today's events with anyone at all."

The escort, who had just endured a thorough and humiliating body search, nodded silently, not responding to the promise of reward or the implied threat. She let her legs uncross and smiled at him. "Do you want me to leave now, or …. "

Her nerve made him chuckle. "I don't allow others to dictate my actions. Go back to the bedroom and wait for me. I feel like using the riding crop tonight. Prepare yourself accordingly.

She nodded and smiled in return, stood up in a single lithe motion and walked towards the bedroom door, which was unlocked again. "I'll be waiting," she said, closing the door behind her.

Werner knew the chief researcher assigned to investigate the werewolf artefacts always worked late so when he called the laboratory he wasn't surprised when Dr. Wright answered. With his eyes focused on the apparently useless door of his office, Werner said, "Where are you with the project?"

"Quite frankly, unless you approve my latest proposal, I can't see us making any progress at all. Whatever was injected into their systems, it is invisible to our instruments," the scientist replied bluntly.

"So you believe that focused radiation bombardment will work?"

"It's possible. Enough radiation might damage whatever it is enough to stop or reduce its ability to function and so make it visible to us in a blood sample." Then as if it was a minor consideration he added, "Naturally, that degree of radiation is likely to be fatal to the test subject."

Werner tapped his fingers on the table. His supply of test subjects was unlimited, but the alien applicators were not. "You have my approval to try it on two subjects. Report your results to me before going any further than that."

Both pleased and relieved, the researcher smiled broadly as he replied. "Yes sir. I'll get on it at once." He had not mentioned that the alien devices might respond in unexpected ways to the deadly levels of radiation, but he considered the risk well worth it. After all, other than the death or some kind of malformed transformation, what could possibly go wrong.

Werner disconnected and placed a call to the deputy head of the Internal Audit department. That man, if it was a man, and the other auditors were on twenty-four hour call, so the time of day was of no consideration. When the man answered Werner said, "All audit actions in the UK are to be suspended until further notice. Is that understood?" He did not choose to explain his decision, nor did he expect to be questioned. Their job was to carry out is orders. Until he was sure of what he was dealing with, the risks of further action in Britain posed too much personal danger to be worth it. The preserved heart, and the fact that it had been sitting on his desk until moments ago was an eloquent and effective warning. There was nothing to be gained by being confrontational at the moment. He had all the time in the world to strike back, and when he did, he would crush his unknown adversary. He imagined sending an assassination team comprised of werewolves and smiled.

Chapter Fifteen

Rowland Harker gazed out of the window, half hidden by the curtain. The bench in the garden was mostly illuminated only by moonlight, but the couple seated there didn't seem to be bothered by the darkness. His brow furrowed in concern and he sighed. "It's inevitable I suppose," he said to himself.

"John is a good man, Rowland. And an honourable one, in the old fashioned sense," Emily said from behind him.

He stepped away from the window and turned to face his assistant and … lover. It felt strange to admit that after all the years of being single since his wife had died. "That's just the thing. Is he a man, or something else?"

"Whatever he is, you have to remember that Tara is becoming like him too," Emily said gently, taking his hand.

"I know, I know. But it's hard not knowing what is truly happening to your own daughter, let alone seeing her with a … man."

Emily looked into his eyes. "You think there is more that John isn't telling us."

He nodded. "I'm sure of it. He's had centuries to work with the nanites, and the legends suggest all sorts of possibilities. What if she changes too much?"

"Whatever he is, John is definitely still a man. He can be harsh, even ruthless, but I think he was that way before the change. No matter what, Tara is still your daughter, and she loves you."

Rowland nodded, biting his lip. "I … I hope so. I truly do."

She put her arms around him. "I love you too. And if you'll come right this way, I'll demonstrate that empirically."

"Your father is watching us."

Tara smiled. "I know. He worries about me. About what I might become." She squeezed his hand. "He worries about you."

"Should I reassure him that my intentions towards you are strictly honourable?" John asked, leaning towards her.

"And are they?" she said teasingly.

"Only if you want them to be," John said easily.

She felt a strange heat growing within her. She was not an innocent virgin, and she enjoyed sex, but this was different. "I think that the vampire aliens got horny too," she said, knowing full well what her words revealed.

He leaned over and kissed her cheek. "That's fortunate, isn't it? It would be terrible if we were overcome by the urge to brood over a clutch of eggs or something."

Tara chuckled. "I don't think there's any risk of that." She lowered her head slightly. "There's more you're not telling me, isn't there?"

"There is. Much more. Some of it is dangerous. But if we are to deal with the vampire clans, a massive outbreak of werewolves, and Viktor's plots, not to mention Werner's inevitable retaliation and the even more inevitable treachery of our own government, you need to be as strong and capable as I can make you."

"I'm not afraid," Tara said.

"No, but for the first time in centuries, I might be," John said, almost reluctantly.

The darkness didn't hide his visage from her and she touched his cheek lightly with her fingertips. "Don't be. No matter what happens, neither of us will face it alone."

"Tara, I..."

She pressed her fingers against his lips. "Hush. I'm not going anywhere. We have all the time in the world to get to know each other." She leaned against his shoulder and looked out across the grounds, her sonar, enhanced vision, and even her sense of smell and the touch of the air against her skin forming a combined image that made the night as clear as day. She understood now that the night was their domain. She had inherited something incredible and the test pilot's spirit within her longed to push her capabilities as far as they could go, and beyond.

The End